The Guardians

STORM OVER WHITWORTH

Richard Williams

authorHOUSE®

AuthorHouse™
1663 Liberty Drive
Bloomington, IN 47403
www.authorhouse.com
Phone: 1-800-839-8640

First published by AuthorHouse 3/22/2011

ISBN: 978-1-4567-4719-0 (e)
ISBN: 978-1-4567-4718-3 (sc)

Library of Congress Control Number: 2011903851

Printed in the United States of America

Any people depicted in stock imagery provided by Thinkstock are models, and such images are being used for illustrative purposes only. Certain stock imagery © Thinkstock.

This book is printed on acid-free paper.

I would like to dedicate this book to my good friend and mentor Sam Balius. His life has been an example to many who follow the path of faith.

CHAPTER ONE

The Calm before the Storm

It was a cold January morning. The sky was clear with the snowstorm now over. DJ was outside waiting for Maggie to meet him. He knew she was still worrying over what they had talked about last fall. Maggie took it really hard when he told her that a storm was headed their way. Even now, although Maggie tried to put it out of her mind, DJ knew it was still there needling her. That was why he wanted her to come outside and play in the snow. He thought it would help to take her mind off things. Maggie liked the cold weather but this was the first really big snow she had ever seen. In fact, the folks around town were talking about how this was the biggest snow they had seen in years. It wasn't that Maggie minded the snow, but she did mind getting her feet wet. Paula watched Maggie as she stood there trying to make up her mind. "Well," she said, "if you're not going to go out, then maybe I should tell DJ to stop waiting on you?"

"Oh no, I'm going, but it's just that… well I don't like my feet getting wet that's all."

Paula reached down and patted Maggie on the head. "Maggie you know I will put towels out for you to wipe your feet on."

"I know," Maggie said. As Maggie looked up at Paula she remarked, "You look so beautiful this morning, Paula."

"Why, thank you Maggie. I feel so big. I mean, who would have thought I was going to get this big?"

"You're not that big, you just feel that way, but your face has such a wonderful glow on it." Paula watched Maggie as she walked outside to be with DJ. She knew there were still times it hurt Maggie that she could never have puppies, but she also knew that she wouldn't trade her life with DJ for ten thousand puppies.

DJ was standing outside with the snow up to his little belly. "Maggie, come over here. The snow is really deep on this end of the yard." Maggie slowly walked over to him. Even with all they have been through, she was amazed that DJ could still be so playful. She jumped over some of the snow and landed right in a large pile of snow. When she picked up her head, she had snow all over her face. DJ was laughing as he walked over to her. He reached out and licked her on the side of the face. "You can be so silly sometimes, my Love."

Maggie shook the snow off as best she could. "Now what is it that you wanted so badly?"

"Nothing," DJ said, "I just thought it would be nice for us to play in the snow together." Maggie put her head down and shook it lightly. "Only you would want to play in the snow." With that, she pushed DJ into some snow and took off running.

DJ popped up and was right behind her, "Boy, are you going to get it when I catch you." Paula was looking out the window at them and laughing so hard that Bill came in to see what was making her laugh so. When she pointed at them, he burst out laughing as well. Bill put his arm around Paula. "You know, we could learn something from them, don't you think?"

"Yeah, a lot, but what are you talking about?"

"Well, look at them now. They would be considered an older couple in dog years. And look how they still play together. They always make time for each other. There has to be a lesson in all of this."

Paula put her head over on Bill's shoulder. "Yes, I think so. You should never grow apart, but you should grow closer together as the years pass by. But as for you calling them an older couple," Paula pushed Bill back and smiled, "I'm going to tell, I'm going to tell."

Bill grabbed Paula, and started to tickle her when he heard Maggie make this grunting noise. "Paula, would you please get DJ and me a towel. Also, Bill, you shouldn't be so rough with Paula, not in her condition."

Paula slipped out of Bill's arms and as she walked out the door she looked back at him and giggled. "Now might be a good time to tell them how old you think *they are.*"

"What!" DJ said.

"Old, who…who are you calling old mister, why I have you know that I'm a young guardian and so is Maggie."

"That's right," Maggie said as she pushed against Bill's leg. "And just think," Maggie continued, "a man of your advance years calling anyone old is beyond me."

Bill sputtered "I…I didn't mean it like it sounded."

"Oh yes, that's what they all say," Maggie piped in.

Paula walked back in and just grinned at Bill. "Have you gotten out of trouble yet?" She asked smiling.

Maggie walked over to Paula and stepped on the towel she placed on the floor. "Come on, DJ, let's wipe our feet and go in here by the fireplace where old folks are supposed to sit." DJ was giggling as he followed Maggie out of the room.

"Just couldn't leave well enough alone could you, Bill?" Paula laughed as DJ and Maggie walked out of the room. "Well, it's Saturday and they will hound you all day about that. So let's see, do you think you started this day off right?"

Bill laughed as he grabbed Paula again, "Ok smarty pants, now whose going to save you?"

They were both laughing as DJ and Maggie lay by the fireplace. "DJ?"

"Yeah, Love."

"When do you think...,"

"Maggie let's not go over that again. Put it out of your mind for now. If we worry about something before it happens, how are we going to be ready for it when it comes? All we would have accomplished is to have worried ourselves into a place of fear rather than faith."

"I know, but I was just hoping it wouldn't happen, that's all."

"I do too, Love, but we need to have our hearts ready, not our heads. Don't let fear rob you of your peace of heart and mind."

"I won't DJ. I mean, not anymore." Maggie reached over and lightly licked DJ's face. He looked at her and she whispered. "That's why you wanted us to play in the snow, isn't it? You were trying to get my mind on something else."

"Yeah, did it work?"

Maggie moved closer to DJ. "Let's sleep by the fire now, and you can figure that out later for yourself."

Bill walked in and found them sound asleep by the fire. He knew something had been troubling Maggie but he wasn't sure what it was. Paula seemed to think it was because she never had puppies of her own. Funny how people can be so close to someone, and not truly understand what is troubling them. Strange, that they never thought to ask. We just take it for granted that we know what the trouble might be, when in fact, we don't know at all. Bill was in his study working on his lesson plans for the next semester when Paula brought him a cup of coffee. "Did you see those two in there sleeping by the fire?"

"Yes, I thought it would be nice to try that ourselves one night."

Paula laughed a little and rubbed her stomach. "You're going to have to wait until after the baby I'm afraid." Bill smiled, "Why, I could make a bed on the floor and..."

"Bill," Paula said, "not until after the baby, it would kill my back to sleep on the floor. I don't care how many covers you put on the floor. It wouldn't be enough. Please try to understand."

Bill got up and moved around to where Paula was standing. "I do understand, and just as soon as it gets cold weather next year, we'll sleep in front of the fireplace."

"Yes, with DJ, Maggie, and the baby, that ought to be just about right."

"Well, maybe on second thought, we'll just sleep in our own bed."

"Maggie was right about one thing though."

"Yeah, what was that?"

"You do look beautiful."

Paula put her head over on Bill's shoulder. "I don't think I will ever grow tired of hearing you say that."

* * * * *

Dr. Pittman was walking to his office to look over the records for the last year. It seemed he never was able to get through with one set of paperwork that another didn't pop up. He smiled to himself as he walked. He had Bill back teaching full time, Jonathan and Dr. Balius were also teaching part time. Yes sir, he had things just where he wanted them. It was going to be a good semester. Nothing could go wrong now.

* * * * *

Jonathan was sitting in his office drinking coffee after he had spent most of the early morning hours drying coffee beans. He was trying to catch up on his paperwork at the bookstore. It seemed he was always working long hours these days. He wondered sometimes if it was worth it trying to teach part time. But he did enjoy the students. And the pain from those days in the past was gone now. He had his good friend back and they did spend a lot of time fellowshipping after school. Yes, that was the one thing that kept him there more than anything else, his friendship with Bill. Jonathan looked at his watch. He knew Bill would go to his office today and that he would most likely stop by on the way there or on the way back. Either way, they would have time to fellowship before the semester got back under way. Yeah, it wasn't so bad being back in the classroom. Why even Dr. Balius loved teaching there.

* * * * *

Irina had taken her maiden name back hoping to hide the fact that she had spent the last three years in prison. She had traveled to the US on a scholarship and had met her husband while she was finishing her last year in college. Irina was five feet nine inches tall, with light brown hair, and eyes that were almost black in color. When she stopped and smiled at you, it always made you forget whatever you were doing. At first she thought she had found the fairy tale. Everything was just wonderful. Jack Holton was a loving husband, or so it seemed. What Irina didn't know, was that he was into running drugs and laundering money. It wasn't until they had been married for about a year that she noticed how the police were always following them. When she started

6

asking him about it, Jack became violent. The first time he beat Irina she tried to run away, but he caught her and told her he would kill her if she ever left him. That was when her nightmare began. The next five years was nothing but a living hell for Irina. She feared for her life more than once, and it wasn't from some of Jack's enemies, but from Jack himself. He was using more drugs, and drinking a lot more, and then it happened. One night he came home and went into a rage. He grabbed Irina, threw her up against the wall, and started beating her. He was yelling that he knew she was cheating on him. "You cheap slut, I know you are running around on me."

Even though Irina tried to reason with Jack, he wouldn't listen to her. The whole truth of the matter was that he was the one doing all the running around. He threw Irina, and she hit the floor. There on the table was a large knife. Irina grabbed the knife, and when he picked her up to throw her again, Irina, stabbed him in the chest. Jack fell dead, but because Irina had never filed a police report about the beatings, Jack's family was able to have her arrested. When she faced trial, all his friends testified that Irina was, in fact, cheating on Jack. So what should have been self-defense was ruled as murder. Irina was sentenced to ten years, but with good behavior, was out in three.

Now, Irina Timkina was facing another problem. While she was in prison, she got hooked up with someone who had promised her they could help her get her child back. All she had to do was to help this person get even with someone. Little did she realize that you can never make a deal with evil, for evil never keeps its promises.

* * * * *

As Bill walked into the *Morning Blend* he could smell the coffee. There was always something about this store that reminded him of Oxford. Bill had been to Oxford for seminars about C. S. Lewis. He always loved the café, and the way it smelled. "Hey, can you guess what blend we are going to drink?" Jonathan called out from the back of the store.

Bill held his nose up in the air trying to guess, and hoping that he would get it right. "Well, let's see it's Saturday, so I'm guessing dark roast blend?"

"You're right!" said Jonathan.

"You mean I guessed it right?" "No, I mean you are guessing, but not right. Do you want to try again or should I just tell you?"

"Just tell me." Bill knew Jonathan loved this game. After all these years of drinking coffee, he would have thought that at least once in a while he could have guessed right. Jonathan came around the bookcase, "it's Indian Malabar." Jonathan smiled at Bill, "Remember what time of year this is? This coffee is available only at this time of year." "Man, you would think I would remember that," Bill was laughing as he said it.

Jonathan pointed over to the table, "Our chess game is still set up, do you want to keep playing this game or start another one?" This was one time Jonathan wished Bill would have given in and started a new game, because although he had Bill beaten when it came to coffee, Bill always beat him when they played chess. The afternoon passed by quietly just two good friends spending time together, drinking coffee and playing chess.

"Hey, did you dry these beans?" Bill asked.

"Nope, I buy this coffee for myself and for my friends."

Paula was laying down taking a nap with DJ and Maggie sleeping at her feet. After Paula had fallen asleep, Maggie whispered to DJ, "Do you think she is resting ok, DJ?" "Yeah, don't worry so much, Love. Paula is alright and so is the baby." He knew she worried because she never had any pups of her own. Maggie put her head down and watched Paula as she slept. It was a long while before she allowed herself to fall asleep too.

* * * * *

Bill walked in the back door shaking from the cold. "Next time I tell you I'm going to walk to the *Morning Blend* in this weather, have my head examined."

Maggie walked by Bill thinking to herself that this would be a good time to get another dig in, "Or, we could just say it was because he was so forgetful and that is why he walked in such cold weather".

DJ put his head down as he laughed, "Man, now that's cold."

Paula was giggling to herself as Bill walked over to her, "Now see what you started." Maggie walked up to Bill and lightly pushed his leg, "I hope you know that DJ and I were just playing with you today, Bill. We didn't mean anything by it, honest." Bill thought to himself how much fun it had been living with DJ and Maggie.

"Oh Maggie," Bill said as he reached down to pat her on the head, "I know you two very well. I knew you were playing with me, and that is what makes it so very special".

"Yeah," DJ said, "and we had better do it now while you can still remember it." DJ erupted into laughter again. "Now Bill, remember, I'm DJ, and this is Maggie."

Paula joined in on the fun as well. "And I'm your wife, remember dear?"

Maggie was smiling as she said, "Yes, that's right, but she can't remember her name either."

DJ hit the floor laughing and rolling, Bill was laughing so hard he had to sit down before he lost his breath. "Hey," Paula said, "I thought we were on the same side."

* * * * *

Irina Timkina arrived in town that night. And even though it was still a week before school started, she was under strict orders to find herself a place to stay and to start making as many contacts as she could. She was supposed to make everyone in town think she was the friendliest person they had ever met. There could be no mistakes here. Everything had to be done, and it had to be done right. All Irina really wanted was to have her little girl back, and to have a chance to start her life over again. She had already made one big mistake. She was hoping this wasn't another one. But if there was any hope of ever getting her child back then she was going to have to trust these people, even though she knew in her heart what she was being asked to do was wrong. Irina knew the pain that came from hurts and broken promises. She didn't want to hurt anyone nor did she want to cause them any pain, but she was told how they had stolen and caused someone to be put in prison. She would be hurting bad people, and maybe, just maybe, it would all work out anyway. "Oh God, just help me to get my little girl back, '*пожалуйста*', please."

Irina is like so many in our world. Even though she had been lied to by her ex-husband, she was taking everything this new friend told her at face value. Irina wanted her daughter so badly that she never questioned what she was being told. Her apartment was only a small one bedroom apartment, but it was enough. She had to get her mind used to the fact that for the next few months, she was working for someone who had promised to help her get her daughter. This had to be right; she wanted it to be right.

* * * * *

Wayne and Cindy Hawkins were both surprised when Irina showed up at their door that Saturday afternoon. They hadn't run an ad in the paper yet about their upstairs apartment, mainly because school was a week away. But there was something about Irina that melted Cindy's heart. "Come on in, dear, it's way too cold to be standing outside." This was the first kind treatment Irina had received in years. Even though Irina didn't have a job yet, Cindy told Wayne that they had to help this poor child. "She's here from another country and she doesn't have any family here, honey."

Wayne whispered, to Cindy from behind the kitchen door. "But we don't know anything about her, and besides dear, she's been in this country long enough to become a citizen."

Cindy's grey eyes matched her gray hair, but when she was upset, you could see fire in her eyes, and right now Wayne was seeing fire. Wayne and Cindy ran the dry cleaners with a one bedroom apartment upstairs over the dry cleaners. Cindy never had any children of her own. They had tried, but after two miscarriages the doctor told them it would be too dangerous for Cindy to try again. Cindy always had her heart set on having a little girl. Cindy stood her ground, "She is staying in the apartment, or here at our house, so which is it?"

Wayne threw his hands up in the air, "I'll get the key to the apartment."

Irina didn't want to cause any trouble, so when they came back into the living room she spoke up, "if this isn't a good time, I can come back tomorrow, or maybe you can tell me somewhere else I can find an apartment."

No," Wayne said, "I'm just not as trusting as my wife. I like to know something about the person we rent to. Please, don't tear up my apartment."

Irina laughed, "Oh no, I'm not a party type." I'm here trying to finish my Master's Degree. I stopped years ago, and now I am ready to get back to work on it."

CHAPTER TWO

One Should Always Listen to Their Heart

Sunday morning was cold. When Paula woke up, she felt like just staying in bed. "Bill," she whispered. "Bill, are you awake yet?" Bill grinned as he lay there pretending he was sound asleep. Paula got closer to him. "Bill, wake up, I need to ask you something." Bill had his back turned toward Paula so she couldn't see him grinning as she kept whispering to him. "Bill, can't we sleep in today? Bill, I don't want to wake DJ, and Maggie."

DJ picked up his head and looked at Paula. "Well, you don't have to worry about that anymore. Besides, Bill is laying there grinning, because he is only pretending to be asleep."

"Hey, whatever happened to us boys sticking together?"

Maggie shook her head and thought to herself, after all this time, he still doesn't understand that DJ loves to sleep late, and besides, what's more fun than telling Paula he is pulling her leg and watching him trying to get out of it.

Paula reached over and pushed Bill, and as she did he reached out and pulled her close to him. "I think sleeping in today would be just fine, and I know Dr. Balius will understand."

DJ rolled back over and went back to sleep, Maggie snuggled close to him so they could keep each other warm. "Yeah, today would be a good day to sleep in," she thought.

* * * * *

Cindy showed up at the apartment early that Sunday morning. She knew she was going to be rushed to get to church, but there was just something about Irina that drew her. Irina's face registered surprise as she opened the door and saw Cindy standing there. "Mrs. Hawkins, please come in. I hope everything is alright. I mean you're not here to ask me to move are you?"

"Lord, no child, I just wanted to drop by and see if there was anything I could do for you." Irina hadn't received such kindness in years. She was a little nervous at first, not sure if this was for real or not. Irina bit her bottom lip as she stood there, not knowing what to say. Cindy could see that she had made this child upset, so she did what she did best. Cindy walked over and hugged Irina around the neck. "It's ok, child, no one will hurt you in this country. Why, we are all just good ole homefolks that's all".

Irina's eyes filled with tears. How could she tell this woman that it was in this country that she experienced her worst nightmare. Irina knew she had to cover up her tears so she said, "You're being so good to me, I don't know what to say. It has touched my heart so much."

Cindy felt a little relieved, but there was still something there that troubled her. It was the look of sadness in Irina's eyes. "So tell me, Irina, were you ever married? Do you have any children?"

Cindy's words cut like a knife through Irina's heart. She had no idea where her daughter was, and the pain she was carrying was the thing that was driving her to do what she was planning to do. "Oh no, I never had any children, I was never married. I guess I haven't found the right man yet, Mrs. Hawkins."

"Please, call me Cindy; why most of this town knows me as Cindy. If they heard you calling me Mrs. Hawkins, they wouldn't have a clue who you were talking about."

Irina stood there still not knowing what to say. The question about children had hit her hard. She only hoped she had hidden it from Cindy. Cindy hugged Irina again, "Well I need to get back home to finished getting ready for church. Tell you what, next Sunday, if you feel like it, why don't you eat lunch with us after church? Why, you could even go to church with us if you wanted to."

Not knowing what to say, Irina agreed to go and to have lunch with Cindy and Wayne next week. As Cindy was walking to her car she thought about Irina's reaction to the question she'd asked her about having children and the look of sadness that was evident as she tried to answer. Then it dawned on Cindy where she had seen that look before. She remembered that look coming from her own eyes after each miscarriage. No, Irina was hiding something. She had lost a child most likely. Maybe the poor girl had gotten herself into trouble. Yes, that had to be it. Well, there wasn't any use in telling Wayne about any of this. Men never did understand these things. Cindy prayed for Irina as she drove home. For her it felt something like what a mother must feel when her daughter needed her, but didn't know how to ask for help. It's alright dear, Cindy thought, "I'll be here for you."

* * * * *

Dr. Balius was sitting at his desk going over his sermon for that morning. It was cold, and he knew that many of the elderly would not get out in the cold weather. He chuckled to himself as he thought, Lord, I don't like getting out in this kind of weather myself. But we're here to serve you, not ourselves. Sam was never one to come down too hard on his members for missing services when it was bitterly cold outside. He remembered the time he was caught out in a rainstorm in South America, and came down sick afterwards. He was in the hospital for more than a week, and then in bed at home for two more. No, his heart went out to the elderly, but his patience wasn't that longsuffering with the younger couples who played around with their commitment to the Lord. They were always putting other things before their service to God, and their attendance to church was lacking. "Oh Lord," Sam prayed, "Help me to reach these young folks. Help them to see what freedom we have here to worship you." Maybe that was why Dr. Balius was so well liked. The elderly knew he considered their situation and the younger couples knew that he truly cared for their souls enough to tell them about it from time to time.

* * * * *

Kim was making her rounds at the hospital when Dr Adcock came up behind her. He slowly put his arms around her and kissed her on the back of the neck. "Hey, not here, we're at work, remember." Howard just laughed at his wife. She was the type of woman who never did show her emotions in public, and he knew she would react that way when he kissed her on the back of the neck.

Howard turned Kim around so that she would face him. "Everyone here knows we're married, dear. And I bet they all know we do kiss from time to time."

"Shush, everyone will hear you."

Kim's sister Vickie walked by just about then, and seeing the chance to embarrass Kim, she said. "And they know what else you two do, too."

Kim's face turned three shades of red. She hid her face in Howard's coat and then just turned to walk away. "I have to finish my rounds, Oh God, everyone heard that."

Howard looked at Vickie as she was standing there. "Thanks, sis."

"Glad to help anytime, just trying to do my part to help you two have a happy marriage." The truth was that Vickie loved her sister and her brother-in-law, and she would have done anything for either one of them. Vickie still missed her dad, calling him and telling him what she had just done would have sent him roaring with laughter. Later, she would tell Kim how much dad would have enjoyed her little joke. It was their way of reminding each other of their Father's love for them.

Howard called out to Kim. "Are we still meeting at your mother's house tonight?" Kim turned and looked at Howard. Her sandy brown hair was tied up in a ponytail, but it was her brown eyes that always melted his heart. She looked at him for just a moment before she spoke. "Yeah, but let's not stay too long tonight, ok?"

Howard smiled, "That's a deal."

* * * * *

Clara Pittman was in the bathroom putting on her makeup while Dr. Pittman was sitting on the side of the bed not feeling very well. He had this feeling before but it always passed off. So he was sure it would again. He lay down, and as he laid there, he noticed there was some pain shooting down his left arm, but he was sure it was probably nothing. A little while later when Clara woke him up, he noticed that she had a worried look on her face. "What's the matter, are you all right?" she asked.

"Oh yeah, I'm fine, just was lying down and fell asleep I guess."

"Harry, your color doesn't look right. Maybe we should call the doctor."

Dr. Pittman shook his head, "No dear, I'm all right. I just stayed up too late last night, that's all."

Clara looked at him with such a deep look of concern. "I think you should see a doctor, and you should go today."

Dr. Pittman rose up and kissed Clara very lightly on her lips, "Not today, my dear, I'm fine and besides if we miss church, then Dr. Balius will think we are some of those old folks who can't stand the cold. Or even worse, he'll think we're like some of those younger couples who miss church for just any reason."

Clara got up and walked back into the bathroom to finish combing her hair. After she walked out, Dr. Pittman rubbed his left arm. The pain was just about gone now. He put his shoes on and thought to himself, "See, if it was something the pain wouldn't go away." Like so many, even the best and brightest can fail to see the signs of trouble ahead.

* * * * *

After lunch Paula went downtown to pick up a few things at the store. She normally didn't shop on Sunday, but they were out of a few things and Bill had forgotten to get DJ's, and Maggie's food. As she was getting out of her car, Paula looked across the street. She saw this young woman walking toward the store. It was Irina. There was something about her that made Paula afraid. Something inside of her was trying to tell her that this woman was going to cause them more trouble than they could ever imagine. But Paula just shook her head and thought; "I must be really going through some changes, now I see trouble everywhere I go." Paula walked in the store, not knowing that her own heart was trying to warn her. If only we'd learn to listen to our heart. If only we'd slow down enough to hear what our own heart was trying to tell us, how many heartaches would we avoid?

CHAPTER THREE

Preparing For School

Bill had just walked into his office from a meeting that morning with Dr. Pittman and the rest of the staff. It was one of those meetings that Bill knew they were going to have every year at the beginning of the semester. Although no one really liked those meetings, Dr. Pittman always managed to make them interesting. Bill had so much work to do to get ready for the next semester. Normally by now he would have already been finished, but he had just spent too much time with Paula and the pups. This was his family now, and he was enjoying every minute of it. As Bill sat there looking over the list of his new students, there was a light knock on the door. "Yes, come in, it's open," Bill called out. As Bill looked up he saw this tall beautiful young woman walk into his office. Irina was dressed very plainly, but her beauty still shone through. As Irina walked toward his desk, Bill stood and reached out his hand, "I'm Dr. Thomas, is there anything I can do for you?"

Irina stood there for a moment not knowing what to say. Could this man be the monster that he was described to be to her? Could he be such a man as to have innocent women thrown into jail? Irina felt for the first time that something was wrong, but then she thought about her little girl, and she quickly put it out of her mind. "Yes sir, you can, I need you to sign this so that I can get into your class. I am wanting to study more about C. S. Lewis, and I am told no one knows more about him than you, sir."

Bill smiled to himself, "Oh no, there are a lot of men who know more, I'm sure," he said as he signed the paper.

As Irina walked out of Bill's office he stood there watching her leave. There was something about her that made him feel uneasy, but he promised himself that he would always try to help everyone who came to him for help. Still, there was that feeling; maybe he should have put her off. Bill shook his head. "My goodness, here I go again seeing ghosts from the past. When will I ever learn to let the past go?" Bill couldn't quite put his finger on it, but that feeling had moved him. He overlooked a warning he was receiving from his own heart attempting to make him remember how he had shut his eyes to that feeling once before, and it almost cost him everything.

* * * * *

Father David Grissom was walking across the parking lot of his church when he remembered that he had promised to go and put up some more candles for the service next Sunday. Father Grissom laughed at himself, "Well now, if I hadn't stayed up so late playing chess with Dr. Balius, maybe I would have remembered. But he wanted to beat me so badly, and after all these years, maybe I should let him win just one game." Father Grissom's hazel eyes seemed to sparkle as he thought about it. "Nope, if he wants to beat me, then he will just have to learn to be a better chess player." If someone had walked by they might had wondered why this priest was laughing to himself as he walked back to his car, but then friendships such as his with Dr. Balius can make you laugh like that.

* * * * *

Jonathan was walking across the campus when he saw this beautiful young woman walking just ahead of him. Irina wasn't aware of Jonathan walking up behind her. She had an arm full of books and was just about to drop them when Jonathan stepped up and helped her with them. "Here, let me give you a hand there. You know most students wait until after the first day of class before they buy their books. That way if you don't like a teacher or if the class is full you don't buy a book you don't need."

Irina looked into Jonathan's eyes, and she saw such kindness. It would have melted her heart at any other time, but not now. She couldn't let herself fall for anyone or trust anyone ever again. She stepped back taking her books from Jonathan. "Thank you so much, Dr. Wedgeworth, for your advice. I have your class on Mondays and Thursdays. Maybe I should rethink it before I buy that book." With that she turned and walked away. Jonathan stood there watching her as she left. He knew she was running from something painful in her past. That look in her eyes was proof of it. Jonathan stood there and prayed for this woman who had without knowing it touched his heart, something that he thought would never happen again.

* * * * *

Bill met Paula for lunch at Bob's Easy Fixings. It was a short order restaurant, operated by Bob Boswell. Bob had been one of Bill's students years ago, but then his wife had twins during his first year of college and he had to drop out. Bob's dad ran a short order restaurant his entire life. Bob said he would never work in one again. But after working for a while at the hardware store, he decided to open his own place of business. And the truth is, he loved it. Now he understood why his dad loved his job so much. Bob knew just about everyone in town, and by the end of a semester, he knew about half the kids on campus as well. Even though he was only five feet two inches tall, Bob was easy to find when you walked in because of his bright red hair. His wife Mary Ann was also just as easy to spot. She stood six-feet tall with hair about as red as Bob's. Needless to say, both of their boys had red hair. When Bill and Paula walked in, Bob yelled out "Honey, I need two deadbeats with everything on them."

Paula whispered to Bill as they were sitting down, "Why does he have to call them that? I mean why can't he just say I want two chicken clubs with everything on them?"

Bill laughed, "I remember how cute you thought it was the first time we came in here." Paula frowned at Bill, and wrinkled up her nose, "Yes, but I didn't wobble in back then either."

Bob walked up and said, "Paula, Mary Ann said to tell you hello, she would come out and speak but we're kind of backed up in the kitchen right now. Let's see, I ordered you a glass of water, I know how cokes can give you gas when you're getting farther along." Paula put her head in her hands. "Oh, well now, don't worry about that. Why, Mary Ann would get gas so badly with the twins."

Mary Ann came out from the back and said. "She's not deaf either, but if you don't shut up and get back here and help me, Father Grissom is going to be doing a funeral."

Bill just waved Bob off before they had to see Mary Ann kill him. "Was he always like that?" Paula asked.

Bill was still chuckling, "Yes, and no one thought those two would ever make it, but they are just right for each other."

"Yeah," Paula said, "she's big enough to beat him up."

* * * * *

Angelia York was working her shift at the fire station. George Lackey wasn't in today due to a bad head cold he had. Angelia was going to get off for dinner soon, "I can run by and pick up some soup and take it to George before my break is over." Angelia liked George a lot, but his staying out of church and not wanting to talk to her about what was troubling him put a wall up between them. "Maybe if I can reach out to him, then George will be able to open up and share with me what has been troubling him."

George lay in bed wishing he felt better. He wished he knew why things never seemed to work out for him. But that wasn't the reason he held Angelia at a distance. He was afraid if he opened up to her then everything would blow up in his face again. She might find out about him.

* * * * *

DJ and Maggie were just finishing their time of worship. Maggie noticed how DJ had become quiet while they were singing. "Is everything ok, DJ?" Maggie asked. "Yeah, everything is fine. I was just wondering about next school year for Bill's workload. You know he is going to have a lot on him, with the baby coming and all."

DJ didn't want to worry Maggie, but while they were singing he felt this heaviness setting over him. He knew something was wrong, but he didn't know where it was coming from or when it would arrive. Maggie felt it too, but she wasn't going to let DJ know how much she knew. He would only worry more about her if he knew just how much she was feeling too. Maggie walked out of the room behind DJ, but the feeling was still there, the kind of feeling you get right before a big storm hits. It was coming, and it was coming soon.

* * * * *

Mable King walked into Bob's place. "Hey Bob, get me something to go. I need to get back to the store."

Bob came out, "Hey Mable, why don't you sit for a while, and enjoy a meal. I have never seen anyone who works as hard as you, and besides, if anyone needs anything, they'll wait."

Mary Ann came out and gave Mable a big hug around the neck. "Mable, please take a little time to enjoy your meal. You do work so hard."

Mable threw her hands up. "Ok, ok; I know when to give in. I'll stay, but just long enough to eat and then I have to get back to work."

Most people wouldn't know it, but Mable was about the best plumber you would find anywhere. She also wasn't that bad as a finish carpenter either. At forty two, Mable stood five feet five inches tall. Her long brown hair and green eyes were always the talk of the town. Although Mable attended Friendship Baptist Church, she was known to go over to the Catholic Church to hear the hand bell choir. "It's not the name on the door," she always said, "but what a person has in his or her heart that counts."

When Mable got back to the hardware store, she found Cindy waiting for her. "Cindy Hawkins, don't tell me that I forgot to pay my dry cleaning bill again?"

"Lord, no, Mable," Cindy said. "We need some work done on our apartment, that's all." "Sure, what kind of work do you need?"

* * * * *

As Cindy walked out of Mable's, she knew Wayne wasn't going to like having a new shower put in the upstairs apartment. But it was about time they did some fixing up, and besides, there was something about

Irina that was pulling at her heart. They were having cold weather, and the girl needed a new shower, and that was all there was to it. Wayne was just going to have to understand. Cindy walked back to the cleaners. It was getting late. She knew they would be closing soon. Cindy couldn't help wondering if Irina had enough food to eat. Maybe she would stop by the store on the way back and pick up a few things. Yes, that is what she would do.

Irina stood in the window watching Cindy leave. She didn't know just what to think about this lady. What did she want from her? Why was she being so nice? Irina was more confused than ever. About that time her cell phone rang, "Hello. Yes, I'm already here in town and I have an apartment. Yes, I have met some people already. In fact, the apartment owner's wife seems to like me. She has been so nice to me. I just don't know what she wants from me."

The voice on the other end was cold, "That's not your concern, you just do what you're told and you will be back with your little girl soon enough. You say the owner's wife likes you? That's good. Now, I want you to get real close to her. Make her think of you as one of her own children. That way when the time is right she will be on your side."

"Are you sure there isn't some other way?"

"I told you that you're not being paid to think, just do what you're told. Or would you rather never find out where your little girl is?"

"No, please, I'll do what you ask, just help me get my daughter back like you promised." The phone call left Irina with this sick feeling, but then talking with that person always had that effect on her.

CHAPTER FOUR

Past Fears

Irina was walking toward the downtown area. It was almost one in the afternoon already, and she didn't want to be late for her first Thursday's meeting. She was hoping no one would see her. She had to report in to her parole officer. This was the one thing her friend forgot about. How was she going to come across so innocent with a parole officer? And why did he have his office in a church of all places? As Irina walked up to St. Paul's Catholic Church, she felt a little strange going inside. It had been years since she had been inside a church, and now her parole officer had his office here. Maybe, she wouldn't have to see the priest. She would just pop in and out. Irina walked in and there mopping the floor was a man she thought to be the janitor. He had on an old pair of pants with an old blue shirt. "Excuse me; I'm looking for a Mr. Grissom."

"Well now, and just what would you be wanting with him?"

Irina rolled her eyes, "I don't think that is any of your business, sir. Now, is he here or should I come back later when he comes in?"

Father David smiled as he looked at Irina. What could she have done that would have landed her in jail. "I guess you must be my one o'clock then, I'm Father Grissom. And I think I'm your parole officer."

Irina's face turned red as she realized that she would have to meet with a priest every week. "I'm sorry, Father, I didn't know you were a priest, I mean"…., flustered, Irina didn't know what to say.

Father Grissom reached out and took her by the arm, "Come on child, let's go into my office where we can talk. The reason I'm dressed like this is because I like to work with my hands and what better way to serve the Lord than by mopping the church?"

Irina sat down in the first chair she came to. She was so nervous. What would she do if word got out and messed up their plans? She might never see her daughter again. Father Grissom could see that Irina was afraid, so when he spoke he tried to put her fears to rest. "Now child, this doesn't have to be a bad time for you."

"But you don't understand Father, I'm trying to get my life back together, and if the people here find out I went to prison, well then, no one will ever trust me."

Shaking his head Father Grissom, said, "No one here is going to judge you child; we're here to help you."

"But why does everyone have to know? Can't I just live my life in peace?" Irina's voice was shaking as she spoke. Tears were filling her eyes and beginning to run down her face.

"I'll tell you what. Why don't you come to church on Sunday morning and if you need to talk with me then we can arrange a time for that. As long as we meet, that's all that matters. If you come by a few minutes before the service, I think I could call that our meeting time and still be on the up and up."

"You, would do that for me?" Irina asked.

"Child, I worked in prison for years before I came here. Why, this was the first church I've pastored that didn't have men with guns standing around in it. But you know when it comes to the time we take up the offering, I wish I had a few then. Maybe I could take in more money for the church that way." Irina was laughing now. She was feeling a little more at ease. "I would like to ask you one thing if you don't mind, Irina? Your file has just arrived, so I haven't had time to read all of it."

"Sure Father, what is it?"

Father Grissom stopped for a minute, "Well, it states here that you.., hmm, well."

"I killed my husband Father, is that what you're trying to say?"

"Yes, you're such a nice girl, what happened, child?"

Irina told Father Grissom as best she could about her marriage. A few times she had to stop for her crying, but when she left there she knew her secret was safe with Father Grissom. "Why, couldn't I just have my daughter, and the both of us live here without having to get involved with Dr. Thomas" she thought. A sick feeling came over her as she walked back to her apartment. She had to do this or risk never seeing her daughter again.

* * * * *

George Lackey was cleaning one of the fire trucks when Zachary Kerr walked up. "Hey man, are you feeling any better from that head cold?"

"Yeah, I don't know how I came down with that. I mean I never get sick."

Zackary patted George on the back, "it's a sign you're getting older, my friend. What you need is a good woman in your life. That would help to pick you up. Now, take Angelia York, she's cute, and she likes firemen."

George turned and walked away without saying a word. He knew he couldn't say anything. He had to keep it hidden. Zachary stood there watching George walking away. "Man, I wish I knew what he was so afraid of. Most men I know would kill to have Angelia liking them, and he acts like he doesn't even know she's alive."

* * * * *

Annette Kerr was at home cleaning house. She had already put up her signs in the Student Hall that she would type papers for anyone. She didn't charge that much and it helped with the bills. Micah was in the first grade, while David was in the second grade. Their oldest son Robert was in the third grade. Annette said that God gave her, her own stairs to climb when He gave them three boys so close together in age. Annette liked living in a small town like Whitworth. Nothing ever happened there. Why, last year there was only one fire and that was someone's field, where a fire got out of hand. She could go to sleep every night without any worries. Whitworth was a sleepy little town. She even had Zachary going to church with her again. They liked going to Christ Community Church, and Pastor Greg Vice was a fine man. He and Zachary had even become good friends.

* * * * *

Father Grissom was sitting in his office later that evening going over his notes on his first meeting with Irina. He had listened to a lot of men in the past tell him how innocent they were, but there was something about this young woman that told him she was telling the truth. He could tell there was something troubling her, something that she was keeping hidden. One thing about secrets like that, Father Grissom thought, "God always has a way of bringing them into the light. Let's see, I think I'll preach on the love of Christ this coming Sunday. I think Irina just might need to hear that message." As Father Grissom was typing his notes, he stopped and just shook his head, "Poor child, she came all the way over here looking for love and found only heartache and jail. That's a far cry from being the Land of Promise. How many lives end up broken because they look to someone or something for love and not from the true source? Irina was like so many today, she looked for love but never realized that love doesn't come from a person, it has to be received from the true source before it can flow out to others. DJ and Maggie were sitting together singing when DJ stopped. "What is it, DJ?" Maggie asked.

"I'm not sure, but someone is coming into our lives soon." DJ looked at Maggie, "they are going to need our help, Love, even though they may be the very one who is going to cause us the most pain."

Maggie put her head next to DJ, "Just as long as we're together, DJ, that's all I ask." "Me too, Love, me too."

* * * * *

Early Friday morning Mable King was knocking at Irina's door. Irina was still half asleep when she came to the door. "Yes, what is it; I mean what do you want?" Mable could see why Cindy liked this young woman. Irina still had a friendly smile, even though she had been through so much.

"Hello, Irina. I'm Mable King, and Cindy asked me to put in a new shower for you." Irina was so confused. Why was Cindy being so nice to her?

"But it works just fine," Irina stated.

"Well, I make my living by running a hardware store and doing odd jobs on the side. I never ask those questions. All I know is that I am suppose to replace the one that is in there with a new one."

Irina stepped back and let Mable into her apartment. Mable knew where the bath was and after taking a few measurements she walked back to the living room. "OK, I have one in my store that will work, so I'll tell you what I am going to do, I will come back tonight after I close my store and I should have it done in a few hours."

As Mable walked out Irina had the feeling that this job wasn't going to be as easy as her friend thought it would be. Already there were more and more people coming into her life. How could she pull this off without going back to jail? Irina picked up her coat and went for a walk. Maybe the fresh air would help her think.

* * * * *

Robert Locklear was a teacher at the University who taught in the English and Literature Department. He had hoped he would get the job of chair for that department, but Dr. Pittman always found a way to fill it for a year or two with someone else. Everyone knew he was trying to keep it open for Bill Thomas. The more Robert thought about it, the madder he got. After all, he wanted that job. Maybe it would open the door for something even better. He had high hopes of getting Dr. Pittman's job when he retired. Now all that was up in smoke. The more Robert sat at his desk and thought about it, the more he hated Bill Thomas. If there wasn't any way he could get the school board to see him as the better choice for department chair rather than Bill Thomas, he just might have to try it again.

* * * * *

Bill stopped by the *Morning Blend* to pick up Jonathan on his way to school. "Hey, we don't need to be late today, you know. This is our last meeting before classes begin on Monday."

"Yeah, I know," Jonathan said as he poured himself and Bill a cup of coffee. "But if we don't have at least one cup of coffee then how are we going to stay awake through the meeting?" Bill laughed, knowing how much Jonathan hated meetings, but even more than that, it was their last weekend before classes resumed. Jonathan looked out the window taking a sip of his coffee.

"What is it?" Bill asked.

"Oh, nothing, well, I saw this girl the other day while I was on campus, oh it's nothing." Bill laughed as he walked up beside his friend. "If you are this quiet about it, then it has to be something. Who is she?"

"Her name is Irina, and I think she is taking one of your classes."

"Yes, I remember her now. She came in wanting me to sign a late slip giving her permission to join my class. I told her I didn't think it was full yet but she said that she didn't want to run the risk of it filling up. She wants to learn more about the writings of C. S. Lewis, so she is taking my class on The Life and Writings of C. S. Lewis."

"Yeah, I wish now I had that class," Jonathan said.

"Now, now my boy," Bill said, trying to sound like Dr. Pittman, "you wouldn't want to get mixed up with one of your students."

"Hey, that's right, maybe it's better this way. You can tell me all you learn about her and that way I will know what she likes."

Bill lifted one eye and looked toward Jonathan. "Ok," Bill said giving in. "What did you say to her? I mean you must have said something that didn't set well with her?"

Jonathan filled Bill in about his first meeting with Irina, Bill laughed more than once at how Jonathan was able to put his foot in his mouth.

One thing that was obvious to him though, he had never seen Jonathan so taken with a woman. Ever since Jonathan came to Whitworth he had stayed away from any woman who might have shown an interest. Bill thought to himself. "This is something I need to really pray about."

* * * * *

May and Fay were both working hard feeding the breakfast crowd. "Fay, did you see Dr. Thomas come in here this morning for breakfast?"

"Nope, I think he must have stopped off at the *Morning Blend* for coffee."

"How in the world can he teach when all he does is drink coffee in the morning?"

"Oh, shush, May, you know Dr. Thomas isn't going to stop coming in here. Why, he has always been one of our very best customers."

May walked out with a plate of pancakes. "I know, but he's about to be a daddy and he needs to take care of himself."

"Well then, why don't you talk to him the next time he's in here?"

May set the plate of pancakes down on the table and started back toward the kitchen. "Well, I will. I'm not afraid to speak up to a friend," she said as she walked through the kitchen door.

Fay just shook her head, "That sister of mine will not mind her own business."

May came out of the kitchen, "I heard that."

* * * * *

Rusty and Teresa Eldridge were walking across the campus together. They weren't saying a lot that morning. There had been another disappointment in their life. One more time, Teresa went to the doctor only to find out that it was a false alarm. "Are we ever going to have a child, Rusty?"

Rusty knew how much Teresa wanted a baby. He did too. But with each disappointment, it seemed Teresa was getting more and more down in her own spirit. She wasn't laughing as she used to. He put his arm around her and held her close to him. "I'm sure it will happen in good time, dear. Besides, you mean more to me then ten kids."

Teresa stopped walking, "But I want to have a child of my own. You don't understand how much it means to me. Women are made different than men. It means more to us!"

Rusty turned Teresa around so that he could look into her eyes. "My dear, nothing would make me happier than to have a child with you. And I do believe it will happen in God's time, but we can't let this tear us apart."

Teresa tried to hold back the tears. "Yes, but when will that be? I can't wait forever." They stood there and just held each other for a moment before heading on to the meeting. Rusty knew his wife's heart. He knew she was hurt over the news, but he also knew she would bounce back. She always did, and she would this time as well. Little did he realize the depth of pain she was carrying. Her desire for a child had grown so that she was allowing it to blind her to the point that the Enemy could come in and cause them trouble down the road.

CHAPTER FIVE

Staff Meeting at Nine

Dr. Pittman was waiting for everyone to show up for the staff meeting. He knew that there would be one or two people who would be late. He had already heard about of Rusty and Teresa's disappointment, so if they showed up a little late that would be understandable. As Dr. Pittman stood at the window looking out over the open courtyard, he saw Shirley Crowe walking toward his building. He had worked with Shirley for years, and she was one of the best librarians he had ever met. Shirley had her gray hair pulled back into a bun, and she was walking as fast as her short legs could carry her. She could never tolerate any student playing around in the library, nor did she allow any noise there either. She had three very simple rules: One, walk in quietly, and two, don't make any noise after you are in the building. Her last rule was an all out must, you must take care of every book you check out and return it in the same condition. Dr. Pittman chuckled as he thought about the time Shirley had a student who was six feet tall, backed up to the wall shaking her finger in his face telling him that he was not going to break any of her rules. Shaking his head, Dr. Pittman thought, "I could have sworn that boy was just about to start crying when I got there."

* * * * *

Coming from across the other side of the courtyard was Philip and Polly Blanks. Polly worked in the library with Shirley. She was a little bit nervous when she was around Shirley. Philip was a fine music teacher who loved classical music and old rock & roll. Philip always said that the first time he saw Polly with her black hair blowing in the wind, and her grey eyes, that her beauty took his heart captive, and he just had to marry her. Polly was only an inch shorter than Philip. She stood five feet and four inches tall, but it was his constant teasing her about how much taller he was than her that finally won her over. Polly loved running her hands through Philip's reddish brown hair, but it was his sad puppy dog brown eyes that she loved the most.

* * * * *

Jerome Reinhart had lived in Whitworth all his life. He was five feet and ten inches tall, with black hair that was peppered with gray. Jerome had his Ph. D in music composition and theory. He had taught at the university for twenty years, and was a good friend of Dr. Pittman's. Annie was walking beside her husband. Annie was an art teacher who still loved to paint and draw. She stood only five feet three inches tall. She said it was Jerome's blue eyes that she loved most about him.

* * * * *

Chip Corey had only been teaching art for about eight years. He was thirty-one years old, and not married. But Nita Cotton had caught his eye for sure. The first day Nita walked on campus she caught Chip's eye, but what he didn't know was, that he had caught hers as well. Nita's red hair and hazel eyes seemed to brighten her face every time she smiled at you. Chip had stood more than once not knowing what to say when she asked him a question. But what Nita liked about Chip, besides the way he kept falling all over himself every time she was around, was his blue eyes and brown hair. Already she had thought about how their children might look, that is if Chip could ever get up enough nerve to ask her out on a date. Nita was a faithful Christian, and all she wanted was to fall in love and have a family. She was hoping Chip just might be the right man.

* * * * *

Rebekah Corey was one of the science teachers at Whitworth. Chip's dad had died a few years before, leaving Rebekah and Chip alone. Rebekah had gray hair that lightly touched her shoulders, and her blue eyes would shine when she smiled. Chip was always proud that he had his mother's eyes, but he did wish he was taller than she was. Rebekah stood five feet seven inches tall, while Chip was five feet six inches tall. That one inch was something Rebekah loved teasing her son about. She would always remind him that she was the tallest one in the family, so he had better listen. But what she loved the most was watching Chip fall over his words every time Nita came close to him. Rebekah laughed to herself one day as she watched Chip just almost choke trying to get his words to come out right. "Yeah, he's that much like his dad." Rebekah liked Nita and thought she would make a good wife for Chip, but even more a good daughter-in-law for her.

As everyone was filing in, Dr. Pittman looked for Bill and Jonathan. Now where could those two be this morning? Just about the time the meeting was getting started, in walked Bill and Jonathan. "Well, well," Dr. Pittman said. "I have your two seats waiting for you as he pointed to the two seats on the front row." Bill turned and whispered to Jonathan

41

as they were sitting down, "I told you we didn't have time for the third cup of coffee."

Jonathan chuckled, "Teacher's pet," he whispered back to Bill.

* * * * *

Irina was standing off to the side of one of the buildings as she watched Bill and Jonathan walk into the Administrative Offices. There was something about Jonathan that drew Irina, but she knew all too well that she couldn't allow her feelings to get in the way of what she had to do. If there was just the slightest hope of getting her daughter back, then she would walk through fire if she had to. Standing by Lewis Hall, Irina could watch as teachers showed up, but she wasn't seen by them. Irina hated living this lie. She had lived with a man who lied to her, and then beat her when she would ask him any questions. And now, she found herself following down the same path. But, she reminded herself, she was doing it for her daughter. She had a good cause to act this way, or so she thought. Isn't it funny how we can justify anything when it's what we want to do? As she stood there like stone, her cell phone rang, "Hello, yes, I'm here at the school watching what is happening. They are in a meeting of some kind is all. Why?"

* * * * *

Leander Philips was minding the store while his wife Sandy was out. They both worked at the drugstore together, and when the day came that their daughter was ready to take over the business, they were going to turn it over to her. Sandy was walking down past St. Paul's Catholic Church when she ran into Vickie Eldridge. "Vickie, Hi, how's your mom?"

Vickie pushed her hair back out of her face, her blue eyes sparkling as she smiled at Sandy. "Oh my mom is just doing fine. Why, just the other day she was telling me that she needed to call you."

Sandy slowed down her pace as she walked. "Tell you what I'll do, I'll head over there right now and pay her a visit."

Vickie waved her hand as she picked up her pace, "I know she'll love that. I have to run now. I have to get back to work."

Sandy watched Vickie as she hurried on toward the hospital. "I hope that young lady can find herself a nice husband some day."

* * * * *

Irina was walking back into town again. She was upset after receiving the phone call. How did the person seem to know just when to call? It was as if she was being watched. With that thought, she stopped in her tracks. Her hand went up to her face. Yes, that had to be it. She was being watched. Fear seemed to grip her. She started to tremble. "Oh God, who have I gotten hooked up with, and will they even keep their promise to me?" Not knowing what to do, Irina just kept on walking. She didn't know where she was going or why, she just walked. It was then that she found herself at the door of the *Morning Blend*. Without knowing who owned the cafe, Irina walked inside. The young girl behind the counter was sitting down reading a book. "Oh, hello, and do come in. Why, I haven't seen anyone all morning. What can I get you to drink?"

Darlene Chisolm worked at the *Morning Blend* on days when she didn't have morning classes. But since school hadn't started yet, she was trying to get as many hours in as she could. Irina stood there, not knowing what to say. She thought this was just some kind of bookstore that she could hide in for a while. "I don't have a lot of money right now," she said. "Well, to be truthful, I don't really have any money. I'm still looking for work."

Darlene just threw her hand up and said, "Don't worry about the money, I'll buy you a latte if you'll stay in here and talk to me. Why, I get homesick, and I just wish for someone to talk to who understands what it means to miss home." Irina eyes filled up with tears. That was the one thing she did understand. She missed her family and home, but she knew she could never go back now. Darlene walked out from the back of the counter. "Don't cry, all I meant was that I could tell by your accent that you weren't from around here, that's all."

Irina wiped the tears from her eyes and laughed a little. "No, I'm from the Ukraine, and there are times I miss my home so badly that I feel sick inside."

Darlene made Irina a latte and they sat down and just talked for a while. It was the closest thing to feeling at home that Irina had felt in years. She enjoyed just sitting there and talking with Darlene. "Hey, tell you what," Darlene said.

"What?" Irina looked up not knowing what she was going to say next.

"Well, you're looking for some part time work while you go to school, and my boss is looking to hire someone else. So, what about it? Do you think you could handle work in a coffee shop?"

Irina threw her hands up over her mouth. "Do you think he would hire me?"

"I just did," Darlene said. "I was told to find someone and it looks like you got the job." For the next hour Darlene was showing Irina how to make all the different latte and cappuccino drinks. Irina laughed at Darlene as they worked together. She hadn't allowed herself to get close to anyone in years. Now she felt like she might have found a good friend.

"Do you think your boss will mind you hiring me?" Irina asked. "Why don't you ask him yourself? Here he is." The door opened and Irina turned around. Her heart stopped for a moment. There stood Jonathan, the man who had so stirred her heart.

"Hey boss, look who I hired to work here."

Jonathan just smiled, "Welcome to the *Morning Blend*, Irina, I hope you'll like working here while you attend classes."

* * * * *

Paula was getting ready to head into town so she could go to the store. Maggie was sitting by her side just watching her and wanting so badly to ask if they could go with her. "Maggie, why are you sitting there staring at me?"

Maggie put her head down, "I wasn't aware I was staring at you, Paula. I was just sitting in here with you, but if you want me to leave?"

Paula felt so bad that she had spoken that way to Maggie. "No, I don't want you to leave, it's just, well, I can't explain it but sometimes I can't control how I feel."

"You're pregnant," DJ blurted out.

Maggie gave DJ one of her 'watch it' looks. "Boys, they never do understand what girls go through."

Paula was laughing by now. "Well, I guess he is just calling it as he sees it, Maggie. And let's face it, I am at that."

Paula walked toward the door heading out, when Maggie spoke up. "Could we go along too? I mean no one would even notice us."

Paula reached down and patted Maggie on the head. "Now tell me again, just how are we going to get you two in the store without anyone noticing either of you?"

"Oh, ok, I see your point. Come on DJ, let's go in here by the fireplace and just wait like we always do. I mean we can pray or do something to make ourselves useful."

Paula shook her head. Here was Maggie, she thought, taking up DJ's habits. "It's cold outside, so I guess it wouldn't hurt, if ya'll stay in the car. The ride and fresh air would do you good."

DJ just barked and said "I knew that would get her, Maggie."

Maggie bumped into DJ. "Well, thanks for keeping it to yourself."

Paula opened the door. "Let's go before you two start something."

* * * * *

Paula didn't notice the car parked down the road, nor could she have seen the person inside the car. But inside the car was her worst fears come true. "It won't be long, and I'll turn your pretty little world upside down. And you will never know who did it to you, or why. I won't stop until I destroy you and everyone you love." Once a soul has given itself over to hatred, the darkness that takes over is hard for someone to understand unless they have walked there themselves. The sad thing is that few who walk this path ever find their way back home again. They can't find it without help, but you have to want help first.

CHAPTER SIX

The Day Before

It was early Sunday morning, and DJ and Maggie were in the living room by the fireplace quietly worshipping. "You know DJ," Maggie said, "I think this is a good idea. I mean, our getting up early to spend time worshipping before we watch church on TV. It helps to prepare our hearts for the service."

DJ shook his head in agreement. "Yeah, and it gives me one more time to hear your sweet voice sing." Maggie walked over and lightly pushed DJ. "You can be so sweet when you want to be." Maggie stood there for a moment not saying anything. When she looked up, DJ could see such sadness in her face. "What is it, Love?"

Maggie put her head down again, "I'm too ashamed to tell you. It's too awful. You'll think badly of me."

DJ walked over and put his face next to Maggie's. "There is nothing in this world that could ever make me think badly of you, my Love."

"Oh DJ," Maggie sighed. "It's Paula and her baby. I'm so ashamed of myself, DJ, but I get jealous.

Maggie looked up at DJ. "I'm not saying that I would rather have been with any other guardian, DJ, I love you, and living with you has been my greatest joy. But I would have loved to have given you some pups, and maybe even some guardians you could have trained."

DJ knew Maggie was broken hearted over that fact, and he knew that it was coming from her love for him. "I would have loved to have had pups with you, my Love, and they would have been very beautiful, as well as smart." DJ just stood for a few moments with his face next to Maggie's. She loved him more than she knew how to say. He was her life, and living with him had been her greatest joy. "Now," DJ finally spoke up, "since I think Bill and Paula have overslept, it's our duty to go and wake them up in time to go to church." DJ smiled at Maggie. "Are you with me?"

Maggie grinned. "What are you up to?"

"Just follow my lead," DJ said. With that they both raced down the hallway and ran into Bill and Paula's room, barking as loudly as they could. Then DJ yelled out, "Bill, it's Monday morning, and you have overslept for work."

Bill jumped out of bed. "Oh my goodness, I can't be late on the first day. Why didn't you two wake me sooner?"

About that time, it dawned on Paula what day it really was. And there was Bill running around the room like a chicken with his head cut off, not knowing what to do. Paula just bursted out into laughter, "Bill, they got you good this time, honey. It's still Sunday morning, dear."

Bill just stood there not knowing what to say. "Oh, very funny, give a man a heart attack. I'm glad you all find this so very funny."

DJ, and Maggie were both laughing, Paula was sitting up in bed laughing so hard she got up and ran to the bathroom. "What's the matter?" Bill asked.

"Oh nothing, I was just about to wet all over myself from laughing so hard, that's all."

* * * * *

Irina walked into St. Paul's Catholic Church. Father Grissom was waiting for her in his office. As she knocked on his door, he spoke, "Come on in my child, the door is open."

How was Irina going to tell this priest that she was falling in love? How could she keep from him the darkest secret in her life? As she walked into his office, Irina silently prayed within her own heart. "*Пожалуйста бог, помогает мне получить мою дочь назад.*" "Please God; help me get my daughter back."

* * * * *

It was half pass nine when Curtis walked outside the fire station. He never went to church. His life was filled with bitterness, and he had never let it go. His wife had left him for another man, and as far as he was concerned, it was God's fault.

Angelia York was pulling her shift, but if things looked like they were going to be slow, and it usually always was on Sunday, Curtis would from time to time allow her to leave and attend church. "Curtis? Do you think it would be ok if I went to church this morning? I'll be right back, and if you need me."

"Yeah," Curtis said, not giving her time to finish. "Just hurry back." Angelia hugged Curtis around the neck. "Thank you." She was headed toward her car when she ran into George Lackey. "Hey, George, Curtis said I could take off and attend church. I'm sure he wouldn't mind you going with me."

George just snapped at Angelia. "If I wanted to go I would go, but I don't."

Angelia thought that if George could just go with her one time, maybe he would forget whatever it was that was troubling him. "I won't mind asking him for you."

George turned around and just snapped. "I said no!"

It wasn't just his tone of voice, but the look on his face that cut her to the very deepest place in her heart. Hurt and angry, Angelia just yelled back. "Well, fine then, don't go you hardheaded fool."

With that she ran out of the station toward her car. As she was pulling out, Angelia looked up and saw George standing there with the saddest look on his face. He mouthed the words, "I'm sorry." Held up his hands and walked away.

Angelia couldn't help but wonder what it was that was eating at him so. It was like every time he let his guard down, he would pull it back again. He wasn't letting anyone in. "How long God, do I keep reaching out to him, and why do I feel this way toward him?"

* * * * *

Harry Pittman was still in bed. He was having pain in his chest again, but he wasn't about to tell Clara. "Lord, please give me two more years. That's all it should take to get everything ready for Bill to take over. That's all I need."

Clara walked into the room. "Why haven't you gotten up? Harry! You don't look good. I'm calling the doctor."

"Not now, I'm all right, I was just laying here praying that's all. Tell you what, why don't we stay home today and sleep in. I mean, when was the last time we missed church?"

Clara looked at her husband. "You know it was when Bill and Paula were in the hospital. Before that, you haven't missed in over twenty years."

Dr. Pittman pulled the covers back, and reached out and took Clara by the hand. "Well then, don't you think it's time we stay home together?"

As they laid there, Harry Pittman fell asleep, Clara held on to him and silently cried. "God, why is my husband so hardheaded, and prideful? I know it's his heart, and he needs to go to the doctor. Well, if he won't go, then, I'll go and talk to the doctor myself." Clara only had a few faults, and one of them was that she loved Harry Pittman more than her next breath. She wasn't about to sit around and do nothing. Tomorrow she was going to the hospital and talk with the doctor for herself. This way she knew he would have to do something.

* * * * *

Rusty was getting ready for church when he called out to Teresa. "Honey, are you still in bed?" Teresa hadn't moved since Rusty got up an hour earlier. She had tried to pray, but every time she did, the pain became so unbearable. "What's the use of going to church anymore she thought, God isn't going to answer my prayers. He just sits up and there finds all this funny somehow. I guess making me cry is going to help me grow in some way. I'm just tired of it all."

Rusty walked into the room. "Honey, you're going to be late for Sunday school if you don't go ahead and get up."

Teresa just rolled over in bed and turned toward to wall. "I'm not going today, ok?"

Rusty started to speak, but something inside told him that now wasn't the time to speak. He walked over and put his arms around her. Teresa tried to pull away, but Rusty held on. "No," he whispered, "I'm not going to let you build a wall between us"

Teresa turned and looked at Rusty. Tears were running down her face uncontrollably. "Why don't you go and find you a wife who can give you what you want? You know you want children as much as I do. So why don't you just leave me and find someone else?"

Teresa words were like a knife going through Rusty's heart. He tried to speak, but the words didn't seem to come out. He felt the hot tears running down his own face. He stood and turned to walk out of the room. Never had Teresa said anything like that to him before. He had never heard her use that tone before. It sounded as if she hated him. As he reached the door, he felt her arms wrap around him as she broke down and cried even harder. "Oh God, what have I done? Please forgive me, darling. I'm sorry for saying that to you." Rusty turned and together they stood there and cried. They wouldn't attend church that morning. But what Rusty didn't realize was that the pain which caused Teresa's outburst wasn't gone. It was just pushed a little deeper into her heart; Rusty was going to have to face this monster again.

* * * * *

Bill turned as he was walking out the door. "Now, when I get back, we're going to have to have a little talk about this morning."

"What!" DJ said.

Maggie started giggling, "Well, it was funny. I mean watching you run around the room not knowing what to do next."

"See, that is what we're going to talk about. You two, and your Sunday morning tricks."

Paula reached out and took Bill by the arm. "Come on dear, you loved it just as much as they did. Your only problem is that you weren't able to pull it on me."

Bill smiled, "Well, I can't now, but maybe later."

Paula pitched Bill's arm. "How dare you stand there and act like you're going to fuss at those sweet little darlings, knowing good and well that if you had thought of it, you would have gotten them to help you pull the same trick on me."

Maggie just shook her head in agreement. "Yeah, he would too. He's just the type."

Bill's mouth fell open, "I guess I know who my true friends are."

Paula pitched Bill's arm again. "Now, what's that for?"

"For..., well, I can't think of a reason right now."

DJ smirked, "How about because he would use us to help him. Which would be causing us to be bad?"

Maggie thought to herself. "That boy opened his mouth and put all four of his feet right in."

"Caused!" Paula said. Feeling her emotions starting to give way, "why you two would have jumped on that idea without giving it a second thought."

DJ turned and looked at Maggie as if to say, "What did I say wrong?"

Getting up, Maggie walked back toward the den where they listened to church. "Come on DJ, now you've gone and hung all of us with that statement."

Bill reached over and kissed Paula. "Hey," he said, "We're all just playing with you."

"Oh, I know. It's just sometimes I can't control my own emotions."

Bill pulled Paula closer to him. "It will get better I promise you. And after the baby is born, you'll be back to your old self again."

"I would watch how I use that word old if I were you, mister." Laughing they walked to the car. Neither of them noticed the car parked down the road, watching every move they made, hating every moment of their happiness, looking and waiting for the right time to tear their world apart.

* * * * *

Robert Lee Locklear was sitting in his office. He worked harder than anyone else at this school. He should be the head of the English and Literature Department. Bill Thomas should have stayed away. Why couldn't he have stayed in the bottle anyway? Why was he thrown free from the car? If he had been wearing his seatbelt like he was supposed to be, then everything would be just perfect right now. It took months to plan, and then it didn't turn out right. But if Bill had stayed away, it would have still been just as good. But no, he had to pick himself up and come back. The same thing wouldn't work again. How could he get rid of Bill this time?

* * * * *

Angelia was sitting in University Baptist Church. She was trying to listen to pastor Frank Robbins preach, but all that kept going through her mind was George. "Why was he the way he was? And what was he running from that made him keep everyone around him at arm's length? "It seemed that the more she reached out to George the more he tried to hurt her. The song director stood and told everyone which page to turn to for the closing hymn. Angelia was upset with herself. "Here I have sat through church and I couldn't tell you one thing the pastor said." As she drove back to the station, Angelia made up her mind that she was through with George Lackey. "If he wants to die an old man and all alone, then let him. It's time I move on with my life." Now all she had to do was to live up to that promise to herself.

* * * * *

Dr. Travis Null was making his rounds that Sunday morning. He didn't mind it when it was his time to pull a Sunday. Sundays were always quiet. He remembered one Sunday that he read most of the day. He made his rounds and then he went to the break room. He told the nurses where to find him if they needed him and he just sat back and read the whole day. It embarrassed him when Vickie Eldridge came in and said that he had stayed past his shift, but this morning he knew that she was working the morning shift. He had planned on seeing her if he could. Vickie worked hard at her job. She liked what she did, and when it came to taking care of her patients, Vickie gave everything she had into her job. That was the one thing Travis liked about Vickie. She put her heart into her work. Vickie was coming out of a room when Travis walked up behind her. "Good morning Vickie. I see you have the Sunday morning shift as well."

Vickie smiled. "Yes, it's my turn, but I don't mind. I do miss going to church and sitting there teasing my sister and her husband, but I'm sure they will make it through the day without me."

Travis knew all too well about Vickie's teasing. Dr. Howard was one of his best friends. Travis grinned, "Yeah, I'm not sure they'll miss you teasing them while the sermon is going on though."

Vickie's face turned red. "What did they tell you?"

"Oh, nothing, but I don't think I would have had the nerve to do that in church. I mean even though no one else knew about it, still, it was in church."

Vickie threw her hands over her face, "Oh my God. I'm going to kill my brother-in-law."

"Who said he was the one who told me?"

Vickie turned and walked away as fast as she could. Travis laughed as he watched her duck into a room. Now Howard was going to owe him big time. Howard never told him what she did. All he said was for Travis to act as if he knew. That would be enough to make Vickie's face turn red. Tomorrow Howard was going to tell Vickie that they never told Travis anything, but now, how was he going to keep from having to tell her himself. Howard had finally gotten the best of his sister-in-law. Maybe her days of pulling pranks were over.

* * * * *

Jonathan Wedgeworth was walking home from church, which was something he did almost every Sunday that the weather permitted. He was walking through the park heading toward the Heartland Grill. Jonathan was glad that May and Fay opened the Grill for the Sunday after church crowd. They went in early and got most of the things ready, but then hurried there from church to add the finishing touches. Jonathan liked walking through the park on Sunday afternoon like this. Most people were either at home or headed somewhere else. It gave him the park all to himself. As he was getting close to his own place of business where he would cross the street and head toward the grill, he saw Irina walking toward him. She had her head down so she didn't notice him standing there.

"Hello, Jonathan called out. "How about you joining me for lunch today?"

Irina stopped and looked up. Why did she have to run into Jonathan now?

"Oh no, I couldn't. I mean that wouldn't be right, seeing as how I work for you."

Jonathan laughed at the way Irina looked so nervous. Was it possible that it even made her more beautiful? "Tell you what. Why don't we just forget that you work for me today and that way you can have lunch with me. I get kind of lonely eating by myself all the time."

There it was that look of sadness that came across his eyes. It wasn't there always, but she knew it was there, deep inside of him. Irina opened her mouth to say no, but heard herself telling him that she would love to.

Jonathan reached out and took her hand in his. For just a second, Irina almost pulled away. But then she felt that spark, it shot right through her heart. Why was she falling for this man? Wasn't he just like all the rest? However, Irina found herself taking hold of Jonathan's hand, and in that one act, she felt a warmth that she thought no longer existed.

*　*　*　*　*

Parked up the road by the University Baptist Church, a pair of eyes was watching with pure excitement. "What luck, if that little slut gets Bill's best friend to fall in love with her, I'll be able to not only tear his marriage apart, but cause him to lose his best friend to boot. Who said you can't have your cake and eat it too?" Slowly the car drove away. There were going to have to be careful plans made here. Irina didn't know she was being set up to go back to jail, which didn't matter anyway. She was only a player in the game. Bill was the one to get even with. Now he was going to pay for all the trouble he had caused.

CHAPTER SEVEN

Bill was trying to hurry as he went through the house making sure he didn't forget anything. Paula stood back watching him work himself up into a frenzy double checking everything. "Dear, I think you have checked everything about three or four times already."

Bill stopped what he was doing, and sighed, "I know, but if the two, whom I won't mention, hadn't scared ten years off my life yesterday I might not be doing this now."

DJ was sitting there watching Bill run around the house. He looked at Maggie after Bill's comment, "Now, Maggie, please tell me again, just how is all of this our fault? I mean, we both knew yesterday was Sunday when we woke up, so why didn't Bill?"

Bill stopped again, and looked at Paula as if he was wanting her to come to his aid. Paula threw up her hands and said, "I have to stay with these two all day. No sir, you're not going to get me in the middle of this. It seems, they have acquired some of Rocky's traits."

Maggie stood up and said, "Come on, DJ. Now they are just being mean."

"But Maggie," DJ said. "I liked Rocky so there isn't anything wrong with taking on some of his traits. He was my friend."

Maggie kept walking toward the living room, "Well, if you need a friend so badly, I'll buy you a pet rock."

Bill stood there laughing at both of them. "Sounds like you had better go in there and make it up to her."

"Yeah, but what did I say that was wrong?"

Paula reached down and rubbed DJ's ear. "You called Rocky your friend, when you should have said, that he was your second friend because Maggie was that very special friend."

"Women," DJ said. "She knows that's how I feel about her."

"Yes, but when was the last time you told her that." Paula smiled as she spoke to DJ.

DJ shook his head, turned and walked toward the living room. "Maggie, you know how I feel about you. Why are you playing with me this way?"

Bill laughed. "I'm not so sure she's playing with him."

Paula reached over and took Bill by the arm. "You know, I still like to hear that too. I know I am this big cow now…,"

Bill kissed Paula and held her close to him. "No you're not. You're my wife and you are carrying our child. I couldn't be happier."

* * * * *

Wayne Hawkins was opening the cleaners when he saw Irina coming down the side stairs. "Well, good morning, Irina. I hope you like the apartment."

"Oh yes, it so roomy inside. And thank you for putting in the new shower."

"Hmm, oh, yes, think nothing of it." Wayne thought to himself, "Cindy and I are going to have a little talk when she shows up for work today." Wayne knew all too well that Cindy was trying to make Irina fill the emptiness in her heart by taking Irina in. But he was also afraid that it could very well be the thing that could cause her even more pain. He didn't know why, but for some reason, there was just something about Irina that made him feel uneasy. It was as if there was something in the air, much like the smell of rain before it comes in the spring.

Irina walked on by him and was headed toward the campus. She was looking forward to her first day. After yesterday she had almost forgotten why she was even here in the first place. All she could think about was Jonathan. The warmth of his touch still lingered in her mind as she thought about how he took her hand as they walked together. Without realizing it, Irina was falling in love again. She had made the one mistake she should have never made. Now, even that was going to be used against her. Her dreams of happiness were far from coming true. She had joined in with evil, and evil never allows you to just walk away.

*   *   *   *   *

Clara walked into the hospital and asked where Dr. Howard Adcock was. Yolanda Weir, a young black woman, worked behind the information booth. She answered all the incoming calls, and told anyone who needed to know, what room a patient was in. "Good morning Mrs. Pittman. I think Dr. Adcock is in the break room now. You're not sick are you?"

"No, I just needed to speak with him about something, that's all. Thank you for your help."

The last thing Clara wanted was for everyone to know she was at the hospital. She walked into the break room and saw Dr. Adcock sitting there drinking coffee and reading the morning paper. When he saw the look on Clara's face, he put his paper down and stood up to meet her. "What is it, Clara?" You look as if you're about to fall out."

"Oh doctor," and with that Clara broke down and cried.

Dr. Adcock put his arms around her and held onto her as he led her to a chair. "Please sit here and let's start from the beginning."

* * * * *

Nita Cotton had arrived at her room early that Monday morning. She always liked being ready for the new students as they returned to school after the Christmas break. As she was going over her list of new students, she heard footsteps at her door. Chip was standing there trying to figure out what would be the best way to start a conversation.

"Why, good morning Chip," Nita said with a smile. She knew he had times when he just couldn't seem to get his mouth and mind working together. Nita stood and walked toward the blackboard. "Would you mind helping me write some assignments on the board?"

"Yeah, I mean sure, hum, ok." Chip walked over to Nita and took the chalk from her hand. It was as their hands touched that Chip's heart seemed to jump ten feet high. He knew this was the woman he wanted to marry. He only needed to get past his fear of saying something that would make him look stupid. This was what he was doing every time he got around Nita and couldn't get his words out in the right order. Chip was lucky Nita thought it was sweet, and that it made him look even more like the man she had been looking for.

As Nita handed Chip the chalk, she walked toward the door. "Hey, where are you going?" Chip asked.

"Oh, I have to run down to the office for a minute, if you can't help me…,"

"No," Chip said with a smile. "I'll be glad to help you, Nita."

Nita walked out the door and slipped her shoes off. She quietly stepped back and peeked into the room. There was Chip writing as fast as he could. He had to be in his own class before the students showed up. When Nita put her shoes back on she turned around and there was

Rebekah Corey. "Why good morning Nita, I thought I saw my son walk into your room a minute ago."

"Why yes, Mrs. Corey, he did and he is helping me while I go to the hmm, office for a minute."

Rebekah peeked into the room and saw Chip writing as if the world was coming to an end. "Hmm, it seems to me that you are pulling something over on my son."

Nita sheepishly looked down at the floor. "Every time he comes around me he just mumbles something I can't hear, or he falls all over himself trying to talk to me. So, I thought that maybe if I put him to work and walked away, he'd get his nerve up to speak to me."

Rebekah looked at Nita and smiled. "He will. It worked on his father, although, it did take a few times before he found his ability to speak."

Nita's mouth fell open. "You mean you pulled the same thing on Chip's dad?"

Rebekah turned and walked away. "Yes, I did, and it worked like a charm. Chip is just like his father, so I hope you realize what a good young man you are going to get."

"Oh, I do." Nita said.

Rebekah stopped and walked back to Nita and put her arms around her. "And if this thing between you two works out, then I will get a wonderful daughter also." Rebekah lightly kissed Nita on the cheek. She turned and walked away heading toward her own room. Nita stood there not knowing what to say. Everyone knew Rebekah Corey as a no nonsense type person around the school.

Without thinking about what she was doing, Nita ran back into her room. "Chip, you won't believe what just happened."

Rebekah smiled as she walked away. "Yeah", she mused, "Young people, they were so predictable."

* * * * *

Curtis was driving into the fire station that he knew all too well, and today was the first day of classes resuming again. It always put him in a bad mood. He hated the school and he wouldn't care if it burned to the ground. Every time he thought about the school he saw his wife, falling in love with another man. The anger would burn within him so that there were times he felt like maybe he needed to move to another city to live. Curtis was afraid that one day his anger would take control of him and he would do something he would regret for the rest of his life. He got out of his car; maybe if he got busy he would forget what that school did to him. Curtis had his own secret that he had kept hidden for years, no one knew about it and they never would.

* * * * *

Kim walked into the break room. She saw her husband standing there looking out the window. "Honey, was that Mrs. Pittman I saw leaving?"

"Is Travis in yet?" Howard inquired, looking as if he had to leave that instant.

"Why yes, he arrived just a moment ago. Why?"

"Tell him that I am going to have to leave the hospital for a little while and that he needs to be ready in case something happens while I am gone."

Kim walked to her husband's side. "Sweetie, what's troubling you so?"

Howard looked into his wife's eyes and saw the look of concern. "I can't talk about it right now, but I promise, I'll fill you in just as soon as I can." With that he kissed Kim, and walked out. Kim knew something was troubling Howard, but she also knew that he had asked her to do something for him and she never let him down. She walked down the hall to where she had seen Dr. Travis earlier.

* * * * *

Dr. Pittman was sitting behind his desk. He had gotten up early that morning so that he could get as much work done as possible. He always loved walking around the campus the first day the students were back in class. His phone rang. "Yes, Oh yes, send the good doctor right in."

Dr. Pittman was wondering why Dr. Howard was there. It was so unlike him. In fact he never remembered him coming on the campus for any reason. The door opened and in walked Dr. Howard. His face had a look about it that spoke volumes. "Dr. Howard, what on earth is troubling you, sir?"

"I'll tell you what's troubling me. It's an old fool who is breaking his wife's heart, that's what troubles me."

Before Dr. Pittman could give his defense, Howard said, "I have already spoken to most of the board members and as it stands right now, you are on sick leave until I give you a clean bill of health."

Dr. Pittman reached for the phone. "There has to be a mistake here, where is my wife?"

Howard reached over and took the phone out of Dr. Pittman's hand. "My car is outside sir. You'll ride back to the hospital with me."

Harry Pittman was angry with Clara for going to Dr. Howard without telling him. What he was really angry about was the fact that he had been caught, and now he was afraid he wouldn't be able to see his plans through.

* * * * *

Jonathan was walking in Lewis Hall when he looked up and saw Irina walking across the campus heading toward the library. He watched to see if she would look his way, and as soon as she did he waved at her. Irina waved back and smiled. Bill was getting out of his car in the parking lot and he saw Jonathan and Irina waving at each other. "Hey," he said. "What was that all about?"

Jonathan just smiled at his friend. "You know I'm not the one to kiss and tell."

"What? Did you take her out on a date? When did all this happen? Man, come on talk to me."

Jonathan smiled as he walked into the building. Bill was still standing in the parking lot by his car. He yelled out, "I told you about Paula being pregnant." Bill looked around and saw students walking by laughing under their breath and pointing at him. "Well now, if this just isn't going to be dandy, I can hear the students now. There goes the nutty professor."

Jonathan wasn't in the mood to talk to anyone about taking Irina out to eat yesterday. Even though they only shared a meal together, something happened inside his heart. Jonathan wasn't aware of it yet, but the springs of love had already begun to reopen in his heart once more. No, this was something he was going to keep to himself as long as he could.

* * * * *

Cindy walked into the Cleaners to a room full of people. It seemed everyone in town wanted their clothes cleaned. She quickly came around and started helping Wayne fill out tickets for everyone's clothes. "I'm sorry. I was late getting here this morning. I don't know what happened to the time."

"Well, maybe if you weren't so busy having new showers put in the apartment upstairs, you'd know what time it was."

Cindy stopped and looked at Wayne, "I was going to tell you about it, but it just slipped my mind. Besides that shower was old, and needed to be replaced."

"I checked it two weeks before Irina moved in and it worked just fine. So, please tell me why on earth you had a new one put in?"

"Wayne, she's alone with no family here. Someone needs to look out for that girl."

She ain't no girl. She is a grown woman and every time you go out and take in some stray, you always end up getting hurt."

Cindy's eyes filled with tears. She put down the clothes she was filling out tickets for. Wayne shook his head. "Now come on mama, you know what I mean."

Cindy yelled back at him. "Stop, calling me that, I ain't anybody's mama, and I never will be." With that she ran out the door leaving Wayne alone with a room full of people, including Alma Smith and Christine Gully. Why on earth did they have to be in here today of all days? The whole incident might as well have been on the evening news.

* * * * *

Dr. Howard walked back to where Clara was waiting. "Clara, we were able to open two of the main arteries, but I don't know how long it will last. Harry needs surgery. Why did you come to me and then tell me if I could do anything other than surgery, to do it instead?"

"Clara spoke softly, "Because I love that old fool more than my own life, and I know what he is working toward. I know what he is planning, and if this will buy him the time he needs, then by all means let's do it."

"Well, it's done now, but I just want to go on record as telling you that I think you made a big mistake."

Clara walked into the recovery room. Harry Pittman was laying there so still it seemed. As she walked up to his bedside he asked, "What did the doc find?"

"You'll get to go home tomorrow, and you should be able to go back to work in a few weeks, but light work only. The doctor said that you should take it easy for a while. Then you could go back to your daily routine. You need surgery, but he was able to open the arteries so that you won't have to have it right now."

"Why didn't he go ahead and do the surgery today?"

Clara's voice cracked as she spoke. "Because I told him to buy you as much time as he could, so you can do everything you need to do and get it done now. Then you are going to have this surgery and come home to me where we are going to grow even older together, do you hear me now, Harry Pittman?"

Dr. Pittman reached out and took Clara's hand. "That's a promise."

* * * * *

Bill drove into the driveway. He was worn out. He could tell it was the first day of classes. He did remember how Irina seemed to be smiling a lot in his class. He was still wondering what Jonathan meant, and whether or not they did indeed go out on a date. He didn't know where Dr. Pittman was today. It was so unlike him not to be walking over the campus and into the classrooms to meet the new students and those who were returning. Everything today seemed to be a little bit off. DJ and Maggie were waiting by the door to hear all about Bill's day. They loved hearing about the new students and about the books that the school was using in each class. DJ told Maggie that he knew Bill was going to buy them some more books to read.

* * * * *

Irina was walking back to her apartment from the Morning Blend when a car pulled up beside her. A voice yelled out, "get in and hurry up about it." Fear filled Irina's heart as she was driven down the back roads of the county. When they came to an old barn, the car stopped. "Get out and go inside." the man ordered. Irina didn't know who this man was, but he seemed to know a lot about her.

As she opened the door there stood the one who brought her here in the first place. "Well, I hope you had a wonderful day at school. But it seems to me that you are losing your focus and that you are forgetting why you are here. I didn't bring you here to jump into bed with that bookstore owner."

Irina felt her face blush. "I haven't been in bed with anyone, do you hear me?" Her voice was getting louder as she spoke.

"If you think you are going to yell at me when I have done so much to help you, well, then good luck finding your daughter and getting her back without my help."

"No," Irina cried. "Please, all I want is to find my daughter." She stood there crying helplessly. Never had she felt so much pain and confusion in her life. Finally she had met a man she could fall in love with, but even that was not within her reach. If she could just get her daughter back…

"So, do we still have a deal?"

The voice was cold and hard. There was no evidence of love ever having been in that heart. Irina only thought she had seen cold, hard people in jail, here before her stood one who cared about nothing or no one. "Yes, we still have a deal." Irina didn't know why, but at that moment, she felt like she had just lost her daughter for good.

Chapter Eight

Irina was walking across the campus Wednesday morning thinking to herself about how it seemed like she always made the same mistakes over and over again. It was as if the path she was on kept her heading in the same direction all the time. "Can I ever get off this path I'm on?" she thought to herself. Irina was like so many in our world today. While she went to church, she didn't understand what it meant to really have peace in her heart. She had never fully given her heart to God, but was always holding back, thinking that maybe just going to church would be enough. Her first day was so happy. Now after her meeting with the person who had promised to help her get her daughter back, it seemed as if a dark cloud had settled over her.

Jonathan had tried talking to her, but she always said she was too busy to talk. Even when he went to the Morning Blend, she was always rushing around cleaning or reading if there wasn't anyone there for coffee. Was her one big mistake going to follow her all the days of her life?

Irina walked into Bill's classroom, the room was already almost full and she had to sit near the front of the room. "Good morning Irina," Bill said as she took her seat. Why was he so nice to her? Why couldn't he be that monster they told her he was? How could she get close enough to him to do what she had to do? She also discovered the other day that his wife was going to have a baby. Irina sat there and bit her bottom lip. What was she going to do?

* * * * *

Dorothy Eldridge was sitting at her desk trying to work on her books. She just couldn't get it out of her mind what had happened Monday morning. Cindy Hawkins came in her store crying so hard that she didn't think she was ever going to stop. Cindy said she was through with Wayne, but Dorothy realized it was only the hurt talking. "Tell me now, what has he done that is so bad that you are going to leave him over it?"

Cindy looked up through tear filled eyes, "He has hurt my feelings for the last time. All I wanted to do was to help the girl who is living in our apartment over the cleaners."

"Oh, I see." said Dorothy, "But if you promise not to get mad at me, may I inject something here?"

"Sure, what is it?" Cindy said drying her eyes.

"Well, it does seem to me that maybe Wayne is only looking out for your own welfare. Now hold on, and don't get upset. Remember the last young girl you took in? Why, she stole over a thousand dollars from you." And you cried for more than a week. See honey, all Wayne is doing is trying to take care of you, even if he isn't being the most sensitive person."

Cindy put her head down. "Have I been taken in that easily before?"

Dorothy reached out and put her arm around her. "All that means is that you have a trusting heart. You just need Wayne to help you not get into trouble these days. Remember, you do live in a different time than when we were growing up."

Cindy sat there and talked with Dorothy for most of the morning. Dorothy just put up her *Not Open for Business* sign and they talked on into the afternoon.

When Cindy did return to the cleaners, she ran into Wayne's arms and cried all over again. "I'm so sorry, dear. Please forgive me."

Wayne brushed her hair back and said, "We needed that new shower in there anyway, and dear; let's try to help this child. Who knows but maybe we can reach this one."

Cindy felt like her prayers had been answered even before she had asked. Dorothy was glad to hear that Cindy and Wayne were on speaking terms again. She knew all it would take was for someone that Cindy trusted to show her how Wayne was only looking out for her and she would run right back home again, which was just what she did; and now it seemed that Wayne had taken leave of his senses as well.

"Oh well, what's the use of living," Dorothy's mother always used to say, "if you can't make a few mistakes along the way."

* * * * *

George Lackey sat up in his bed with cold sweat running down his face. It was the same nightmare that had been plaguing his sleep for years. He sat there with tears running off his face as he tried not to break down and cry, but each time the nightmare appeared, it seemed it was becoming even more real. It was as if he was reliving the incident all over again. If only he had kept his mouth shut. Why did he have to go on and keep mouthing off when he knew better? And what if anyone here ever found out about his past? George got out of bed and poured himself a drink. He knew he was drinking way too much these days, but if he wanted to go back to sleep he would have to drink himself into a stupor. He looked at his watch, thankful today wasn't his shift. He sat in a chair and started drinking. As he was taking his third drink, he thought about Angelia York. He put his glass down, his hand stopped shaking. For the first time, George realized that he loved Angelia York. But how could he ever face her with what he had done.

* * * * *

Robert Lee Locklear was walking across his bedroom floor. He had heard rumors that Dr. Pittman was sick, but with Bill Thomas back, Robert Lee knew that Bill would get the job if Dr. Pittman wasn't able to return to work. Robert Lee stood with his feet planted in one spot and shook his fist toward heaven and cursed. "If it's the last thing I do, I'm going to get that job. I don't care what I have to do or who I have to step on to get it. That's my job, and I am going to have it one way or the other."

* * * * *

In an old barn out in the country there stood a soul filled with hatred. Smoke from the cigarette was rising overhead. "How much longer am I going to have to wait until that stupid girl makes her move on Bill? All I need is for her to act like he tried something. Can't the little tramp do anything right? I guess I am going to have to hold her feet to the fire. She thinks she's falling in love. Well, let her. I'll use even that against her." The laughter that followed would send cold chills down the spine of any man. Here was a person who was completely given over to hatred. There wasn't anything too low, or even too hateful, just as long as the results were the same; the destruction of Bill Thomas' life and marriage. When the laughter stopped, the figure walked over to the window, lighting another cigarette. The dark figure stood alone. Taking in a deep drag from the cigarette, once again the laughter started. "I'll break him this time. He'll pay for what he did to me. And he'll never know who did it to him."

* * * * *

Bill and Paula walked into the hospital together. As they walked up to Dr. Pittman's room, Paula stopped and took a deep breath. "Bill, why didn't Clara call us?"

Before Bill could answer, Clara opened the door. "Shush," she said. "Harry is asleep now. Let's go down the hall where we can talk." Bill felt like he knew the reason, but hearing it was only going to make the pain even worse. As they took their seats, Clara started. "I know I should have called you both, but Harry was at his wits end and was afraid word would get out and then the rumors would start."

Bill looked up at Clara. "He put it off because of me didn't he?"

"Now see, there you go blaming yourself for something that has nothing to do with you at all."

Bill stood and walked across the room. "Really, it has nothing to do with me? You mean to tell me that Dr. Pittman didn't put off seeing a doctor because he was waiting to see if the board was going to go along with him on the idea that I would be the right man for the job when he stepped down."

Paula got up and walked over to Bill. "I'm sure that's not it, honey. You know how Dr. Pittman hates to take time off."

Paula looked over at Clara waiting for her to agree with her. But instead, she saw tears falling down to the floor. As Clara looked up, you could see the pain and hurt that was tearing her heart apart on the inside. "Bill," she spoke in a soft voice. "What I'm about to tell you must never be repeated to anyone. Do you both promise me that?"

* * * * *

As Bill walked into his classroom, it felt like he had been kicked in the head, twice. Even though Clara did her best to try and take the responsibility off him, he knew better. Was his mistake always going to follow him? Yes, he left school in mid-term. But had everyone forgotten about his wife and daughter dying? They didn't have to try and get back to a car that was burning out of control. For over a year he could still hear their screams. That's why he drank all the time back then, and the drinking still didn't stop their cries in his head. It wasn't until DJ and Maggie came to live with him, and he said something to DJ about the dreams stopping. DJ told Bill that every night when they prayed, they sang a song just so he would sleep at night. It was then that the nightmares stopped. Now he knew it was the presence of God filling his house as they sang. That's what drove the nightmares away. So why now; why did he have to face something that was tied to his past? Why couldn't it all just go away?

* * * * *

Annie Reinhart was looking out the window of her classroom. She had dropped her son Josh at the daycare before coming to school. Josh was five now, and already she could see his father in him. The way he did things, the way he laughed. Annie made the doctor promise that he wouldn't say anything to Jerome, until they knew for sure. "I'm not hiding anything from him," She said to herself, "When I know, I'll tell him." Taking a deep breath, Annie wiped the tears from her eyes. "My mother didn't live much longer than her fortieth birthday. Oh God, please give me more time."

CHAPTER NINE

Trying to Walk Away From the Past

Friday morning was cold as Irina walked across the campus heading to her English Literature class. At first she had planned to take that class under Robert Lee Locklear, but after meeting him in the hallway, Irina changed her mind and enrolled in Jonathan Wedgeworth's class instead. Irina had been keeping her distance from Jonathan ever since that person came and confronted her about how she wasn't doing what she had agreed to do. During the last few days Irina had thought a great deal about what she was being asked to do, and about the promises that were made to her. First of all, she didn't have any possible way of knowing if these people could even find her daughter. Nor did she even know for sure they would help her get her daughter back. She could very well help them to mar Bill Thomas' name, only to find them gone when it was all over. No, she had to put the past behind her. The very thought of it drove such pain through her heart that she had to stop walking for a moment. Tears filled her eyes as she thought of the little girl she would never see again. "Am I doing the right thing?" she thought. "Can I walk away from any chance of ever seeing my daughter again?" Irina sat down on a bench and cried. How could her life have gotten into such a mess as this?

* * * * *

Bill was getting ready for school when DJ walked into the room where he was. "Bill, Could I talk with you for a moment?"

Bill looked down at DJ. Here was this little creature asking him for a moment of his time, after all they have done for him how could he say no? "Sure, but I can't talk too long. You know I have a class in just a little bit."

"Oh, yeah, I won't take too long. You see, I'm a little worried about something and I thought that maybe you could help me with it."

Bill's eyes were wide open. "You mean you need my help with something?"

"Yes, but you can't tell Maggie."

About that time DJ heard Maggie say. "Can't tell me what?"

DJ turned and looked at Maggie. "Oh Maggie, you are always listening to things you shouldn't. Just forget it then." And with that, DJ walked out of the room.

Maggie looked at Bill. "What did I say?"

Bill laughed, "I'm not sure Maggie, but I have to run now. You two will have to work that out yourselves."

* * * * *

George Lackey walked up to Angelia York as she was finishing up some paperwork Curtis had asked her to do. He sat on the desk and looked down for a moment. "Hey, would you like to go and get something to eat later?"

Angelia stopped what she was doing. It hit her like a ton of bricks. Here she had tried being nice to George for months, and it seemed that every time she got close he delighted in hurting her. Angelia stood up so fast that the chair fell to the floor. "No," she said. "I have tried being nice to you and all you've ever done is hurt me, George. So, please tell me why I should trust you now?"

George slowly stood to his feet. Had he thrown away the only hope he might have had for happiness? "I guess there isn't one, not a good one, anyway. I'm sorry for the way I treated you. I know it was wrong, and maybe one day I will be able to tell you why I acted the way I did. But I can't right now. I'm sorry."

With that George walked away. His heart was breaking in two and he didn't know what to do about it. He had hurt Angelia more times than even he could count. But when he was doing it, he honestly thought he was doing it for her own good.

* * * * *

Maggie walked into the room where DJ was standing. "Why did you get so upset with me?"

DJ looked at her with such a sweet look upon his face. "I'm sorry, Love. I just had something I needed to talk to Bill about that's all." "But DJ, why couldn't you talk to me about it?"

DJ didn't know how he was going to keep this from her, but he knew he had too. "Maggie, it was just something that I needed Bill to do for me, now please don't ask me anymore questions. It's nothing wrong, Love. I promise."

Maggie got up and walked over to DJ. She very lightly licked him on the side of his face. "DJ, you know I trust you, and if you say that there isn't anything to worry about, then that's all I need to hear." Maggie turned and walked toward the door. She stopped and turned around. "I think Paula has a doctor appointment today, so we are going to be here most of the day by ourselves. Do you want to go outside later and play in the snow that is still on the ground?"

"Why yes, that is a wonderful idea. I'll be right there, Love." As Maggie walked out DJ couldn't help but think how lucky he was to have her in his life. He just had to get Bill to go along with this idea.

* * * * *

Jonathan noticed that Irina did at least make eye contact with him today while he was teaching. And was that a smile he saw on her face as she was leaving? Did she look back at him and smile? Jonathan sat there not knowing just what to make of it. He thought he had put the past behind him, and then when Irina started acting like she didn't want to have anything to do with him, it all came back with the force of a savage storm. He found that he was sitting up at night wondering what he had done wrong, and wondering why Irina was treating him that way. He even thought about picking up everything and moving again. But where would he go? This was his home now. He had the store and now that he was teaching part-time, his life did seem to begin to make sense again. "Maybe," he thought, "things just might work out between us after all." Jonathan looked out the window and watched Irina walk toward her next class. There it was again. Love growing in his heart. A heart that he had thought was too cold for love to ever grow there again. But here it was. Pushing its way into the very core of his heart, and for the first time since that painful day Jonathan was glad it was there.

* * * * *

Teresa Eldridge was sitting at her desk, just staring out the window. It seemed this time the depression wasn't going away as it had in the past. Teresa found more and more reasons to work late at night. Almost every night she went to bed hours after Rusty. "How could he want me?" she said to herself. "I can't give him any children so why shouldn't he want someone else instead?" Already Teresa's mind was starting to play tricks on her. With the lack of sleep, and the constant pushing herself, Teresa's health was starting to wear thin. Little did she realize that it's when we are at our weakest that the enemy of our soul will come in very quietly, working his lies, to our own undoing.

Rusty taught biology at the school and was in his classroom working to get everything ready for the next class. Not sure what to do, and with Teresa telling him that she just had a lot more paperwork this semester, Rusty didn't see the signs that should have been a warning to him. Instead he just threw himself more into his own work and hoped it would all work itself out before too long. The one mistake we always make is just hoping things will work themselves out for the better. It's only by prayer, and standing in faith in prayer that we can see situations change.

* * * * *

Darlene Chisolm was walking across the campus when she saw Irina slowly walking by herself. "Hey, wait up and I'll walk with you." Irina looked back at Darlene and was glad to have the company.

"Ok, I'm headed to the grill to get something to eat. Do you want to come along?"

"Sure," Darlene said. "I'm about half starved myself."

Both the young women broke out laughing. Darlene, because she thought she should lose a few pounds, and Irina, because she knew what it was like to really go hungry. But here in this land of plenty, she had a job and was going back to school. Yes, maybe putting the past behind her was the only thing she could do. Together they walked and talked, no one saw the lurking figure standing over by the side of a building watching. And with every moment the anger grew.

Darlene reached for the door, and as she opened it she asked Irina if she could work for her that afternoon. "I know this is your afternoon off, but I have this paper that is due in three days and it is going to be a killer."

Irina smiled at her new friend. "Sure, why not. I don't have any papers due until next week. I'll be glad to work for you."

* * * * *

Dr. Pittman sat in his chair at his house waiting for the day the doctor would let him go back to work. "You know," he said. "I think Dr. Adcock is letting his position go to his head. Why, I feel just fine and I don't believe it would hurt me to go back and do some light work."

"That's the problem though," Clara said. "You don't understand what he is talking about when he says light work. To you that means anything that isn't running over five miles. No sir, you stay right there where I can see you, or I'll lock you up in the basement."

"The basement!" Dr. Pittman sputtered.

"Yes, the basement. We don't have a sixth floor here in this hospital, so if I need to... "in the basement you go." Clara stood there with her hands on her hips. "So get any idea of trying to sweet talk me out of your head, mister, because it's not going to work this time," Clara walked over and softly kissed Dr. Pittman's forehead. "Besides you old goat, I have a flower bed we are going to work on just as soon as the doc gives the ok."

"But, my work at the school Clara, I can't let it just keep piling up." With that, the doorbell rang.

* * * * *

Dr. Travis Null was walking down the hall of the hospital when he felt a sharp pain in his right arm. "Hey, what's that for?" He asked as he turned to see Vickie Eldridge standing there with her fist ready to hit him again.

"That's for making me believe you knew more than you really did."

"Now wait a minute. What are we talking about here?"

Vickie's eyes flamed as he said that and she hit him again in the arm. "You know good and well what we're talking about. The other day when you said my brother-in-law told you what I said in church."

Travis just grinned at Vickie. "Now wait just one second, sweetheart. I never said I knew for sure. I just acted like I knew. That way you would be embarrassed and Dr. Adcock would have settled the score."

Vickie's mouth flew open. It was one of those moments when you just knew you had said the wrong thing, and Travis was having one of those right now. Vickie turned to find her brother-in-law and sister when she felt Travis' arms around her and he picked her up and carried her into an empty room. "Hold on now, Vickie. You do your share of teasing them. So now it's your turn to take what is dished out to you." Travis smiled at Vickie which made her madder than ever.

"I'll have you know that this is none of your business."

With that she tried to pull away, but instead Travis pulled her back into his arms and he kissed her. Vickie stood there shocked. She didn't know what to say now. What could she do? Her face turned red from embarrassment. She pulled away and turned to walk out when Travis reached out and took her by the arm. "Vickie," he said quietly. "If I didn't feel something for you, I would never have kissed you. I thought you should know that."

Trying to find the right words to say, Vickie found herself speechless, which was something Travis had never seen before. Then as if she knew what to do, Vickie grabbed Travis and kissed him as hard as she could. When she backed away, Travis felt his face turning red now. With that, Vickie smiled. She had come out on top after all.

*****

Dr. Pittman heard Bill's voice as Clara let him in. "Harry is back here in his office." Bill walked into the room and sat down in a chair near Dr. Pittman. "My boy, you have got to reason with my wife. She has it in her head that I need to take a few weeks off. It will take me the better part of a year to get caught up on my paperwork."

Bill chuckled, "No sir, it won't. You see, I am working every evening a few hours to keep things up to date for you."

"And here all this time I thought you were my friend." Bill laughed again. Then he reached out and took Dr. Pittman by the arm. "Sir, when I needed you, you were there for me. You and Clara stood by our side when we needed you. I owe you, sir, more than I could ever hope to repay."

Dr. Pittman patted Bill's hand. "My boy, I wanted to be there."

"I know that sir, and I want to help you now. Clara said that you need two years before you can retire. But Dr. Pittman there are a lot of good men and women who could fill your shoes right now. Sir, you could go on and retire now."

Dr. Pittman got up and walked over to a window. "No, there is only one man for that job, and the board wants to wait until you have been back two years before they offer it to you, son. So you see, I need two years, because I know you will take care of my school."

Bill sat there not knowing what to say. "Sir, I'm sure there is someone else who could do a better job than I could."

"Maybe, but no one will care for the school as you will. I remember when you used to work every weekend helping raise money for this school. I never had to ask you either. No Bill. You're the right man for this job. It's just that foolish school board is afraid you might pick up and leave again. I told them you had a good reason for leaving as you did back then."

Bill shook his head. "No sir. I left because I couldn't face the pain of living without my wife and daughter. And even though I am back here now, with all that has happened in my life, I would do it the same all over again. What I thought was running from God, turned out to be running right where He wanted me."

Dr. Pittman stood by Bill and put his hand on his shoulder. "Any man who could learn that lesson is the right man to take my place."

$$* \quad * \quad * \quad * \quad *$$

Irina was working that afternoon for Darlene. It was a slow day, because it seemed everyone was somewhere studying either for a test or working on a paper to turn in. Irina was washing some cups, and as she did, she started to sing. It had been a long time since she washed dishes and sang while she worked. All she had known in the past was hurt and pain. Now that she had made up her mind to move on with her life, it seemed as though she was finding it in her heart again to sing. Irina was so caught up in her singing that she didn't hear the door open. As she turned around, Jonathan was standing there smiling at her. "I don't remember when I have ever heard anything more beautiful. Please don't stop.

Irina felt the blood rush to her face. "I'm sorry, Dr. Wedgeworth. I didn't know anyone was here."

Jonathan walked closer, "Well, I'm glad I came in." He stood there not knowing what he was feeling. It had been so long since he had allowed his heart to feel anything for a woman. Yet, here he stood, looking into the eyes of Irina and it felt as if he could take wings and fly.

"I'll be through cleaning in a little while and then I'll get out of your way."

"You could never be in my way, Irina. To be totally honest with you, I was hoping you would stay and we could just talk for a while. I would really like to get to know you better." With that, Irina felt a little fear in her heart. What about her past, what if he asked too many questions. Jonathan could see the fear that ran across Irina's face. "Or, we could just take it from here and let the past be the past. God knows, there are things in my past I want to forget." Irina moved back a few steps; she was biting her bottom lip. Jonathan moved even closer to her. "Please, don't run from me. I'm not going to hurt you."

"That's not what I'm afraid of. I'm afraid I'll hurt you."

"You, how? I don't believe you could hurt a fly." Irina started to cry as Jonathan spoke. How she wanted to fall in love. How she wanted to have someone in her life that would love her and take care of her.

Jonathan reached out and gently took Irina's hand. "See, I won't hurt you, and I know you would never hurt me either." As he pushed her hair back from her eyes, Irina did something she had no plans on doing. She stepped closer to Jonathan and kissed him. As she stepped back Jonathan pulled her closer again and lightly kissed her again. It was as if he was afraid he might bruise her. He was trying to put her fears to rest about his ever hurting her. It was at that moment that love grew between them. Neither of them knew just what was ahead of them. If they had known, they might have turned and run away. But here they stood, looking into each other's eyes, with the fire of love burning brightly in both their hearts. They sat and talked on into the night. Both talking at the same time and then laughing at each other for their words running together like they were. For Jonathan, this was a dream come true. For Irina it was her only chance for love.

Neither of them saw the car that drove by repeatedly. How could they? Love had pulled them into its own world. While they sat there in love's sweet embrace, they didn't realize that just outside hatred was raging. For every time the car drove by, curses filled the air. "If she thinks for one moment that she is going to break her word to me, I'll get even with her. She is going to do what I want her to do and then I'll leave her to end up in jail for the rest of her life."

CHAPTER TEN

Walking on a New Path

The Monday morning sun rose with a clear sky and much colder weather. But for Irina it didn't seem cold as she walked to school. Even though Jonathan asked to pick her up in the morning so that she wouldn't have to walk in the cold, Irina told Jonathan that she liked the walk and it gave her time to get awake before her first class. She did promise that on days it was raining he could pick her up, however. For Irina it seemed as if the whole world had changed. She had walked out from under a dark cloud that wasn't allowing her to see things as they truly were. The day would come when she would look back and see that many people walk through this life under such a cloud with the darkness so blinding their eyes that they can't see what is right in front of them. As Irina walked toward the school the wind rippled through her light brown hair. Yet, today, it didn't seem to bother her. There was a sense of freedom in the wind it seemed. Irina could not remember when she had felt so at peace with herself. She was even thinking about telling Jonathan about her first marriage and how she went to jail. She was going to wait a little longer to be sure, but she just knew he would understand.

* * * * *

George Lackey was loading a truck when Angelia York walked up behind him. She reached out and lightly touched his shoulder. George turned around and to his surprise it was Angelia. Before he could speak, Angelia reached out her hand. "Hello, I'm Angelia York. And if there is anything I can ever help you with, please, just ask."

George looked down at his feet. He knew what she was doing. She was trying to say let's just start all over again and go from here. He looked up into her blue eyes. "Thank you, Angelia. I'm George Lackey, and yes, I could use your help with a lot of things around here." When Angelia smiled back at George, he could have sworn her red hair turned just a little more red and her blue eyes seemed even bluer than the sky. That day was one of the best days in George's life. For a time he had allowed himself to put the past behind him. The fears and the pains of his past were no longer kicking at the door of his heart. Maybe he could put it all behind him after all.

* * * * *

Curtis stood over to the side looking down from an upstairs window. He had known for some time that Angelia liked George, but he never thought anything would come of it. Now it seemed as if things might take on a different turn than he had hoped. Did he dare let Angelia know that he had hoped she would one day look at him as she did George? Curtis walked away from the window and over to his desk. From a bottom drawer of his desk he pulled out a file. In the file were all the things that George had hoped no one would ever find out. All of his greatest fears were in the hands of a man who had planned how he could keep George and Angelia apart. Even if she never liked him, at least he would see to it that George never had her. Why should George find happiness? He hadn't, and it looked now as if he never would.

* * * * *

DJ was outside sitting in the sun and enjoying the cold morning air. He had tried to talk to Bill again, but he said that he was busy. It seemed to him that Bill was too busy these days. DJ was getting worried. If Bill didn't slow down, the enemy might find a way in and cause him trouble. Maggie walked up behind DJ and pushed him with her nose. "Now I know you were in deep thought if you didn't hear me walking up behind you. What were you thinking about, DJ?" "It's Bill, my Love. I'm worried he is allowing himself to get too busy. Have you noticed how he hasn't worshiped with us in weeks?"

"Yes," Maggie said. "And Paula is also following his pattern. Why, she is always so busy fixing up the room for the baby." Maggie looked at DJ. "Please don't think I'm being too hard on Paula. I know she wants things to be nice, but DJ, how much more can she do to get things ready?"

DJ shook his head. "My Love, I think they have lost sight of the most important thing."

Maggie looked with a question upon her face. "What's that, DJ?"

"They have lost sight of the fact that it's not the event that is so special, but rather the birth of the child itself. Humans it seems, Maggie, get caught up with doing things. They love to do, and they will do things when it might be better to enjoy the moment instead."

Maggie sat by DJ. "You mean like how some people can't enjoy life if someone has a bigger house then they do?"

"Yes, that's it. People are easy to become slaves to things, Maggie. And that is what always pulls them away from the Creator. They allow other things to fill their hearts, and there is no room left for Him."

Maggie smiled. She liked it when she and DJ could have their talks. "Just think, DJ. When the Creator came to this Earth He was born in a feeding trough."

"Yes, my Love. The greatest gift to man came through the lowest beginnings. He was born without a nice house or a painted room. Yet, never has any one's life so changed the world."

DJ and Maggie sat out in the backyard for some time talking. When Paula looked out the window to see where they were, she felt for just a moment a sense of guilt. She knew how she had not been reading her Bible nor praying. But surely everyone knew how busy she was. Bill and Paula are like most of us. They always have their reasons for why they don't do what they know they should do. But excuses are never reasons; they are after all, only excuses.

* * * * *

Bill hurried into the Heartland Grill to pick up something to go. As he closed the door behind him, he heard May call out to Fay. "Fay dear, you can call the bank and tell them that we'll be able to make the house note this month. Dr. Thomas is back."

Bill knew that with these two you never knew just what they might say, so there was no getting around it. He had to take his lumps for not coming around sooner. "OK, I know I've been away for a while, but really ladies, your house note?"

Fay walked over to where Bill was standing. "Oh, it's ok if they throw us out in the street because people stop coming in here, why I'm sure the Morning Blend's coffee is all you need to get you through the day anyway."

Bill knew he wasn't going to win this one. He raised his hands, "I give up, from now on I promise you two will see me in here more often."

May turned and smiled at Fay, "It works every time just like a charm."

* * * * *

Annette was still typing as Zachary was sleeping in their bedroom. He had just pulled his two day shift and was still in bed. Annette had stayed up most of the night typing for some students who didn't know how to type or they didn't want to wait until they could get to a computer. Annette laughed to herself. "Most of them are just afraid of Shirley Crowe, the librarian. Good thing for me too. This way I always have more typing than I can handle."

Annette always thought about going back to school, but with their children keeping her so busy, she knew that this was what she should be doing right now. "One day, I'll go back. Now, let's see if this student's spelling is as bad as the last one."

* * * * *

Bob Boswell was in the kitchen with Mary Ann working to get everything ready for the noon crowd. "Hey honey, do you want to go out tonight?" Mary Ann looked over at Bob and sometimes she wondered just what he was up to.

"Sure, all we have to do is to find someone who has lost their mind, and get them to agree to keep our two little monsters." Bob laughed.

"What would you say if I told you I have found someone?" Mary Ann laughed.

"Well, I would possibly say that if they agreed to keep our two kids, then they weren't fit to watch anybody's children so why are we going to trust them?" Bob grinned as he winked at Mary Ann. "Just remember you said it, not me."

She turned her head and looked at him with that look she could give him. "Bob, just what in heaven's name are you up to this time?"

"Oh nothing, but when your mother shows up this afternoon, I'll tell her you said she was unfit to keep the grandkids."

Mary Ann threw her arms around Bob's neck and gave him a big kiss. "And if you do! I'll kill you myself." They both laughed as they finished preparing the food for the lunch crowd.

Mary Ann smiled as she thought that only Bob would send her mother a ticket to fly over so that they could have a night off together. But why, she wondered, didn't he wait and do it on a Friday night. It seemed he was always one day short of a full week when it came to timing.

* * * * *

Dr. Pittman was walking across the campus heading toward his office. He had promised Clara that he was going to just sit in his office and answer the phone. He wanted to tell her that he just had to get out of the house, but didn't want her to take it the wrong way and get her feelings hurt. In the very depth of his heart, he felt that if he could get back to work, then just maybe, he could talk some sense into the school board.

The cold wind blowing against his face felt good to him this morning. As Dr. Pittman came around a building, he ran into Irina. "Oh, I'm sorry dear. I'm afraid my mind was a hundred miles away this morning and I didn't see you." Irina was a little afraid of Dr. Pittman. Every time she had seen him he was either walking hurriedly to get to a meeting, or he was talking with one of the teachers. Irina thought that maybe it was because of her past that she felt this way around him.

But running into Dr. Pittman like that just about unnerved her. Dr. Pittman reached out and patted her on the shoulder. "Now, now child, you don't have to be afraid of me. I'm not the one giving you your test." With that he walked on chuckling as he walked.

* * * * *

Robert Lee Locklear watched from a window as Dr. Pittman headed toward his office. "Why couldn't that old goat just die?" He knew that Dr. Pittman had set up a meeting with the school board the first of the next week. "I can just guess that he is going to tell them Dr. Thomas is the best man for the job. Well, we'll see about that. I'll find some way to stop him this time. That job is going to be mine one way or the other."

He walked back over to his desk and sat down. Even though Robert Lee Locklear put in more hours than anyone else, he was the most disliked teacher the school had. In every way his bad attitude came across in whatever he said and did. What he didn't know was that it was Bill Thomas who had in the past gone to bat for him more than once. He kept asking Dr. Pittman to give him more time to see if he could make the adjustment to being in a small school. What Bill didn't know was that wasn't Robert's problem. He wanted more than just a teacher's job. He wanted Dr. Pittman's job.

* * * * *

Chip was walking toward Nita as she was heading to her first class. He didn't know why he felt so nervous every time he got around her. It seemed as if his mind filled up with more words than his mouth could say. Nita could see the nervousness already coming across his face. She thought to herself that this morning she was going to really unnerve him. Nita stopped right in front of Chip. "OK, now please tell me just when, if ever, you are going to say something to me about how you really feel. I mean, I'm not getting any younger, you know."

Chip's hands were sweaty, his mouth was dry, and his mind was being flooded with more words than he could ever hope to say correctly.

"Well, Chip? I'm waiting." Nita said with a smile. Then it happened, it was one of those moments that came out of nowhere. Chip reached out and took Nita by both of her arms, pulled her close and kissed her long and hard. Then he turned and walked away as fast as he could.

Nita stood there with her mouth wide open, not knowing what to say or do. "Hey, wait a minute," she yelled as she followed after Chip in a fast walk. Nita couldn't see the smile that was on Chip's face. Now he had finally turned the table on her. Now the nervousness was gone. Nita caught up with Chip and took his hand in hers. "You're not going to just walk away, are you?"

"Nope, I was waiting to see if you would follow me, that's all."

Nita moved closer to Chip's side. "I'll follow you wherever you lead."

Rebekah stood over to the side of a building watching the whole scene unfold. "I'm glad I left his father's old college journal out where he could find it the other day. Seems he read what his father did when I pulled the same stunt on him. And I would say it has worked again. I've never seen Nita walk so fast in my life."

Rebekah turned and walked toward her own classroom. Tears were running down her face as she remembered the love of her own heart. "How I wish..," She said out loud, knowing that her life was going to be filled with loneliness and with joy. Her joy would come from watching her son find the love of his heart, and loneliness because she was going to miss even more the love of her own heart.

* * * * *

DJ and Maggie were sitting in the backyard watching the sunset. DJ looked over at Maggie and thought to himself how beautiful she looked with the light of the setting sun upon her hair. Maggie turned and looked at DJ. "What is it DJ, you're looking at me as if you wanted something?"

Slowly he shook his head. "No, Love. Not wanting something, I have something. I have you in my life. What more could I want?"

Maggie lightly pushed him with her body. "I feel the same way about you too." Maggie's eyes sparkled as she spoke. "DJ, tell me one of our ancient stories."

"But Maggie, you know them as well as I do."

"I know, but I love it when you tell me a story. Please, tell me one when one of the guardians told his master the truth about guardians."

"Hmm, let's see. Well, there was this one story, but no. That one isn't right for this occasion."

"DJ," Maggie said.

DJ grinned at Maggie. "OK, I have one. Once in Scotland way back in the Eleventh Century there lived this man who was a sheep herder. Now, Innes Mac Call didn't have a large herd of sheep, but he was as proud as any man could be of what he did have. And he loved his wife too. Even though she did have the devil's own temper; it happened on a cold night. Much like this night is going to be."

Maggie turned to DJ, "We're not going in until you finish the story."

DJ reached over and licked Maggie on the side on the face. "Now, as I was saying, it was a very cold night and the guardian was outside in the field watching Innes' sheep. He was used to spending long hours alone, but his heart was breaking because he felt as if he couldn't reach his master with the truth about God's love. Oh, Innes was a good man and even went to church on Sundays, but there was something missing in his life: an ole Tip Ear, that is what Innes named him."

Maggie giggled. "Now why did Innes name him that?"

DJ frowned. "Because only one of his ears was tipped Maggie; you know that. Anyway, Tip Ear was out in the field watching the sheep when all of a sudden Innes came walking up the hill. He flopped down right by Tip Ear as if it was something he had done all his life. That's when he started talking to Tip Ear. Not that he knew anything about Tip Ear. People always talk to their dogs when no one else is around. 'By the heavens above, I swear it seems as if I can do nothing to make that woman happy. Why, all I said was that she might have burned the stew. I wasn't saying she was a bad cook. Lord knows how many blue ribbons she has won at the county fair. But you know if you don't stir the pot of stew, it can burn on you' Innes put his head in his hands. You know Tip Ear, the truth of it is. I'm not happy. No sir, not at all. I talked with the priest and he said that I was baptized as a child; therefore, I was a child of God. But, shouldn't you feel something inside of you that will let you know it? I mean, I have asked the Almighty to give me a sign, or something, but I haven't received any as of yet.'

It was then that Tip Ear knew what he had to do. He looked up at Innes and said, 'Well, just maybe today is your lucky day.'

Innes jumped up and said, 'By what foolishness is this?'

Tip Ear, knowing how superstitious Innes was, stood and said. 'Please sit down and I'll tell you everything about me. But you'll have to promise never to tell a living soul.'

'But why, I mean how can you talk?'

Tip Ear calmly said, 'I have always been able to talk. There just was never any need to talk to you until now. Please, sit down.' Well, they talked on into the night and were still talking as the sun rose the next morning. But by the time the sun was coming up, Innes had the witness in his heart he was looking for. He had found the love of God to be real and it had changed him. He even became a better husband to his wife; even though he always was a good husband. Now he was able to be more understanding of her and her ill temper. In the end, Bonnie Mac Call also found the love of God.

"Yes, that is one of my favorite stories, Maggie. Ole Tip Ear put his life on the line that night, but it paid off in the end."

The backdoor opened and Paula called out. "It's getting late; don't you two think it's about time you came on inside?"

CHAPTER ELEVEN

Blue Skies and Happiness

It was late Thursday afternoon as Irina was hurrying across the campus. She had been so busy this week. With all the studying she had to do, in addition to writing two papers, she had only seen Jonathan while she was in class and one afternoon when she had to work. The sun was setting and the sky was a beautiful reddish-orange color. Irina stopped to watch the sun setting, when she felt an arm go around her waist. Jonathan whispered, "I have missed you, you know."

Irina put her head over on Jonathan shoulder, "I have thought about you every day." As she looked into Jonathan's eyes, he saw for the first time a love pouring out of her toward him, and it almost knocked him off his feet. "Tell you what? Why don't I take you out to eat, and then you can get back to your studying."

Irina reached her hand over under his arm and pinched him on the side. "Is that all you teachers care about? Studying?"

Jonathan started to speak but the words just wouldn't come to his mind. "No, I mean, yes. I mean no."

"It sounds like to me you're not sure yourself." Irina said with a smile.

Rebekah Corey walked up behind them. "Honey, you have him so beside himself right now. I doubt Jonathan could tell you what day of the week it was."

Irina stepped back and let her arms drop by her side. "Oh, no, I wasn't, I mean, we were just talking about an upcoming test."

Rebekah's blue eyes just danced as she looked back at the two of them. "I was in love once too you know."

Jonathan had recovered himself, "Oh, no, Mrs. Corey. I'm not."

Rebekah held up her hand and stopped Jonathan from speaking. "First," she said. Let me say that Irina is way past being a child, and never say you're not in front of the woman you love."

With that Rebekah walked away. Irina looked at Jonathan. "What did she mean I was way past being a child?"

* * * * *

Bob Boswell was cleaning up after the noon crowd when his wife walked up to him and asked. "How long is my mother going to stay with us?"

Bob smiled, thinking to himself that Mary Ann had left herself wide open for this. "Hmm, tired of your mother already?"

Mary Ann's mouth flew open. "Why Bob, you know that's not what I meant. I just wanted to know if we were going to get to go out some more before she left."

Bob smiled, it was one of those times when his face turned about as red as his hair. "Well, I thought about taking you out tomorrow night, but you have to promise not to hurt me anymore."

Mary Ann, put her hands on her hip. "Just please tell me when I have ever hurt you?"

Bob's face turned even redder as he smiled. "I seem to remember one night long ago, when a certain someone pushed me out of the bed and dislocated my right shoulder."

"Why, Bob Boswell, you know it was a spider in the bed."

"Yes, but it was also our wedding night and I got to spend it in the ER, and just think what people would think if I told that story."

Mary Ann reached out and pulled Bob closer to her. "They would think how natural he looks lying there." With that they both started laughing, and Mary Ann kissed Bob and held him close to her. Her mother had given them the time they needed together. With school starting again and the twins, it seemed as though they never had time for each other.

*   *   *   *   *

Cindy and Wayne Hawkins were closing up their shop when she asked Wayne, "Have you seen Irina this week?"

Wayne thought for a moment, "Yeah, I saw her the other day walking down the stairs. I asked her if she wanted to come by and eat with us one night but she said, that she had a lot of school work this week. Said she might see us this weekend. I think she is seeing Jonathan Wedgeworth."

Cindy looked at Wayne. "She is, and I think he is the best thing for her. She has seemed to come out a lot more since they started seeing one another."

"Yeah, Wayne said. "He has a business and he teaches part time at the school. What more could a girl want?"

Cindy's eyes flared. "How about love? I think she would want that as well."

Wayne knew he had Cindy going. When she saw him smiling she picked up some old clothes and threw them at him. "Oh, you, I should have known you would be pulling my leg."

* * * * *

Ann Reinhart was sitting on the couch by Jerome. He was talking about his classes that week and how he thought this was going to be his best year yet. The very words he spoke caused a pain to shoot through Ann's heart. She still hadn't said anything to him about the other test, and now the doctor's office called today and said that there was something there, but they couldn't be sure until they ran one more test. But, they cautioned, she shouldn't get her hopes up too high. It looked like a tumor and they thought it was cancer. Ann was just rubbing her hands together as Jerome spoke. How did she tell him that she was so afraid that she couldn't sleep at night; that every time he reached out and touched her, it caused her such pain. She was going to leave him; she knew it, just like her mother did, and the pain caused her to hurt all the way to her very core. "Honey, did you see the sunset this afternoon? Why it was beautiful, it made me think of you."

Ann turned and looked up into Jerome's faces. "I have something to tell you that I should have told you long before now. But I was too afraid."

* * * * *

Dr. Travis was filling out paperwork when he felt a sharp pain in his side. He turned to see Vickie Eldridge standing there with her fist ready to hit him again. "Now wait a minute, I thought we had things worked out between us."

"Yeah, so did I, then you went off and haven't spoken to me for days."

Travis smiled, "You know, we're going to have to work on your communication skills."

Vickie's mouth fell open. "What did you say?" She swung with her right fist trying to hit Travis in the head this time.

Travis moved back which caused Vickie to lose her balance and fall right into his arms. "Now, see, I knew I could get you back in my arms if I got you to take a swing at me."

Vickie tried to stand up straight but Travis held her close to him. "Let me go!"

"Oh, I plan to," he said, and with that Travis spun Vickie around and kissed her right in front of everyone there. All the other nurses quickly turned and looked toward the other end of the hallway.

At first Vickie tried to push away, but then she put her arms around Travis and held him tight. Suddenly she heard her sister say, "My, my, look whose being so forward these days. Why, you just never know what you're going to see in hospitals now do you?" Vickie pushed back away from Travis; her face was redder than it had ever been.

Kim looked over at her husband Dr. Adcock. "Have you ever seen anything like this in a hospital?"

"Nope, well, now that you bring it up, I did see something like this in some third world country once."

"What," Vickie said. She looked over at Travis who was enjoying it all until he saw the look on her face.

"Now, Vickie, I didn't know they were even around here. You have to believe me."

But before he could say anymore, Kim added. "I wonder what mom is going to think about all this?" With that Kim turned and took off running down the hall with Vickie right behind her, yelling for her to stop, and that she had better not say anything to anyone.

Dr. Adcock walked over to Travis and put his arm around him. "Welcome to the family. Hope you can put up with those two. They are always going at it like that."

* * * * *

Rusty Eldridge was at home grading papers. He was worried about his wife Teresa. Her depression was getting worse it seemed, but she wouldn't go to the doctor, nor would she talk to anyone. Teresa was pulling more away from him. She was sleeping more in a chair in the living room. She told him it was because she wasn't sleeping much, so she didn't want to keep him awake all night. Rusty had thought about talking to his sisters, but then they always hit things head on, and right now Teresa needed a gentle hand. "Hey, honey, why don't we go out tomorrow night and see a movie."

Teresa was washing the dishes, so her back was turned to Rusty. She was mad at God, and now it was starting to even turn toward Rusty. "Ok, if you want to. What's showing?" Teresa thought to herself: "I'll eat popcorn and say that it made me sick when we get home. That way I can stay out here in the living room." For a moment, there was a sick feeling in her heart. Teresa still loved Rusty, but her depression and lack of sleep was working on her emotions to the point she wasn't even sure what was real anymore. As she finished the dishes, Teresa walked toward the table where she was going to spend the next few hours grading papers. She had put it off as long as she could, this way Rusty would go to bed before her.

* * * * *

Jerome told Annie that he had to go and get milk for Josh. Oh, he told her that everything was going to be alright, that she wasn't her mother and that they had come a long way with the treatment of cancer. But what Annie didn't know was that Jerome's car only drove two blocks before he had to pull over. He sat there and cried as if his heart was going to break. Never had he felt so helpless in his life. Why was this happening to them? How could he face life without Annie? Jerome tried to pray, but all that came out was tears. All he could do was cry.

* * * * *

Jonathan and Irina had sat in Subway for hours. They ate and then just sat there talking. Irina told Jonathan that he had made her the happiest woman in the world. "Sweetie, we're in a Subway. It's not like I took you to the best place in town."

Irina reached out with her hand and lightly touched his face. "But I'm with you and that's all that matters to me." Irina thought about it and then she looked at Jonathan. "I need to tell you something about my past."

Jonathan placed his hand over her mouth. "Tell me when we're rocking the grandchildren, ok." He saw it again. A sharp look of pain shot across Irina's eyes. "What is it, dear?"

Irina thought how lucky she was to have this wonderful man in her life. But she also thought about her little girl. How she needed a father like Jonathan. She just knew he would be good for her. "I really do need to tell you something."

Again Jonathan placed his hand over her mouth. "Remember, we said that we were going to let the past be the past."

Irina bent down and kissed the back of Jonathan's hands. Looking up her eyes were filled with tears. "I don't deserve you, you're so good."

Jonathan laughed. "Honey, I cheated on a third grade test once. I'm not that good."

Irina looked at him, and then they both just about died laughing. Neither of them noticed the car that was parked across the street. It had followed them and had been sitting there watching them the entire time.

"I hope that little tramp is happy. I'll fix her. She'll wish she had never tried to double cross me. I won't rest until I get her and everyone else who did me wrong. They will all pay for what they did to me." The car started up and drove away. The driver reached for the cell phone. "Hey, yes, it's me. Now you owe me big time and unless you want me to tell everything I know about you, you're going to help me. Here is what I need you to do." With that, plans were being made to pull Irina back into the trap she had walked out of. By her not telling Jonathan about her past, she had left a door wide open to be used again. She would learn one day that being open with those you love is always the best way to be.

* * * * *

Curtis was sitting at his desk. He had watched George and Angelia York work together all day. Why they had cleaned just about everything in the fire station. And the laughter, it was making him sick just to think about the way she was following behind George. He remembered how his ex-wife used to be when she came home from class. She was always laughing about what this one student said when they were in the break room, or in class. Curtis stood up and hit the top of his desk. He told her that he didn't want her to have anything to do with that school. He told her that she belonged at home. He just couldn't understand why she wasn't happy staying there taking care of the house while he was away. Curtis walked over to his desk and opened the bottom drawer he pulled out the file he had on George and a bottle. He knew he wasn't suppose to drink when he was on duty, but since he was the boss, what did he care what anyone thought. Curtis drank until the bottle was just about gone. Then he put the file back along with the bottle. George's day was coming. He'd see to that.

* * * * *

It was late when DJ and Maggie went out the pet door into the backyard. They went out there so that they would make sure not to wake up Bill or Paula. There was a full moon out and the wind was blowing Maggie's hair as they sat there and sang. DJ looked over at her and in the moonlight she looked more beautiful to him than he had ever seen. Maggie stopped singing, "DJ, why did you stop singing?"

He smiled at her, "Well, when I saw you in the moonlight, I was so taken by your beauty that I found myself breathless."

Maggie slid over close to DJ and pushed him with her body. "You know I love you too."

DJ laid his head over next to Maggie's, "I'm glad we decided to come out here at night while it's cold. I like the cold air, but being out here makes the presence of the Creator even closer. Don't you think so, Maggie?"

Maggie nodded her head. "Yes, and I also think you look very beautiful in the moonlight. DJ, I don't have that same feeling I had. I mean maybe something has changed. Maybe this time nothing bad is going to happen."

Looking at her, DJ had to admit to himself that he had not felt the same, but he knew that you could never go on just feelings. "I haven't had that feeling either Mag. But let's not get careless here. While I hope the trouble has passed us by, we still need to be ready just in case."

Maggie smiled at DJ, "I like it when you call me Mag." She rested her head over on him as they continued singing. The next hour was a wonderful time for those two. It was going to be time well spent, for the days ahead were going to be filled with trouble for the both of them.

CHAPTER TWELVE

Evil is Persistent

It was very late that Thursday night as the car drove down the mountain. The weather was cold and there was a misty rain falling that made driving even more difficult. But it wasn't the rain or the cold that was the problem of the driver. It was the condition of the heart. For the heart of the driver was filled with hatred and revenge. Within this heart all pity had died out, there was no room for love, nor any thoughts of charity. Anger was burning within the driver as they drove down the mountain that night. "I'll make them all pay for what they done to me, yes, Bill Thomas is going to get what he deserves, and his sweet little wife is going to hate the day she ever fell in love with him."

The driver reached over for the cell phone in the seat next to them. After dialing a number that had long been put to memory, the phone rang on the other end. "Yeah, who's calling at this time of night?"

The voice was cold as the driver spoke, "I thought you would have been glad to hear from me."

"I thought you were, I mean."

"Shut up you fool. If I wanted your opinion on anything, I would have asked you for it. Now, I need you to tell me where I can find an old friend of mine. I know she used you to find her the next old fool on her list. So, where is she?"

You could hear the hesitation in the voice of the man on the other end, "I'm not sure I should tell you that. She doesn't want you to know where she is."

Laughter came across the phone, such that it made even his cold heart chill. "I hope she's afraid. But if you don't tell me what I want to know, I'll remember where I hid those files I had on you. You remember, the one's where you blackmail families to keep certain information from falling into the wrong hands."

"I thought those files were destroyed?"

"No, never, and if you don't give me what I want, I'll see you burn, do you hear me you sorry piece of trash?"

"Ok, you can find her at this place."

* * * * *

Lisa Ainsworth was living in a quiet little town with an ocean view. She was dating this older man who had more money than he knew what to do with, so she decided it was time she helped herself to it. She was living on St. Simons Island in Georgia, and people around town heard that she paid a little over two million for the house she was living in. No one knew where she was from or anything about her really. All they seemed to know was that as soon as she moved in, she was dating the richest widower in those parts. Lisa had turned many a men's heads before. She knew just how to dress and to walk into a room so that everyone would notice her. Her brown eyes and blond hair was the talk of the town with all the menfolk. This was going to make husband number five, and he was the richest one yet. When this little game was over, she would be worth around thirty million dollars herself. Then maybe, just maybe, she would try marrying for love; if there really was such a thing.

* * * * *

Lisa was sitting in the backyard with her new friend watching the sunset. Old Jake was falling head over heels for this beautiful young woman. And with Lisa still in her mid thirties, she still retained her beauty. Jake reached over and took Lisa's hand, "I don't know when I have ever been so happy. Why, just being here with you makes me feel young again."

Lisa reached over and kissed Jake ever so sweetly, "Why Jake, you're the man of my dreams; I think I have been looking for you all my life."

"Yeah, now tell him how wonderful he is in bed, and then I'll go on and throw up."

Lisa turned around to see Jane standing there with her hands on her hips. "What are you doing here?" She yelled.

"I'm here to pick up some things of mine that you seem to have forgotten about."

Poor old Jake stood up, "Now, now, young lady, I'm sure you must be mistaken here. Why, I doubt my dear little Lisa would know a woman like you."

Jane threw her head back and laughed, "Yeah pop, for your information, you're number five on her list, or is it six? I can't seem to remember, so let me fill you in on something. All of her husband's never live more than two years after she marries them. I'm doing you a favor old man; now get out of here before I kick you out of that chair."

Lisa turned to Jake, "I'll call you later dear, let me take care of some unfinished business with Jane here."

Jake's face registered such shock, "No, Lisa. I think its best we never see each other again. It seems you're not the person I thought you were." With that Jake got up and walked back toward his car.

Jane looked at Lisa, "Oh well, easy come, easy go."

* * * * *

It was late Friday afternoon and Rusty was waiting for Teresa to get home from school. He was going to wait and ride home with her, but she said that she had some paperwork to get done before she could leave. "You go on ahead, and I'll see you back at the house."

As Rusty was walking out of her room he turned, "We're still on for the movie tonight, right?"

"Oh, sure dear, just let me finish this up and I'll be right on." What Rusty didn't know was that already Teresa was thinking about how she didn't fit in with his family and that she maybe didn't fit in with him anymore. As Teresa left the campus, she drove off toward a little bar on the outside of town. It was known to be a place where some of the college kids hung out. Teresa wasn't brought up this way, but with her depression and the lies she was beginning to believe, she was out to do just about anything. All she ever wanted was to have a happy home, and now she was putting it at risk.

* * * * *

Robert Lee Locklear was sitting in his car on the side of the road about twenty miles outside of town. Another car drove up and a man got out and walked over to Locklear's car and got in the back seat. "Now, why did you call me, and why did you have to see me this afternoon? You know I don't meet people during the daylight hours. What if someone comes by and sees us? You are putting us both at risk here." Locklear was wanting Dr. Pittman's job so desperately that he was just about ready to do anything to get it. "Well, for starters, you never finished the job I paid you for. Bill Thomas isn't dead, and now he is back here."

"Well, now doesn't that just make you want to cry, but it isn't my problem. I did what you paid me to do. It's not my fault, I can't be held accountable if the man doesn't wear his seatbelt and he is thrown free."

Locklear was just about to lose it. "I want him dead, do you hear me, dead!"

The man opened the door, "Then you had better do it yourself. I never go after the same man twice. If he lived through that, then maybe he is supposed to live. I don't know, but that has always been my rule. And I never break my rules for anyone."

Robert Lee Locklear felt helpless. What was he going to do now? Could he pull it off by himself? One way or another, he was going to get Bill Thomas out of the way.

* * * * *

Lisa had walked into her house with Jane right behind her. "I don't know why you had to come back now of all times!"

Jane's eyes flared at Lisa, "Maybe I missed all the fun we use to have, or how about my overseas bank book you were holding for me? I need my money and I have come to get it."

Lisa poured herself a drink, "You seem to forget that your little mess cost me some money. I had to leave in a hurry and I was just hooking up with this really nice older gentleman."

"Save it." Jane yelled at her. "I could care less about some old goat you have tied to a rope. I want my money and I want it now."

Lisa made the one mistake that so many make, she thought Jane was the same woman she knew before. She looked at Jane and smiled,

"Oh dear, I just can't seem to remember where I placed it. I'll tell you what. Call me in a few days and I'll send it to you."

Jane reached in her purse and pulled out a 38, "I know how to make you remember." With that she pulled back the hammer on the gun.

Lisa's heart jumped, "Now, wait a minute, I didn't say I wasn't going to give it to you. You know how I don't like to be pushed around."

Jane shot the glass on the table next to Lisa. "And I hope you know now that I not am leaving without it. At least not with you alive, that is. Now what is it going to be?" My bank book or do I put a hole in you as well?"

Lisa knew she had to do something to get Jane out of this frame of mind before she handed her the bank book. "Ok dear, it's right here. But tell me, who are you going after that you need so much money? I thought our goal was to get their money, not spend our money on them."

Jane's eyes were still burning, "You fool. I'm not going after anyone's money. I'm going to get even with Bill and that tramp wife of his."

Lisa reached in her purse and handed Jane the bank book. "You know that is only going to cause you more trouble. Why don't you let it go and go after some nice man with more money than brains?"

"Do you think I'm going to let him get away with what he did to me? No, he is going to pay big time for it. But I need to find someone, and I need the money to pay the right person to find them."

"Hmm, well then, I might be able to help you there, my dear." Lisa walked over to her desk and there in a folder she had a pad, she opened it and turned a few pages. "Yes, here it is. Now this man did some work for me once, but I didn't like him. He's mean Jane, and they say he is very dangerous. There is a rumor that he even killed someone he was doing work for once."

116

Jane took the paper from Lisa's hand and folded it up and put it in her purse with the 38. As she turned to walk away she stopped and looked back, "It's also rumored that I killed someone when I was in prison, but no one could ever prove it."

With that, Jane walked out and went back to her car. Lisa just sat down in a chair next to the window. She watched Jane drive away, and for the first time in her life, she had to take a good look at herself. It was as if Jane had become a mirror, and Lisa saw what she could very well become one day. Her face was ashen as she sat there. She reached over and picked up the phone, "Yes, is this the agent that called me last week? You know you said that you knew someone who really wanted my house. Yes, I know I said that I didn't want to sell, but I've changed my mind. No, I'll take less than what I paid for it. I know it's worth more, but I need to move. No, I'm not going to stay here; things just aren't working out for me. Yes, if you can have the papers drawn up, I'll be by tomorrow afternoon to sign them."

Lisa poured herself another drink. She sat there for another moment and then reached for the phone again. "Yes, tell them I want the boat ready to leave tomorrow night. No, I don't know where I'm going, just anywhere away from here." As she laid the receiver down, Lisa walked over to the backdoor. Maybe it's time I really think about what I am doing with my life she thought.

CHAPTER THIRTEEN

The Sound of Thunder

It was five days before spring break was to begin and Irina thought she had never been happier in her life. She loved her classes and every day she fell more in love with Jonathan. And she had not seen Jane in weeks. Maybe she took the hint that she wasn't going to go through with it. Either way she was gone, and Irina was happy again. Irina loved going over to Wayne and Cindy's house to eat or just to visit. It seemed every day her new life was more like life back home. She had family and friends again, and now she knew she had a man who really loved her. She still couldn't shake the feelings about her daughter, but she knew that she had no way of ever finding her. Irina had figured out that most likely Jane didn't either. She was just lying, trying to use her, that's all there was to it. It was a cool Monday morning, and she knew nothing could go wrong now.

As Irina walked around Stonewall Hall heading toward the music building, there she stood by her black car. Jane's face was hard and cold. "Get in, and hurry up." Irina started to stop and run away, when a man came up behind her. She felt the knife against her back. "Did you think I would come by myself?" Jane laughed as she spoke. Irina got into the car, she was fighting fear and as she looked around there wasn't anyone insight. "What do you want with me?" she demanded. "What I want is for you to keep your promise, that's what I want, dear. But it seems you have forgotten what I did for you that night when those two guards were going to use you for their fun."

Irina's lips were moving slowly. "No, I haven't forgotten. But that was a long time ago."

"A long time ago?" Jane screeched. "It hasn't been that long ago and you know it. Should I tell you what I had to do to one of those guards? He came after me later that night. You remember how they found his body..."

"No," Irina said as she put her hands over her ears. "I don't what to know or hear anything about it."

"Well, it's because of you I had to spend fifteen days in the hole. They were trying to break me and get me to confess. Yeah, fat chance of that ever happening, but you still promised me that you would help me get even with Bill Thomas and you are going to keep your word to me. Do you hear me?"

Irina started to cry, "But he's a good man."

Jane reached back and slapped Irina across the face as hard as she could. "Good? Damn you, you sorry little tramp. He took from me and caused me to go to jail. There is nothing good about him, and I am going to get even with him with you or without you. But if you don't want to see your little girl ever again, well, that's alright by me." With that Jane handed Irina a picture of her daughter playing outside in the backyard of a house Irina did not recognize.

"Where is she?" Irina asked.

"First you have to help me and then, I'll help you." Irina lost all sense of reason for a moment and she grabbed Jane's arm screaming at her. It was then that the man sitting next to her hit her in the side and put his knife up to her throat. Jane reached back and slapped Irina once more. "Maybe I should let my friend here cut your throat. How does that sound to you? Or better yet, I'll let him take you off and have his fun with you before he cuts your throat." Then it was as if a light of evil had come on in Jane's sick mind. "No, I won't do that. I know some men who like to play with little girls. I'll send them over to get your daughter and they can have their fun with her, and when they are through with her. Well, I'm sure her body will wash up somewhere. So, what's it's going to be? Are you going to help me or do I let you go and send someone after your little girl?"

Irina was sitting there crying and shaking so hard that she couldn't keep still. "I know you would do that, wouldn't you?"

Jane smiled, "You can bet the last drop of your daughter's blood on it."

"I've sold myself to evil, and now my daughter's life is in danger. You'll never tell me where she is. I know that now, but to keep her safe, I have no choice but to do what you want."

"That's right, do what I want and she'll live. Don't, and I swear she'll die very slowly and painfully." Irina reached for the door. "Wait, we need to talk and then I'll carry you back to the outskirts of town."

"I know what to do." Irina said. As she was getting out of the car, Irina turned and looked back at Jane. "But if anything ever happens to my daughter. I'll spend the rest of my life hunting you down." Jane knew that Irina was serious; you could see it in her eyes. "No one knows where she is but me, and I have no reason to hurt her if you do what I want." Irina got out of the car. Jane looked at her as if she had lost her mind. "We're a mile from town."

"I know, but I'd rather walk a mile than to ride with you." As the black car drove away, Irina started walking back toward town. Every step was killing her. In her heart she knew that she was throwing away the one man who loved her. But she also knew that if she hoped to save her daughter, she had no other choice. Even though the skies were clear, clouds had moved across Irina's heart.

* * * * *

Jerome was sitting in the music hall waiting for his next class to begin. He still couldn't figure out why Annie had waited so long to tell him, or why she wasn't going to see the doctor about treatments. From his point of view it seemed she had just given up. The thought of Josh growing up without a mother was unthinkable to Jerome. There had to be some way he could get her to see the need to fight this thing. Looking out the window he said out loud, "Why doesn't she fight, why is she just giving up?"

A student walked in just as he was saying that. "Dr. Reinhart, are you ok?"

Jerome turned around and saw the look on his students face. "Oh yes, I'm ok, I was just thinking out loud about something and I guess I didn't realize how upset I was about it until I said it out loud. Hmm, maybe it's time I had a talk with her."

"With who, sir?" the student asked.

"Oh, never mind, it's something I have to do that's all."

* * * * *

The whole town was working to get ready for the Spring Break Yard Sale. Every vender in town and the surrounding area would come and have booths where they sold whatever they made or items they had in their store. Even though Paula felt as big as a house, she had already promised DJ and Maggie that she was going to take them walking through town so they could see everything. As she sat on the side of the bed, she reached down to pat them both. DJ looked up at her, "Paula, if you don't feel up to it this year we'll understand."

"That's right," Maggie joined in. "I know it's hard walking through town with both of us."

Paula looked down at them both, "I gave you my word and I'm going to keep it. We'll take the car and park it and then get out and walk around town. But you cannot beg anyone for food, that's the deal."

DJ just shook his head. "I knew there had to be a catch, and didn't I hear that May and Fay were going to have a stand out by their place? What if they have fried chicken, surely I could beg for just a little bite."

Paula reached down and rubbed the side of DJ's face. "No, but if they do have fried chicken, then I'll buy some and give you and Maggie a little bite when we get back home."

Maggie smiled, and thought to herself. "That's my DJ; he can get food when no one else can." Paula finished dressing and told DJ and Maggie to get ready also, "I thought we might go on and make a run into town today while the weather is so nice."

DJ looked at Paula, "But, I thought we were going next week when all the food, I mean, when all the booths are going to be up." Maggie shook her head. Paula laughed at DJ. "You can't hide it can you, your little stomach rules." DJ just stood up straight, "No, it doesn't, but if I happen to like fried chicken, then what's wrong with that?"

Paula reached out and pulled him close to her and said. "Not a thing in the world," as she kissed him on top of his head. Maggie walked over and held her head close to Paula so she could kiss her too. "Oh, I see, you want in on this loving too."

"Why yes," Maggie stated emphatically. "Everyone likes to be loved, Paula."

* * * * *

Curtis walked up behind Angelia as she was cleaning one of the fire trucks. "George isn't working today is he?"

Angelia looked over at Curtis with a smile. "Well, you make out our schedule, so you should know that better than anyone else." Angelia laughed as she stood up and looked at Curtis.

Looking around Curtis spoke quietly, "Well, I don't want to start anything and please don't repeat this, but you should watch out about getting too close to him."

With a puzzled look on her face, Angelia pulled her hair back from her face. "What are you trying to tell me, Curtis?"

Afraid he might spoil things with her, Curtis backed away slowly. "Oh, nothing, but just don't go and put all your eggs in one basket."

Still wondering what he was trying to tell her, Angelia watched Curtis hurry back upstairs. "What on earth was that all about?" When she thought about asking George, she remembered Curtis asking her not to say anything to anyone. And one thing Curtis knew he could count on, and that was Angelia's sense of honor. She would never betray anyone's trust. "Maybe Curtis is just having a bad day," she said as she went back to work washing the truck. Curtis looked out his window at her while she worked. Little did he realize that his feelings for her were becoming an obsession to him.

* * * * *

Teresa was sitting in her classroom waiting for her next class when Rusty walked in. "Hey," he said. Teresa looked up at Rusty and wondered why he would even bother coming in there to speak to her after the way she had been treating him. "Look, I think we need to talk this thing out. Honey, I love you. Can't you see that?"

"Rusty, I have students about to show up; can't this thing wait until after school?"

Rusty was starting to get a little annoyed with Teresa now. "No, it can't. You seem to forget that you have started going to a bar after work! I want you to stop acting like a fool and come back to your senses. Why are you trying to hurt me?"

Teresa had tears in her eyes as she spoke. "I just want to be left alone, that's all. Why can't you understand that?"

Students started coming through the door and some of them stopped, not knowing if they should come on in or not. Rusty turned and started to walk out of the class. Then he stopped and did something he had never done in a classroom before. He walked back to Teresa's desk reached down and picked her up and kissed her. "I'm not going to stop loving you if that is what you're trying to do here, I'm not." Rusty walked out, heading toward his own classroom. Teresa just sat there and cried, while her students sat there not knowing what to do.

Rusty stood in front of the blackboard without moving or making a sound. The students were wondering why he just stood there. One student asked him if everything was all right. "Yes, tell you what, today why don't you just read the next chapter and we'll call it a day. While they sat there and read, he looked out the window, not sure what was going to happen next.

* * * * *

Irina was back at her apartment sitting and absentmindedly looking out the window. She knew that what she had to do was going to hurt so many people in this quiet little town. Why couldn't Jane just leave her alone? She had faced the idea that she would never see her daughter again and for the most part, had come to grips with it. But now, there was the picture of her daughter playing out in the yard. So, Jane did know where she was. But she would never find her. Irina knew that if she didn't go back to jail, she would have to leave this place. Looking up toward heaven she asked. "Will I always have to pay for my sins? Can't I find some peace and someone to love me?"

Her heart was breaking as she looked at her watch. She knew she had missed her classes that day and she had called in and asked Darlene if she could work for her. "I just don't feel well that's all. No, don't come over, I might be coming down with some bug or something."

It wasn't anything Irina said, but the way she said it that caused Darlene to wonder what was wrong with her. When Jonathan came into the Morning Blend that afternoon, he asked Darlene if she had heard from Irina. "Oh, yeah, she called me and asked me to work for her. Said that she was going to bed early, thought she was coming down with something."

"Hmm, I wonder if I should go by and see how she's doing."

"I wouldn't, she was real plain that she didn't want anyone coming around her right now."

Jonathan thought for a moment, "Well, I'll call her tomorrow and see if she feels better."

* * * * *

Bill was working late at his office; he had been doing some paper work for Dr. Pittman all week trying to get ahead before Spring Break the next week. He knew Paula understood his working late, but there were times he could tell she wanted him home earlier than he had been arriving there lately. His cell phone rang. "Hello honey, yes, I'm still here. I know, but I should be through in about an hour and then I'm headed right home. I love you too, bye."

Paula put the receiver down, why did she feel this way? Was it just because she had gotten so big? It was that old fear coming back again; that uneasy feeling that something wasn't right. No, Bill wasn't that type of man and she knew that. Everything that happened before they were married was just because he was so confused, that's all. Maggie walked in there were Paula was standing. "Sweetie, is everything all right with Bill?"

"Oh yes, he is just working late helping Dr. Pittman out, that's all."

"Hmm, then why are you still standing here with that worried look on your face?"

"Me? I'm not worried Maggie, just tired that's all. Who would have ever thought that being this far along would make you so tired."

Maggie walked over to Paula and put her head up next to her leg. "It won't be long now dear, and then you'll have a little baby to run after all the time."

"Maggie, do you think I can do this?"

Maggie giggled, "Why sure you can. See how well I run after DJ and keep him in line?" They both laughed and Paula sat down in a chair while Maggie told her one of their old stories.

DJ was standing outside the door listening in. He knew Paula needed Maggie right then, which is why he sent her in there without him. "Sometimes girls just need to talk among themselves. Which is what Bill and I are going to do when he gets home, I know he has to work long hours sometimes, but he has to remember that his wife needs him now also."

DJ walked back to Bill and Paula's bedroom, there he felt it. That presence of evil, DJ stopped. All the hair on his back stood up. He hurried in where Paula and Maggie were, and whispered to Maggie to stop talking. "Something is wrong outside."

DJ whispered to Paula. "Call Bill and tell him to hurry home now. Tell him I said so."

* * * * *

Jane had walked back to her car and was just sitting there. She hadn't heard DJ or Maggie talking, but she was keeping a record of the times Bill wasn't home, when he left and when he came home. "Who knows?" she said to herself. "This might come in handy, if I decide to do something to that wife or child of his."

Jane drove off and was already gone when Bill drove up in a hurry. He ran into the house. "What's wrong, what's going on?"

DJ looked at him. "I'm not sure, but there was such a presence of evil outside your bedroom that I felt you needed to get home as soon as you could."

Bill walked outside but he saw nothing amiss. "Look DJ, I know you can sense things that we can't, but are you sure you didn't miss it tonight? I walked all around the house and I didn't see anything."

Maggie walked up and pushed Bill's leg with her body. "If DJ said there was something there, you had better listen to him." "Now, I wasn't saying…

"Bill," Paula said. "I think we should both listen to them. If I have learned one thing, it's that they do know more about what's happening around us. It's their gift and we would be foolish not to listen."

"Ok, ok, I'm listening. What should we do?"

DJ tried his best to explain to Bill and Paula that he didn't know everything, but that he had this feeling that something was coming their way. He could tell by Bill's reaction that he really didn't understand, or just didn't want to believe it.

* * * * *

Frank Robbins, the pastor of Christ Community Church, walked into the hardware store. "Mable, I need a washer or something; that sink is just about to drive me crazy the way it drips all the time. Why, my wife asked me yesterday how much I thought our water bill went up because I hadn't fixed it yet." Mable took one long look at pastor Robbins. "Now tell me this. If I were to give you the right washer or whatever it is you think you might need, would you know how to fix it?" A look of knowing came across Frank's face. "I see what you mean. How about you coming over tomorrow to take a look at it?"

Mable smiled, "Let's see, this is Monday night and if I am correct, your wife just about always cook's chicken and dumplings."

"Yes sir, the best in the whole state."

"Tell you what, feed me, and I'll fix it for free."

Frank pulled out his cell phone and hit the number to dial his home. "Hey dear, Mable said that if you would feed her some of your chicken and dumplings, she would come over and fix the sink tonight free of charge. Yes, I think that's a good idea too. What do you mean you doubt I could have ever fixed it?"

Mable reached out and took Frank's cellphone, "Don't worry dear, I'm on my way now. I was just about to close up shop and go home and eat some peanut butter and crackers. This sounds a whole lot better to me"

* * * * *

Annette was typing for some of the students, "You know honey, with everyone having computers nowadays, I'm still surprised I can find students to type for. Now this one here that I have been typing for, Irina, you can tell she is from another country because sometimes she gets her verbs backwards."

"Well, to us maybe, but remember dear, not everyone grew up speaking English." Zachary walked over to where Annette sat. He put his arms around her and held her close. "How much longer are you going to be up?"

Annette hit the save bottom and turned around, "I just finished, dear."

Zachary reached his hand out to Annette, "Come on and let's go outside and sit on the porch. It's a nice night and it's not too cold."

Annette smiled, "Only a fireman would want to sit out on the porch when it was cold outside."

"Yeah, but then you have to sit close to me to stay warm."

* * * * *

Jerome walked into the room where Annie was working. She was trying to finish some paintings she had started. She wanted to leave them to her son. "Now," he said. "I'm only going to say this once and that's all, and there isn't going to be any fussing about it one way or the other. I talked with Dr. Howard and he said that you caught this early enough if you do something now, but if you keeping putting it off then it will be too late."

"But my…" Jerome walked over to where Annie was sitting and sat beside her. "I'm not going to take no for an answer. Do you hear me? We are not giving up without a fight. I love you and I don't care if it cost all the money in the world. We're going to fight this thing together."

Annie was crying by now, "I never meant to hurt you. I just didn't want to put you through some long drawn out ordeal that in the end didn't help."

"If it had given me just one more month with you then it would have been worth it. I have already talked with Dr. Pittman and he said

130

to tell you not to worry about your class. He knew someone who could fill in for you while you had to be out."

Annie lay her head over on Jerome's shoulder. "You know I'll most likely lose all my hair?"

"Well, then I'll shave my head so that we'll match."

Annie looked over at Jerome and started laughing. "Now, wouldn't we be a sight?" Jerome held her close to him. "But at least we would be together."

* * * * *

Teresa was out on the dance floor dancing with some students. She had been drinking a little and even though she knew what she was doing was wrong, she told herself that Rusty would be better off without her. "Hey," said a young man who walked up to where she was dancing. "Aren't you one of the teachers at the University?"

"So?" Teresa said. Showing that his question was making her more than a little annoyed, "What if I am? Can't teachers have a good time too?"

"Sure, if you want to have a really good time, I have an apartment back in town." Teresa wasn't ready for those kinds of questions. She knew someone might ask her out, but it never crossed her mind that it would be a student.

"Not tonight, I'm having too much fun dancing."

Out in the parking lot Rusty was sitting in his car. He was trying to decide if he should go in and get her or should he give her a little more time. What he didn't realize was that deep down inside, Teresa wanted him to come after her. It was going to take that to prove to her that he really did care for her. Rusty drove away, thinking that maybe if he gave her a little more time she would come to her senses.

* * * * *

Dr. Pittman sat in his office at his house. He had told Clara that he was going to do some light reading, which is what he was doing in one sense of the word. What he was reading was a report that one of the other staff members had given him. In the report it told how Rusty and Teresa had been overheard fighting in each other's classroom, and that she was seen going out to a bar that was known to be a place where students went. Dr. Pittman sat there remembering when they first came to work for him, and how upset they were when Teresa lost the first child. Why she couldn't seem to carry a baby to full term no one knew. But this was unthinkable. He reached over and picked up another list of names. The list contained the names of some male students. "Hmm, I think I might could make this work, if I play my cards just right."

Clara walked into his office. "What are you reading that has you so lost in thought?" "Oh, nothing, just a list of students who aren't doing as well in their school work as I would like to see them do. Maybe there is a way they can get some help with their class work."

* * * * *

DJ and Maggie were sitting alone in a back room spending their time in worship. Maggie thought to herself that for some reason, DJ was putting more feeling into his singing. "DJ, I don't think I've heard you sing with such feeling in quite a while. Why, it was back when we were with Rocky." Just saying it made everything clear to Maggie. Now she knew what DJ had felt, but was glad when that feeling left him for a time. "How long have you felt this, DJ?"

"It went away for a time, so I didn't say anything to you because I thought that maybe we might be spared."

"Your dying is not something I want to face, but you can't hide it from me either."

"But Maggie, it's just a feeling; that doesn't mean anything will happen."

Maggie's voice was shaking now with emotion. "You had that same feeling about Rocky and look what almost happened to him. If that woman had used a bigger gun he would be dead now. Don't tell me it's nothing."

DJ put his head down, "I'm sorry, my Love. I should have told you."

Looking up, Maggie could see the sadness in his eyes. "It's the thought of leaving you that is hurting me so badly. I know how I would feel if I lost you. Please understand, I am going to be very careful." Slowly in a low voice Maggie spoke, "But if it means dying to save Bill or Paula, you would leave me, DJ."

"Yes," he said now with emotion filling his voice. "But that is our calling, Love. To live and die for those we watch over." Maggie lifted her head and sang a song which DJ knew he could not join in. It was the song of death. The death of the one you loved.

*　*　*　*　*

Irina sat looking out her window. It was late and she had turned all her lights off hours ago. She didn't want Jonathan driving by and seeing lights on and stopping to see if she was alright. She had to plan this out to the very last detail or her daughter's life would be at risk. As she held a calendar up to the street light, she knew it had to be Friday. That would have to be the day she flushed her life with Jonathan down the drain for good. Irina had to get her mind accustomed to the fact that she would most likely die in prison. Even if they sent her back to finish out her time, she knew Jane would see to it that someone would kill her. Irina did something that night she never did. She drank, not just a little but until she passed out. It was the only way she could make it through that night.

* * * * *

Father Grissom was in his office going over some of his records. "Let's see, Irina has been coming to Church every Sunday, but the last few weeks she hasn't met with me. I know she is seeing Jonathan Wedgeworth, and I had, let's see here… Oh yes, talked with Dr. Pittman about it four weeks ago and he didn't see anything wrong with it, so I guess I won't say anything to her about it either. But she is going to have to start making her appointments. I have to keep records of all this."

Father Grissom hated talking with Dr. Pittman but he knew that whatever he told him, Dr. Pittman would keep it to himself. He wasn't talking with him as a priest then, but as Irina's parole officer. He did notice that Dr. Pittman was a little concerned when he learned that Irina had been to prison and when he asked him the reason why. All Father Grissom could say was that he wasn't free to discuss Irina's case with outsiders, but that he just needed to know that everything was on the up and up, so to speak, with her and Jonathan. Come Sunday, he was going to have one of his long talks with Irina. If only he had talked with her sooner. If only he had listened to that still small voice telling him that he needed to talk with her now. But it could wait he told himself.

CHAPTER FOURTEEN

Storm Clouds

Irina had missed the last three days of her classes. She had called in sick to work and even called the school telling them that she was very sick. When Jonathan went by to check on her, she wouldn't come to the door. "I don't feel well and I have been throwing up for the last two days."

"Well, then maybe I need to take you to the hospital and let them check you out."

He could hear the aggravation in Irina's voice. "No, I just want everyone to leave me alone. Why can't you understand that I'm not one of those people who likes to have everyone hovering over me when I'm sick. Please, just go home and let me get back to bed."

Jonathan was hurt that Irina talked to him that way, but then he just shrugged it off that she was sick and didn't want him to see her that way so he left. "Alright, I'll leave for now, but if this thing continues then I am going to take you to the doctor whether you like it or not."

Irina heard his footstep as he walked away. She knew that she couldn't stay locked up any longer. It seemed the time had come for her to do what she knew was the wrong thing to do, but then she really didn't have a choice. Or so she thought. For everyone has a choice, if only we are willing to open up and allow others into our lives. If Irina had trusted Jonathan, he could have found a way to help her. But fear never listens to reason.

* * * * *

Jonathan was planning to talk with Bill early that Thursday morning before class. He wanted some input about the way Irina had been acting toward him. It seemed as if everything was going really great between them and now she was starting to act really crazy. His thoughts were on Irina when he looked up and saw her walking across campus. He ran to catch up with her. "Hey, hold up a minute. What's going on? Why haven't you been returning my calls?" Irina turned to look at Jonathan and he could see the conflict in her eyes. "What is it?"

She backed away, "It's nothing you can help me with, so please leave me alone."

"What are you saying? Irina, if you're having trouble let me help you."

Irina knew this was the open door she needed. "Would you help me even if you knew one of the teachers here was putting pressure on me to sleep with him? Would you put your job on the line for me?"

Jonathan stood there shocked. "What are you talking about?" He couldn't believe that anyone there would do anything like that.

"See, that's what I mean. You like having a pretty Russian girl holding onto your arm as we walk around town. But you're not willing to put your life on the line for me." With that Irina pushed Jonathan away from her. "Stay away from me. You're just like all the other men I have known in my life. You're just out for one thing, just stay away, do you hear me?" Irina turned and ran away from Jonathan. She was crying as she ran. She had started down a path from which she could not deviate.

* * * * *

Bob was working trying to get everything ready for the lunch crowd. Mary Ann walked up behind him and put her arms around him. "You know, we could maybe ask my mother to come back again and watch the kids some more. I kind of like having our night's out."

Bob turned around and kissed Mary Ann. "Well, I was thinking about asking my mom to come next month to stay for a few days. That way we wouldn't wear one out with our kids."

Mary Ann laughed, "You mean you think they're that much of a hand full?"

Pulling her even closer to him, he lightly kissed her again. "Well, they are getting a little older, so maybe they're not too much to handle. But I just didn't want to wear one parent out in case we needed them later on."

"Well, if I can get them to bed on time tonight, maybe we can sit in front of the fireplace and watch a movie?"

Bob's eyes just sparkled, "It's a date."

* * * * *

Robert Lee was standing at the window in his classroom watching the students and teachers walk across campus. He had already had two drinks this morning, which was more than his usual. But this thing about Bill Thomas was eating at him. He wanted to get rid of Bill, and he was at the point of doing it himself if he had to. Yes, that was the best idea he had all year. Why pay someone else to do what he could do just as well. As he took a drink of his coffee trying to clear his head before his students arrived, his thoughts kept going back to the last time

137

he tried to have Bill Thomas killed. Yet Bill had made it out alive. No, this time he was going to watch and wait for just the right moment and then, he would be rid of Bill Thomas for good. He saw Irina running across the campus crying. "Hmm, it seems Jonathan isn't as great of a catch as he thought he was. She's running away from him." Robert Lee, in his younger days, fancied himself a ladies' man. "Well, maybe once I have Dr. Pittman's job, I'll take her away from Jonathan and then fire him and send him back to that broken down coffee shop." Robert Lee Locklear was blind to everything going on around him. He was being pulled into a large spiritual battle and he didn't even realize it. His path could only lead him two ways now. And he had chosen the wrong one.

* * * * *

Fay and May were outside working to set up their table for next week's town wide yard sale. "May, now make sure we have those students scheduled all next week. We're going to be busy cooking, so we'll need someone to work outside at our table." May turned and put her hands on her hips. "After all these years, no, in fact every year, you tell me the same thing. And every year I tell you that I have already taken care of it. So, please tell me just when are you going to trust me to do my job?"

Fay grinned as she turned around to face May. "Never, Mama told me to always watch out for you, so until they plant me in the ground little sis, I'll always be checking up on you."

About that time a sweet roll went flying by Fay's head. "Hey," she said, "that was a perfectly good sweet roll you just threw away."

"Well now, I wouldn't say she threw it away" Dr. Sam Balius said as he took a bite out of it. "I mean when you see a sweet roll flying at you then that means it's yours, right?"

May was embarrassed that Dr. Balius had caught Fay and her fussing like they were kids. Even though she knew they were only teasing with each other, she never wanted the preacher to see them doing it. "Now, I can see that the two of you are being such good examples of Christian love, so I guess I won't have to change my sermon for this coming Sunday." Dr. Balius grinned as he took another bite.

"Well now," May piped up. "It seems you haven't minded eating my roll this morning."

"Why my merciful morning, May," Fay said. "And he ain't paid for it neither."

With that, Fay picked up another roll and sent it in the direction of Dr. Balius who caught it and turned quickly to walk away. "I can see my work here is done and I have to get to class. See you ladies on Sunday."

May was laughing as she said, "Only a preacher could get two free rolls out of a deal and still walk away with a sermon text in the mix as well."

"Yeah," Fay said. We're next week's topic, that's for sure."

Alma Smith and Christine Gully walked across the street. "Did we see you two throwing sweet rolls at the preacher?" Christine's lips were poking out as she spoke.

"Now, did you see him eat them too?" Fay asked, even wondering why she was taking up her time answering these two.

"Hmm, then he shouldn't have eaten them if he didn't pay for them." Alma said.

"Why, that's stealing," blurted out Christine.

Fay was just about to lose her cool with these two when May walked up with two sweet rolls. "Here you go ladies, they're on the house."

Shaking her head, Alma said. "I just couldn't eat anything that has been thrown around all morning."

Fay stepped up by May. "I'll have you know..,"

May butted in. "We hope y'all come back next week when we have everything set up."

"Come on, Alma." Christine said. "We need to keep walking if we are going to get our blood flowing this morning."

As they walked down the sidewalk, May said. "Yeah, sure would be something terrible if the blood stopped flowing to your two brains. Why, the rest of us wouldn't have to listen to all the yuck that came out of your mouths."

Fay was giggling as she leaned over on May. "Come on and let's get back to work. I think we've had enough excitement for one day."

"Nope, for a year," May said.

* * * * *

Bill was sitting at his desk looking over some papers. He was unaware that his life was about to be turned upside down. He didn't listen to DJ's warning like he should have. He was just too busy to stop and listen, or to pray. Now the day was upon him and he didn't have a clue as to what was about to happen to him. Irina walked into his room. Bill looked up and said. "Class doesn't start for another twenty minutes, Irina. By the way, are you feeling better now? Jonathan told me that you were sick earlier this week. If you don't feel like making class today, that's fine with me."

Irina just stood there. "Dr. Thomas could you look at this paper for me, I'm not sure I have the verbs right."

"Sure, hand it here."

"No, maybe I shouldn't get close to you."

"Nonsense, I doubt if I'll catch anything from you." With that, Bill got up and walked around his desk. As he got close to Irina she threw the paper down and reached up with her right hand and grabbed her

140

own shirt and ripped it open leaving marks across her breast as she did. Irina had loosened the stitches in her bra on the right side so that it would tear open also. Irina screamed as loud as she could and ran out of Bill's classroom. Students were coming down the hallway running to see what was going on. "Help me! Please someone help me he's trying to rape me." Irina was crying now almost out of control. Not that she was acting. Her heart was truly breaking inside for what she was having to do to save her daughter.

Bill ran out into the hallway after her, not realizing that the very act itself was going to make him look guilty in everyone's eyes. "Wait a minute," he yelled. "I didn't do anything."

* * * * *

It was dark by the time he was released from jail. Dr. Pittman had gone to bat for Bill and on his word that Bill would not leave town they released him into Dr. Pittman's custody. As they walked down the stairs of the Courthouse, Bill asked. "Is Paula alright Dr. Pittman? I swear to you that I never laid a hand on her. Please, you have to believe me."

"Son, you know I do, but it's what everyone else in town believes that is going to hurt you. Already this thing has spread over the whole campus and town. People are being torn apart by this, Bill. Some are siding with you, and some with Irina."

As they reached the sidewalk, Jonathan came out of the shadows. Bill looked up in time to see Jonathan's fist hit him right in the mouth and sent him to the sidewalk. Jonathan looked down at him with eyes filled with boiling rage. "How could you? You, of all people; I trusted you, man. You know why I left England." Bill laid there with blood flowing out of his mouth. He didn't know what to say to Jonathan. He was still having a hard time believing any of it himself. Jonathan turned and started walking away. He stopped and turned back around. "If I ever see you around her again, I'll kill you."

Dr. Pittman sat down on the steps of the Courthouse. He didn't let on that all of this was causing him a lot of pain in his chest. He just sat there and cried. For not only was the town he loved being torn apart, but the school he had worked so hard to build was being torn apart as well. "Are you ok, Dr. Pittman?" Bill asked.

"Yes, my boy. Let's get you home before anything else happens."

Bill said, "I need to explain this to Paula, sir."

"She isn't there, Bill. She is staying with us for a few days. Just give her time. She'll come around."

"And if she doesn't? Then what do I do? How can I go on without her?"

Neither Bill nor Dr. Pittman saw the black car parked over in an alley. But inside the car there was rejoicing going on. Oh it was quiet enough, but rejoicing all the same. "Now Bill, let's see you get yourself out of this one. And don't think that I am through with you. Not by a long shot. I promise you that you are going to pay." Jane was softly laughing as she spoke. Hatred had so filled her heart that she only cried now when she was hurting someone. "Yes, and I am going to tear your lovely little town apart as well. Nothing is going to be the same when I'm through with you. And everyone is going to hate you for it."

* * * * *

As Bill walked into the house, DJ was waiting for him. Bill just sat down on the floor and cried. "Why DJ, please tell me why this is happening to me?"

DJ laid his head down on Bill's leg. "We don't always understand everything that happens in our lives, Bill, at least not at the moment we are going through it. I'm sure that if we keep our eyes on God, then in the end everything is going to turn out alright."

"How can you be so sure? I wasn't doing anything to hurt anyone. All I wanted was to live here and work. What did I want that was so wrong?"

DJ laid there without saying anything. His heart was so heavy that he couldn't find the right words for Bill. Maggie walked up to Bill and placed her head on his other leg. "Bill, I'm so sorry. I wish there was something we could have done to stop this from happening to you and Paula. Have you talked with her yet?"

"No," Bill said shaking his head. "She doesn't want to talk with me right now Dr. Pittman said. Surely she doesn't believe any of this?"

Maggie moved closer to Bill. "She's going to have your baby, but right now her emotions are out of control and her fears are running wild. Remember how you reacted when you first found out about Jane? You were mad at God and just about everyone else too. Give her time, she'll come around soon."

Bill sat there and cried some more. He didn't know, nor could he truly have understood how such hatred could live in one person. His world was turned upside down, but that is sometimes the best thing. For then God can turn it right side up again.

CHAPTER FIFTEEN

Pain and Confusion

It was raining that Sunday morning as Bill sat looking out the window. He had already drank two pots of coffee, and when Maggie started to say something to him about drinking so much coffee, DJ whispered to her not to say anything.

"But why, DJ," she asked when they entered the other room.

"Mainly because he isn't drinking liquor, Maggie. He could be in there right now drunk and passed out. But he isn't. Bill has gone through something very terrible, and he is hurting. He needs us right now more than ever."

Maggie's head was down when she asked DJ. "DJ, do you think Bill is guilty?"

"No!" DJ said sharply. "Maggie, how could you even think such a thing, much less speak it."

Maggie sat down and just held her head down. "I saw Paula crying, DJ. She is hurt so deeply over this and she feels like Bill has been pulling away from her lately."

DJ walked over to Maggie. He knew she was fighting her own battles now. He knew how much she would love to raise a pup of her own. "I know, my Love. But remember, Bill has been working a lot with Dr. Pittman and doing work for him. If he wasn't with Dr. Pittman, he was by himself all that time. Remember, the young lady was Jonathan's girlfriend. So, it seems to me that she must have been spending a lot of her free time with him."

"You're right of course DJ, but… I'm hurt over this whole affair as well, I guess. I never thought we would be facing this. Did you, DJ?"

"No, my Love, but here we are, so let's make the best of it and get Bill and Paula back together."

Maggie pushed DJ with her body. "That's right, let's get them walking in love then we can figure out the rest of this mess." When they walked into the den, Bill had fallen asleep in his chair. They both just lay down and stayed in there with him. When he awoke they wanted Bill to know that they still loved and cared for him.

* * * * *

Paula was sitting in the back bedroom crying. She had tried to stop, but every time she tried, it seemed to start all over again. "How could Bill do this to me?" Paula looked up toward heaven, "Please God, tell me why my husband did this?"

"Have you ever thought that maybe he didn't?" Clara said behind her.

Paula didn't even turn around to look at her. "I knew you would take his side. I would have been better off going home to my parent's."

Clara walked over to where Paula was sitting. She sat down beside her and put her arm around her and just held her close as she began crying again. "My dear child; I'm not taking sides with anyone. It's just that I have known Bill Thomas much longer than you and longer than most people at that school even. I would have to see him doing something like that with my own two eyes before I would believe it."

Looking up with tears running down her face, Paula asked. "But how can you be so sure? I mean I thought he loved me and now I find out that he has been eyeing this young woman. I don't know what to think anymore."

"Well maybe I could help shed a little light on this subject."

Turning to look at Dr. Pittman, Paula asked. "What do you mean?"

"I mean, I have been on the phone all morning with a dear friend of mine and he has given me permission to tell you something that he told me. But understand young lady, you cannot, under any circumstance, tell Bill what I'm about to tell you."

Paula's voice was raised when she said. "But why not? If you know something that will prove Bill is innocent, then you have to tell the police."

Dr. Pittman stood in front of Paula and placing his hands lightly on her arms he said, "Young lady, the man who told me this information has broken his own oath by even telling me. The reason he told me was because I told him how upset you were and that I was afraid you might go into early labor. No, you either agree to not tell Bill or anyone else what I am going to share with you, or it will go with me to my grave. That is what I promised Father Grissom."

It was then that Paula realized the Father Grissom was Irina's pastor and that she must have said something to him while she was in confession. "Dr. Pittman, if you two know something, then you should go to the law with it."

"Neither of us can, nor will we go. I have given my word dear, and that is where it stands. Now do you want to hear it or not?"

Shaking her head yes, Paula said, "I do sir, and I promise never to repeat this to anyone." Paula learned that day what friendship and honor meant to men like Dr. Pittman. As much as he loved Bill Thomas, even as if he was his own son, he would never break his word to another friend. There was a bond there, one that isn't easily broken. A bond that had held men together through tough times in the past; it was rare to see such honor in these days. Paula knew that she had witnessed just such a bond that day. Dr. Pittman sat in the chair across from the bed on which Paula and Clara were sitting and he told them everything that Father Grissom had told him.

* * * * *

Jonathan had been opening the Morning Blend on Sunday mornings so that the students would have a place to go study, and drink coffee while they studied. That morning he brewed two of his favorite coffees. One was from Nicaragua and was called Colibri Azul. Jonathan liked this coffee and always kept some on hand. The next was an Ethiopian coffee called Abyssinian Mokka. As he made the pot of coffee, a sadness and anger came over him. These were the two coffees he and Bill would always drink when they played chess. "Why," he wondered; "did Bill have to turn out to be such a moron." Jonathan turned his back to everyone as he worked. He didn't want to reveal too much about the way he felt.

Chip and Nita were sitting in the back of the room drinking a latte and trying to not talk about what everyone else in town was talking about. Finally Chip spoke up. "You know, my Mom has known Dr. Thomas for a long time and she said that she didn't believe he did anything wrong."

Nita sat there quietly, "But why would that woman lie? I mean if it was some nineteen year old, you could say that she was failing his class and she was trying to get a better grade out of the deal. But this is an older woman, Chip."

"I know, none of it makes sense to me. But let's not get in the middle of this thing. I don't want anything to hurt our relationship. Besides, five years from now, no one will even remember it happened. You know how college kids are these days."

Nita sat close to Chip. "Yeah, but there is something about this that makes me believe everyone will remember it many years from now. But you're right, we don't need to get in the middle of this thing. It's already tearing friendships apart on the campus and in the town as well."

"Yes, I know. Our peaceful little town is in the middle of a meltdown."

*   *   *   *   *

Jerome and Annie were coming out of Dr. Adcock's office at the hospital that rainy Sunday morning. "Thanks for seeing us on a Sunday morning doc," Jerome said.

"That's quite all right, I had to be here anyway. I'm just glad Annie, that you decided to listen to Jerome and go for the treatments. Now, here is the name of the doctor down in Atlanta. They are waiting for you and when you arrive there tomorrow, they will go on and check you in."

Annie was a little nervous when she asked, "When do you think they will start the treatments?"

Dr. Adcock looked at Annie, "I told them to get started the day you arrived. Young lady, we are going to beat this thing and you are going to come back here to finish your career as a teacher."

Annie spoke very quietly, almost in a whisper. "But Dr. Adcock, my mother had cancer and she didn't beat it. Why are you so sure I will?"

Tears formed in Dr. Adcock's eyes as he spoke. "Now, you know that I was your Mother's friend and I always told her the truth. But

Annie, we found it in time, even for the treatments they had back then. Your mother put the treatments off for almost eight months. By the time she made up her mind to fight it, the cancer had spread too far. I begged her to go on with the treatments but she just wouldn't listen. Thank God, you have a wonderful husband who's not going to let you make that same mistake."

Annie's face brightened, "Then I can beat this? I can get better?"

"Yes," Dr. Adcock said.

"Thank you again for taking time with us sir," Jerome said. "Honey, we need to get on the road if we're going to get there before dark." Hand in hand they walked out the door. Dr. Adcock thought to himself, the best care in all the world is someone loving you and Annie has that.

*****

Annette got up from her typing, "Zachary, honey?"

"Yeah, sweetie, what do you need?" Zachary rubbed his eyes as he sat up in bed.

"I'm sorry I woke you, but I just don't know what to do about this."

Zachary looked puzzled, "About what?"

"Well, I did all this typing for that young woman Irina and now they say that she isn't going to her classes anymore, so how do I get paid for all the work I did?"

Zachary pushed her hair back from her face. "Tell you what, why don't you lay down with me and let's get some more sleep, because I'm about dead. We'll talk about it when I wake up."

Annette put her hands on her hips, "Firemen, when you're not working all you want to do is sleep."

"Yeah, I was up all night. Alma Smith's cat was up in a tree. There were power lines by the tree so we couldn't get close enough with the

150

bucket, so I had to climb up the tree and that stupid cat when out on a limb that was too small for me. So, I had to call the stupid cat all night and finally it came to me. To tell you the truth, I just think it wanted to get away from Alma."

Annette laughed, "Even I could have told you that." With that, she turned off the lights and laid down so Zachary could go back to sleep. While Zachary slept, Annette thought about all that was happening in their sleepy little town.

* * * * *

Irina was getting dressed to go the church. Father Grissom had left word that he had to talk with her now. She was afraid to face him. What if she said something that put her daughter's life in danger? How could she keep the truth from him and the rest of the town? Irina was worried that she wasn't going to be able to hold it together. It wasn't even about helping someone get even with another person now. This was about the life of her daughter. No matter what she had to go through, even if she went back to prison, she had to do whatever it took to keep her daughter safe. Irina walked out the door heading toward church. She was more determined now than ever to save her daughter. Even if it cost her every bit of happiness she could ever have.

* * * * *

Dr. Travis was walking down the hall of the hospital when he felt a sharp pain in his side. As he turned, there stood Vickie Eldridge with her blue eyes just beaming at him. "You know," Travis said. "We're going to have to work on the way you say hello."

Vickie's mouth flew open, "Why, I never, in all my life had a man talk to me like that."

151

Travis smiled, "Yeah, but how many men have there been that you bruised their side and arms every time you got around them?"

Vickie smiled back at Travis, "Why none, of course."

"Well, I hope you're not as tough on my heart as you have been on my arms."

Vickie put her hands on her hips, as she shook a finger in Travis' face, "Why I'll have you know that I would never do anything to hurt anyone."

With that, she started to hit him on the arm again when Travis reached out and grabbed her and pulled her up close to him. "Maybe, I should just kiss you here and now."

Her eyes softened, "Well, I thought I was going to have to hit you again to make you think of it."

Travis pulled Vickie close and kissed her ever so lightly on the lips. Kim Adcock walked by about that time. "If my husband couldn't kiss me any better than that, why I would probably hit him."

Vickie just smiled, "That's not going to work today, sis. Just leave me alone."

Kim walked in the office where Howard Adcock was sitting. "Hey, did you know we have doctors and nurses kissing in the hallway?"

"Hmm, let me guess, Travis and Vickie?"

"Why yeah, who else?" Howard smiled at Kim and stood up, kissed her, then picked up his papers to make his rounds. "Well, come on," he said. "We still have to make our rounds, seeing as how your sister has stopped one of our doctors from doing his job."

"Wait a minute, my sister? Why Travis is your friend and he was the one who kissed my sister, I saw the whole thing."

Howard just winked at Kim, "Yes, and isn't it grand?"

Kim put her arm around Howard and looked up at him, "I never do win with you, do I?"

"No, but then again winning isn't everything." They laughed as they walked back out into the hall. Most people would have thought this a strange sight indeed. While the town was starting to tear itself apart, here in one of the most unlikely places, there was an oasis of love and peace.

* * * * *

Polly Blanks was finishing getting undressed from church when she couldn't hold it any longer. "Please tell me why you said to everyone on the sidewalk that you didn't believe Bill Thomas was guilty?"

Philip walked back into the bedroom from the bathroom. "Mainly because I don't believe he is guilty. I know how women are going to stick together, and believe me, this isn't some guy thing either. If I thought he was guilty, then I would have said so."

Polly's black hair fell loosely upon her shoulders and her grey eyes were now flaming. "Well, it sounds like a guy thing to me! How could you take his side?"

Philip spoke now with his voice rising in anger. "Well, maybe because I just can't see Bill Thomas being that kind of man, but let's face it, you don't have to look far these days to find cheap and loose women."

Polly picked up her hair brush and threw it at Philip. "Get out, I don't want to speak to you or even look at you all day; maybe never!"

Philip walked out of the house and shut the door. He got into his car and drove off without telling Polly where he was going. Polly sat on the side of the bed crying. Just the other day they had talked about starting a family, and now this happened. Why did she allow herself to get so mad over Bill Thomas? Did she really care one way or the other about this whole mess? No, she did care. What if some young woman set her eye on Philip? He had to understand how she felt, how this affair at school made her feel. She was now afraid of losing her husband to some teenage girl. Polly cried and wished Philip was back home holding and comforting her.

* * * * *

Paula had sat in her room all day after talking with Dr. Pittman. He had told her all he knew about the young woman, but it still didn't make any sense to her. She went to prison for killing her husband, who was supposed to have been a drug dealer. OK, no problem with that part. He was beating her and was one day going to kill her himself most likely. But what didn't make sense was why was she's claiming that Bill had attacked her. What reason did she have for doing this and why pick Bill out of all the teachers at the school. Clara walked back into the room. "I was hoping you were packing to go back to Bill."

Paula turned around slowly. "I'm not sure I want to go back. I still can't figure out why this woman would choose Bill out of all the teachers at the school."

Clara sighed, "Paula, when you were both in the hospital, there were some newspaper that got wind of what happened to Bill with that woman Jane and about the money he has in the bank. Don't be surprised if this young woman doesn't make Bill an offer to say she was lying for a large sum of money."

Paula turned her head quickly, "What! Pay her for all the hurt and damage she has done? Has Bill said anything like this to you? Please don't hold anything back from me."

Clara walked over and sat down in the chair by the bed. "No, I doubt Bill even knows about the papers picking up the story online. But it does make sense now doesn't it? I mean if you came from a country where you had very little, and after all she has gone through, this would be very tempting."

Paula stood up, "If I wasn't pregnant, I'd show her tempting. I would kick her all the way back to wherever she came from. I'm going home tomorrow. It's time Bill and I had a long talk."

* * * * *

Monday morning Dorothy Eldridge was heading toward her antique store when she stopped off at the Bailey's Bakery. "Why hello Ruth, I was heading to work and well, I know I shouldn't, but let me have a look at what you two have been baking this morning." By the way, did you hear that some folks in town aren't going to use Hawkins Dry Cleaners anymore because of that business with Bill Thomas and that young woman who is staying in their apartment?"

Before Ruth could say a word Roy spoke up, "Yeah, and I'm one of them. I mean how could they allow her to stay there knowing that she set Dr. Thomas up?"

Ruth walked out from behind the counter, "Now Roy, we said that we were not going to get in the middle of this mess. So let's not say anything that might upset them."

Dorothy could feel her blood pressure rising. "I think they are doing what every good Christian should do, help those in need. And from the way it seems to me, that young girl is very much in need. She doesn't have any friends here and no family either."

Roy's face was just about as red as it could get. "Friends, friends, you say; how could she have any friends in this town when she is nothing but a no good liar?"

Dorothy stood straight up and said, "Well, if you feel the need to stop doing business with Wayne and Cindy, then I feel the same need to stop coming in here." With that she turned and walked out.

Ruth looked over at her husband. "If you don't keep your mouth shut, we'll not have a business by the end of the month."

* * * * *

Irina was helping Wayne and Cindy in the dry cleaners. They had to let one of their workers go already and were afraid they might have to let the other one go if things continued as they were. "I'm sorry I have caused you all this trouble. I was hoping to just leave town, but the Chief of Police will not allow me to leave town right now."

What Irina didn't want anyone to find out was that it was Father Grissom who refused to allow her to leave town. As her parole officer he told her that she could, under no circumstances, leave town. "Child, if you leave town this whole mess will tear this town apart for years. No, you are going to stay until we get to the bottom of this thing. But if you take off, I'll be forced to tell the police chief everything about your record and your past. Then it will become knowledge that everyone will have access to. The newspapers, and yes even Jonathan, will hear the truth then." That's when Irina got up and ran out of Father's Grissom's office.

Cindy spoke up. "Maybe it would help if you spoke with Father Grissom. I'm sure he would be glad to listen to you and he might even be able to help you, Irina."

Irina shook her head. "No, I don't think I should talk with him about this. Priest's don't understand things like this."

Wayne said in a low voice, "You might not have to worry about that, here he comes now."

Father Grissom walked into the cleaners and spoke to Wayne and Cindy both. "Good morning, dear folks. I was wondering if I could have a few moments with Irina."

"Why sure Father," Wayne said. "Do you want us to leave?"

"No, Irina and I can take a walk around town and talk, if that's alright with you Irina?"

Sheepishly Irina walked around to where Father Grissom was standing. "Yes sir, that would be fine with me." As they walked for a few moments without either one of them saying anything, Irina finally asked if he was going to tell everyone about her. "You're not; are you Father? You did give me your promise."

Father Grissom looked over at Irina, "Why don't you tell me what happened that day at school."

"There's nothing to tell. Dr. Thomas attacked me, that's all."

Shaking his head, Father Grissom remembered one inmate telling him that nothing just happens. There's a reason for it. "Ok, but why did he attack you? I mean he has a wife and everyone in town who knows Dr. Thomas says that he isn't that type of man. So, why now?"

Irina's voice was starting to get agitated. "I don't know why he did it. His wife has gotten really big they tell me; maybe she wasn't being a wife to him. I don't know. He started asking me to go out with him, and when I said no, he attacked me. Maybe his blood was just boiling over that day. I don't know and I don't like talking about it."

"Hmm," Father Grissom said, "You see I worked in prisons for years. I think I know something about men getting out of control. I can't see that being the reason. Can you, my child."

"So, you are going to take his side against me as well?"

"I'm not here to take sides, Irina. All I want is to hear your side of the story and try to figure this whole mess out. Can't you see what it's doing to this town? Over a third of the booths aren't even up yet. This big city wide yard sale has been one of the biggest things this community has ever done and now it's falling apart."

"I'm sorry Father, but what can I do about it?" Without saying a word, Father Grissom looked over at Irina. "I don't want to talk about it anymore today, Father. May I leave and go back to work, please."

Without saying a word, he shook his head. Irina turned and walked away. She thought to herself that she had pulled that off ok. He doesn't know a thing. Father Grissom started back to his church office. "Now, I know she's lying. But I just don't know why." Years of working in prisons had taught him how to listen, and to recognize the way someone's voice would change when they were lying. Heavy hearted, he walked slowly back. What he knew, he could not prove. And even if he could, he couldn't tell anyone. "Sometimes, it's hard being a priest, O Lord."

* * * * *

Rusty was sitting on the side of the bed when Teresa woke up. "Good morning, how are you feeling this morning?"

Teresa held her head. He knew how she felt. She was sick from being out drinking all night. Before she could answer, she jumped up and ran into the bathroom vomiting. As she sat on the floor she thought to herself, "How can this be so much fun? Those kids keep talking about all the fun they are having, and then the next morning you're in the bathroom throwing up your toenails." She felt a cold wet rag across her forehead.

Rusty gently picked her up and carried her back to bed. As he laid her in bed and pulled the covers back over her, he whispered so very softly, "I'm not giving up on you. We're meant to be together for the rest of our lives. I don't, and I could never love anyone but you, Teresa." Kissing her forehead he walked out of the room.

Teresa buried her face into the pillow and cried. Rusty stood outside the door listening to her cry. It gave him hope, for as long as Teresa was still crying over the way she was acting, he might still be able to reach her.

* * * * *

Rebekah Corey was walking around town looking at some of the booths that were set up when she ran into Irina. "Oh, I'm sorry." Irina didn't know what else to say. Her mind was a thousand miles away, trying to find some small measure of peace.

Rebekah's gray hair was shining in the sunlight, and her blue eyes were very deep and penetrating. "Nice little town we have here, isn't it?" Before Irina could answer, Rebekah said. "That is before all this misunderstanding happened." Her eyes softened a bit, "Look child, I've known Bill Thomas for a long time; why when my husband was still living…" Her words were cut short; tears filled her eyes as she tried to speak again. "All I'm saying is that we spent a lot of time with Bill and his wife and daughter. There was never more a family man than Bill Thomas. And with his wife Paula about to have their child, I can't believe he would throw it all away. Not Bill, not even if his wife wasn't going to have a child. He just isn't that type of man."

Irina stepped backward a few steps. "Sure, you'll believe Dr. Thomas, and you'll think the very worse of me. What makes you so sure I'm the one lying?" Irina wasn't aware that her voice was being heard by everyone standing around. But as she spoke, something happened, she felt like the biggest liar. She felt dirty and unclean. Irina started crying and ran away toward the cleaners.

Rebekah stood there watching her run toward the cleaners. "Hmm, let's see, if I remember right it says something about the Apostle Peter remembering, and then running out into the night crying. Or into your upstairs apartment as it were. Your guilt isn't going to go away, Irina. I don't know why you're doing this, but believe me, your guilt isn't going away."

CHAPTER SIXTEEN

Howling Winds

The police station was hopping early Tuesday morning. Alissa Tidwell, the dispatcher, called out to the chief, "They're bringing her in, but it's taking both of them."

"Bringing who in, and why is it taking both of them?"

"They're bringing in Mable King, Brad."

Brad loved being chief of police here where nothing ever happened, but now it seemed as if the whole town had lost all its good sense. "Well, what on earth did Mable do to get herself arrested?"

Alissa smiled, "She knocked out this tourist, did it with just one blow to his jaw."

Brad threw his hands up in the air, "Has everyone in this town gone crazy?"

"Well," Alissa said. "He said something about Bill Thomas. Said he heard we had a wild teacher at our school here, that he wouldn't send his daughter here for anything."

About that time the front door flew open. You could hear Mable's voice over everyone else. "Les Tidwell, if you don't let me go and take these handcuffs off me, I'll kick your rear end all over this town."

Holding his jaw Les said, "Brad, Mable tried to knock me out too."

"Oh Mable, now why on earth did you go and do a thing like that? You know you can't go around hitting a police officer. Now, I'm going to have to lock you up for sure."

Mable's eyes flared, "You're what? I hope you have more help coming; because it's going to take more than the three of you to put me in that cell."

Floyd O'Neal walked in behind Les and Mable. "Chief, this whole thing is just a mess." Brad shook his head, "Well, what ever happened to the man Mable punched out?"

Floyd walked up to Brad so he wouldn't be heard by everyone. "Dr. Balius got to him before anyone else and helped him up too. Then that ole fellow started mouthing off about how this town was filled with nothing but scum. Then Dr. Balius pushed the man; why if it hadn't been for Father Grissom grabbing him, I honestly believe he would have decked that fellow. Then Dr. Balius and Father Grissom had words and they both were yelling at each other."

Brad looked as if he had seen a ghost, "Well, what happened next," he said as his arms flew up in the air.

"Oh," Floyd said. "The man got in his car and took off. I don't think we'll ever see him again and Father Grissom walked away from Dr. Balius. But they both were still upset when they parted."

"Why didn't you arrest Dr. Balius for pushing that fellow around?"

Brad was wondering if he was going to live through this. Floyd's eyes got as wide as plates, "No sir, not me. I'll never arrest a preacher. No sir, that has to be a sure ticket to hell."

"Speaking of which," Mable yelled out, "I mean you had better let me go and do it now. You heard that guy ran off, so he can't press charges."

"No, but you still hit one of my officers and that is going to get you at least one night in jail Mable. You can't go around hitting my officers."

"Look, his mother told me when I was a teenager and I used to babysit him that I could hit him, so what's the difference now?"

Brad's face was turning red as his temper was starting to get the best of him. "I'm the police chief here and what I say goes, does everyone hear me?"

"I hear you, dear," Leah Payne, Brad's wife said as she walked through the doors. "But what you don't seem to remember is that we have this broken pipe at home and Mable was on her way to fix it when that tourist fellow mouthed off. Now, he's gone, so let her go."

Brad pointed toward the door, "Leah, just go home. This is none of your business."

Leah was only five feet tall, but when she was mad, her bluish-grey eyes could look as if they were on fire. She walked up to Brad, her head coming nearly to his chest, "None of my business, well please tell me that not having any water at home right now is none of my business. No sir, what you are going to do is let Mable go, so that she can come and fix my pipe. And just maybe, I'll let you back in the house tonight."

Floyd had already walked into the other room. Les was reaching for his keys. "Ok, let her go, but Mable, if you do anything like this again, nothing is going to keep you out of jail. I don't care if I have a hundred busted pipes."

Mable rubbed her wrist as she walked toward Leah. "I guess I'll have to help Leah fix your supper tonight. Any man who's smart enough to know that his busted pipes need attention should get supper, I reckon. But Les, if you ever grab me like that again, the next time you open your eyes, Dr. Adcock will be standing over you."

When Mable and Leah walked out, Les asked Floyd. "Why didn't you help me out there with her? I could have used your help."

"True, but then she would be mad at me too. I'm no better at fixing broken pipes than Brad, so why would I want to make her mad at me?" Alissa walked over to Les and kissed the side of his face. "That's going to leave a bruise."

"Feels like she broke my jaw." Les rubbed his jaw as he spoke, "Man, who would have ever thought she could hit that hard?"

Alissa smiled as she walked back to her desk, "The tourist."

*　*　*　*　*

Bill was sitting at the kitchen table when he heard the keys turn the doorknob. Paula walked in and just stopped. Bill was sitting there having not shaved in days and with very little sleep. He was holding his coffee cup in his hands when he saw the look on Paula's face. "No, it's only coffee; I'm not going back down that road ever again."

Paula walked all the way into the house, she put her bags down. "Well, if you had, it would have been partly my fault. I never gave you a chance to explain anything to me. I judged you before I even heard your side of it." Tears were filling her eyes as she spoke. "My God, I treated you just like that woman Jane. I was that heartless to you." Paula was crying now even more as she thought about how she had acted.

Bill got up from his seat and walked to Paula. Taking her in his arms he held her close to him. "No, you haven't. You could never be that mean to anyone. I don't know what prison she is in, but wherever she is she should rot in jail. Believe me, you are nothing like her."

Paula put her head on Bill's shoulder, "You know life has enough bumps already, why should we add anymore? I just lost sight of what God had given me, I'm so huge now."

164

Bill smiled at her, "But more beautiful than ever. I don't know why all this is happening, but, I know the truth will come out one day."

"But how could I act that way toward you? I love you with all my heart."

Maggie spoke up. "I might be able to help you with that, dear. You see, we allow fear to come in and when we do, it will overrun every other emotion we have." Hanging her head, Maggie spoke slowly now. "I know, I have been fighting my own battles throughout all of this." Looking up at Bill and Paula Maggie spoke again. "Please understand, my life with DJ has been, and is still the most wonderful life I could ever hope to have. But with you having this baby, Paula, I allowed jealousy to come into my heart. Can you ever forgive me, dear?"

Paula sat in a chair and patted Maggie on the head. "Oh Maggie, how could you ever think I wouldn't forgive you? You and DJ have taught me so much."

Maggie smiled, "Well, I'm still learning. DJ wanted to, and did pray for Jane. I told him that I wasn't going to, and I didn't. I know I was wrong and I have asked forgiveness for my wrong. We're all learning, dear. DJ has been my greatest strength. I just wish we could have had one pup. I know he would have been such a good dad to it."

DJ walked in and said. "Only if you were there to help me, my Love. Paula, you and Bill have gone through a very bad thing here. And I don't know how, but I believe it will all come to light and that it won't be years, but rather it will happen soon."

Bill sat down on the floor by DJ. "I hope you're right, my friend."

"I am." DJ said. "I feel it so strongly. Something is about to happen, I don't know what. But just you watch; it's going to happen soon."

Maggie stood there watching DJ as he talked. How could she tell him that she was afraid that what was going to happen was his own death. She couldn't shake that feeling, and she knew he felt it too.

* * * * *

It was mid-afternoon when Chip Corey walked into the Morning Blend. He had told Nita that he would meet her there around one. Chip had walked in holding his coat close to him. "Man is it cold out there! I thought the weather man said it was going to be a warm day today?"

Jonathan laughed, "Well, then you might as well learn one very important fact now. Weather men are almost always wrong!"

Rubbing his hands together, Chip looked at Jonathan and wondered how he was holding up to everything, but he knew it wasn't his place to ask.

Nita came in, which broke the uneasy stillness that had settled in the room. "I just love cold weather, don't you Chip?"

Chip looked at Nita with her coat and gloves on; and wondered how she could feel anything with all that getup on. But his heart spoke instead of his head. "Yeah, I do. In fact, why don't we take a walk and then come back for some hot chocolate?"

Nita put her arm through his. "You lead the way and I'll follow."

As they walked out, Jonathan couldn't help the feeling of pain that shot through his heart. He had tried to talk with Irina since everything happened at the school, but she had been staying away from him. Watching Chip and Nita walking off only made the pain that much deeper. His anger burned as he thought about Bill and what he tried to do to Irina. He still wanted to beat the devil out of him every time he thought about it. Why was it he seemingly couldn't find one true friend?

* * * * *

Business at Bob's Easy Fixings was slow, to say the least. Bob was wiping off a table when his wife, Mary Ann, came up behind him and put her arms around him. Some might have thought it strange looking. Mary

Ann was six feet tall, while Bob was only five feet two inches tall. She would rest her chin on the top of Bob's head. "Honey, don't worry. The business will pick up again. Folks are just bent out of shape right now. They'll get over it and then everyone will be back to normal again."

Bob turned around and stood on his toes as he kissed his wife. "I hope they get back to normal soon. I have never seen this time of year so slow. The people who are coming into town aren't staying."

Mary Ann laughed, "Well, could you blame them. It's all over town how Mable King knocked that fellow out with one blow. And then she even hit a police officer."

Bob held onto his wife, but he was shaking with laughter. "I know Mable is a fine lady and a good friend, but heaven knows she has the devil's own temper. I would have given anything to have seen the whole thing."

Mary Ann said, "I think I know someone who got it on tape. We could watch it later."

Bob held Mary Ann even closer. "No, my mother should be here by this afternoon, and she is going to watch the children while we go out. So how about dinner and a long walk in the park?"

Mary Ann stepped back, "How about dinner, and I pay for us a room so we can have one night alone?"

Bob smiled, "It's a deal. I told my mother that was what I was planning. I'm glad I got you to pay for the room though."

Mary Ann pinched Bob's arm, "Just for that you'll pay for the room."

Bob smiled; "I was planning on that as well."

* * * * *

Dr. Pittman was sitting in his office. He knew he had promised Clara that he wouldn't work long hours, but this was something he had to do.

He wasn't sure how he could help Bill and Paula, but he was working as hard as he could to try to figure out something. The board was pressing him to go ahead and name someone to replace him in the event that he had to step down suddenly. Dr. Pittman knew Bill Thomas was the right man for the job, but now he had to get the board to hold off until Bill could clear his name. But how to accomplish that was the biggest question? With what he knew about Irina, they still couldn't go to the police, and there just wasn't anything there to go to the police about. Bottom line, he knew Bill was innocent. He just couldn't prove it yet. The phone rang, "Hello, yes dear. I know I'm working late. No, I haven't forgotten my promise to you. Ok, I'll be home within the hour. I promise."

He rubbed his chest after placing the phone back down. The pain just had to go away.

* * * * *

Dr. Travis Null was having a bad day that Tuesday. He'd spent most of his day in the ER. More people had come in because of fights, or because of couples throwing things and a piece of glass getting into someone's eye. He was beginning to wonder if this town was ever going to get back to normal. Vickie walked up behind him. "Hey, do you want to catch a movie after work?" Travis turned around and the look on his face told her volumes. "What's the matter? Did you lose someone today?"

Shaking his head, "No, I think I could handle that better than all of this upheaval. I have witnessed people that have been friends for years fighting and trying to hurt each other. I have spent my entire day patching people up who have always worked side by side during this time of year while the town yard sale was going on. And now, they act as if they hate one another." The pain and sadness was written all over his face. "I just wish someone could tell me why all of this is happening."

Vickie put her arms around Travis and held him tight. "I don't understand how this thing could get so blown out of hand," she said, "but I believe that if something doesn't happen soon, there won't be a town left."

Dr. Adcock walked up and placed his hand on Travis' shoulder. "I heard what you did for Jerome and Annie. That was a really nice thing to do for them during this time." "What did you do?" Vickie asked.

"Come on in the break room and I'll tell you. But I have to say no to the movie tonight. I'm way behind on my rounds and it is going to take me hours to get caught up."

Vickie's eyes just lit up. "Do you need a nurse?"

"Travis smiled, "Yeah, come on and let's take a break first."

Vickie asked Dr. Adcock. "Howard, where is my sister Kim?"

"She's in the break room. I think this has been the worse day any of us have seen, and I'm afraid it's not going to get better anytime soon."

* * * * *

Annie was lying in bed. Her first treatment was over and she was so very sick. She had been vomiting for the last hour. Jerome had stayed by her side, held her hand and her head as she vomited into the pail he was holding. Annie started crying, "All my hair is going to fall out."

Jerome held her close to him. "Then I'll shave my head, and that way we can match."

"No," Annie said. "You don't have to do that for me." Placing her head on his shoulder, "My dear, I would shave my whole body if I had to, "but I'll look ten years older by the time I'm through with all the treatments." Jerome lightly kissed her forehead, "Ok, then I'll take up worrying, that should add about ten to me as well. We're in this thing together, and we're going to see it through until you are well and back home again."

One of Annie's doctors walked in the room. "You can leave in the morning Mrs. Reinhart, but you have to be back here next week for your next treatment."

"Doc," Jerome spoke up. "We are going to stay here in Atlanta, so could you tell us a good safe place to stay?"

"Oh, wait a minute." Reaching into his pocket he pulled out an envelope which had a note and a key inside it. "A Dr. Travis Null sent this to you. He said for you to stay here while you were in Atlanta, and not to worry about anything, the place belonged to him."

Jerome's eyes were filling up. "See dear, everything is going to be alright. God is taking care of everything ahead of us."

* * * * *

Angelia York wasn't suppose to work today, but she was called to come in because Curtis said he felt like he was coming down with something and needed to go home. "Make sure I left my desk in order. I think I forgot to put up some paperwork I was working on. Just being a scatterbrain today, I guess."

"Yeah sure, I'll check it out for you." Angelia laughed as she hung up the phone. She knew Curtis was one of the most hardworking men she had ever met.

As Angelia was walking up the stairs to Curtis' office; George called out to her. "What are you doing here today? I thought you weren't coming in until tomorrow?"

Throwing her hands up in the air, "Curtis got to feeling bad, so he called me to come on in; besides, I can use the overtime." She turned on the lights in the office as she entered the room. Sure enough, there were about four or more files left out on Curtis' desk. Shaking her head, she thought: "Men; if it weren't for women, please someone tell me where they would end up."

Picking up the files she noticed the one on the bottom as if it was being hid from sight. When she turned it over it read. File on "George Lackey, and his history as a firefighter."

"I wonder what this is all about. Hmm, should I open it and take a look? Looking back toward the door, Angelia opened the file. She sat down and began to read the report written by his last Fire Chief. Her eyes filled up with tears as she read. She wanted to put it down, but she couldn't. It was like some force had drawn her in and all she could do was read. But with every word she read, her heart only broke that much more. "How could he?" She said.

George was downstairs washing one of the trucks, when he felt a hand push him. "Hey," he said turning around. Angelia hit him right between the eyes as hard as she could. Stepping back George rubbed his head. "Hey, what on earth has gotten into you?"

Now her fury knew no bounds. "Don't you ever speak to me again you sleazebag. I thought you might be different, but no, you're just like the rest, aren't you? You sorry jackleg..."

He heard the other names she called him, but his ears and heart didn't want to believe this was really happening. "Please, tell me what you think I did."

Angelia pointed her finger at him as she backed away. "Tell Curtis.., no, I'll tell him myself. I don't ever want to work the same shift with you again."

Angelia was crying as she ran out of the station. George stood there watching her leave. He knew she was upset over something she thought he had done. He had never seen Angelia cry like that before. Looking upstairs, George thought something happened up there. He went up the stairs and found the files still on Curtis' desk. There on top was a file that had his name on it. With trembling hands he opened the file and read what was written inside it. At first fear hit him down deep in his stomach, but then rage filled his eyes.

* * * * *

It was Tuesday afternoon and Philip and Polly Blanks still were not speaking to each other. By the time he came home that Sunday night, he was already good and mad at Polly. It seemed all he did while he was driving around, was just stew over their fight. He never stopped to ask himself why he got so mad, or why he didn't just sit down and talk this thing out. But that's how emotions can allow things to get out of hand. People say things they don't really mean, and then they are too prideful to go back and admit they were wrong.

Polly walked through the house wishing they could talk, but at the same time waiting for Philip to admit he was wrong about Bill and that whole mess. She had her mind made up as to who the guilty parties were, and she didn't need her husband's input. Normally during their spring break they would take walks and do things together, but now all they did was try not to run into each other under the same roof. She looked out the window and wondered if things were ever going to straighten out.

* * * * *

Paula was cooking supper when DJ walked up to her. "Have you seen Bill?"

"I think he is in his office, DJ. Why don't you look in there."

DJ didn't want to talk to Bill. He felt that same evil presence around the house again. He was just trying to figure out where everyone was. He thought about asking Maggie to go outside with him to check and see if everything was ok. But then he thought about how she had been so uneasy lately, so he went by himself. It was dark outside, and there wasn't a moon out. He walked very quietly around the backyard, and then he walked over to the side of the house by the fence. As he got closer, he could feel that same evil presence, but it was much stronger. Quietly he walked up to the fence without making a sound. As he looked, he saw a figure standing and looking into the window of Bill's house. It was then that she turned around.

DJ was shocked when he saw who it was. Before he could bark or do anything, Jane reached down and grabbed DJ. Pulling him up mostly by his hair, she held his mouth so that he could not bark. She hurried back to her car and put him in the trunk. Jane drove off but not too fast. She wasn't going to draw attention to herself. DJ lay down in the trunk of the car. He was afraid; he wasn't ashamed to admit that. He knew Jane was most likely going to kill him. What he had to do more than anything was to keep a cool head about himself now. If he had any chance of getting out of this alive, it was going to be very slim indeed. He had to stay calm and listen with his heart, for only then would he know the right moment and what to do when that time came. With his eyes closed, quietly within his heart he prayed, placing himself into the Creator's hands for safe keeping, even if this was to be his end.

* * * * *

Maggie walked into the kitchen, "Have you seen DJ, Paula?"

"No, well, he was in here a little while ago asking if I knew where Bill was. Maybe he is in Bill's office with him."

"Hmm, he said we were going to go outside and sit for a while tonight. I'll go and remind him."

Paula laughed, "Yeah, tell him that's a bad sign when you start forgetting things."

Maggie walked into Bill's office but she couldn't see DJ anywhere. "Bill, have you seen DJ?" Looking up from the work on his desk, "No, Maggie. I haven't seen him all afternoon. Maybe he's outside."

Maggie shook her head. "If he went outside without me, well, he isn't going to hear the last of that, let me tell you."

She turned and walked toward the pet door. When Maggie got outside, she could feel that something was wrong. Everything was out of place. Somehow she knew deep in her heart that DJ had been taken. Running back inside, Maggie was yelling, "Bill, Paula, help. Someone has taken DJ." Bill was hurrying down the hall, Paula yelled from the back bedroom. "What, who, did you see anyone?"

Bill came into the kitchen, "What happened?"

Maggie was so upset she could hardly talk. "DJ, he's missing from the backyard. Someone has taken him, I can feel it." Bill hurried to the door and walked outside; he looked all around the yard but couldn't see where anyone had broken in through the gate. Maggie was crying out of control when Bill walked back in. Oh, not the type of crying that people do, but even guardians cry when their hearts are breaking.

Bill picked up his phone and called the police station. "I need to report a stolen dog. Yes, you heard me right. Someone came into my backyard and took one of my dogs. His name is DJ and I need someone out here right now." Bill hung up the phone. Maggie got up and started out of the room. Bill spoke up, "Look Maggie, we're going to get him back."

"No," she said shaking her head. "I have felt this coming for a long time, and so did DJ. What's happening to him is because of what's going on in your life Bill. He saw something or someone, so they took him. I've lost him for good this time." Her voice was cracking as she spoke. "O' God, what am I going to do without my sweet DJ?" Crying, she walked out of the room.

Bill stood there in shock, Paula was crying sitting down in a chair. It was as if the very worst fear you ever had came to pass. Bill saw himself unable to keep his promise to Sally; to keep DJ and Maggie safe from harm.

* * * * *

Jane drove up to an old house beside the barn. She was using this place as her hideout while she watched a sleepy little town tear itself apart. The big man that was helping her grabbed DJ and took him inside. He was placed in a cage with bars that were too close for him to get out of. Jane walked over to him, "Well, well. It looks like I have one of Bill's dogs. Hmm, I wish the other one had been outside too. That way I could have gotten both of them. Maybe I would have just shot them both right there, let him run outside to find two dead dogs." Jane laughed as she stood there.

DJ felt a very strong presence of evil in that room. He knew he was in enemy territory now. He knew his life could be taken at any time. He had to keep his wits about him. He laid down in the cage as Jane stood there, towering over him. Her gun was in her hand as if she might shoot him. DJ knew fear, but this was different. This wasn't the same as when he was running from Three Paws, no, this was fear due to the strong presence of hate that filled the room. Quietly he prayed within himself. That was all he could do now. But with that, he felt a peace come over his heart that brought with it a strength that helped him to stay calm. He worried about Maggie though. He knew she was lost without him, as he would be without her. He knew she thought the worst, that he was dead somewhere. His only prayer was to die well, if that was the Creator's will for him. "But please oh Lord, he silently prayed. Let me see my Love again; if it's your will."

Jane kicked the side of the cage. "Hey dog, look at me when I'm talking to you, how would you like to die tonight?"

CHAPTER SEVENTEEN

A Shattered Heart

There was a cold overcast sky when Bill walked in the backdoor that early Wednesday morning. Paula stood there in her robe waiting to see if he had any news. "Well, what did the police say?"

"Oh, let me tell you what words of wisdom our wonderful police chief had for me. He said that most likely it was someone from around here and that they were doing it because of all the trouble I have caused. Not to worry, most likely DJ would be dropped off in our backyard any day now. Can you believe anyone is that dim-witted?"

Paula walked up to Bill, "What are you going to do then?"

"Nothing," they heard a soft voice speak. Maggie walked in the kitchen. "DJ is gone. There isn't anything anyone can do about it now."

Bill shook his head, "No, I don't believe that for one minute, and neither do you, Maggie. I'm not giving up, I'll find him somehow."

Her voice was shaking now as she spoke. "What you are going to find, if you find anything at all it will be his broken body. I could have saved him, but I insisted that we stay with you when he wanted to run away."

"What!" Bill said. "When did all this take place?"

"When we first came to live with you, the first few weeks were rough to say the least. And DJ wanted to try and find our way back to Mrs. Browne. He felt that was our best place to go at the time. But I insisted that we stay on with you and keep our promise to Sally. And now I have lost my DJ forever."

Paula spoke up. "Maggie, how can you say that after all we've been through together? Look at all the good that has come out of your being here with us. We might not be together right now if it wasn't for you and DJ."

"I don't care," Maggie yelled at Paula. "All I want is to have my DJ back." She turned and walked out of the kitchen very slowly, her cries were getting louder with every breath.

Paula looked at Bill. "I can't believe she said that. I'm going to have a talk with that young lady."

Bill stood in the doorway. "Paula, I know how she feels. That's the way I felt when I lost my wife and daughter. Leave her alone for now. I know the grief she is experiencing right now. Leave her be for the moment. There will be time enough for talking when we have found DJ."

"Do you really think he's alive then?"

"I'll stake my life on it. Whoever is doing this wants to hurt us. They're not going to finish it quickly. No, we still have time, but we must hurry." Bill walked over to the phone and dialed a number. "Hello, yes, it's good to hear your voice again too. You know you said that if I ever needed you, all I had to do was call. Well, this is that call." Paula sat as Bill talked for more than an hour on the phone. He described the whole situation and explained how the police weren't even going to look for DJ.

As he hung up the phone, Paula looked at him. "Well? What's going to happen now?"

"Moses and his dad will be here bright and early in the morning, and they're bringing help."

* * * * *

Rusty walked outside and found Teresa asleep in the car. She was just about sick from being out on such a cold night. But the truth was, she passed out after driving into the driveway. The car ran out of gas some time just before sunup. Rusty opened the car door, "Teresa?" He said, fighting to hold back the tears. This was the first time she had stayed out all night; he was wondering if she had been with someone else. "Why are you doing this to us; why can't you just come back home?"

Teresa just barely opened her eyes, "You don't want me, I can't give you any kids."

The tears were running down Rusty's face now. "I don't care about kids, I care about you. I love you. Why can't you see that?"

He picked up Teresa and carried her into the house. Rusty was fighting his own fears that she might have been with someone else. It was later in the day when she woke up that she told him she hadn't been with anyone else. "I'm not a slut you know. I just want to have some fun, that's all. Maybe I'll…"

She never finished her sentence; she wasn't sure what she wanted to say anyway. Teresa knew she wasn't happy living this way. It was causing her a lot of anguish of heart hurting Rusty the way she was. She was just trying to forget her own pain. She wanted children and was told she couldn't have them. Why did this have to happen to her?

* * * * *

Father David Grissom was sitting in his office with the door closed. He couldn't remember when he had felt like such a fool. "I let myself get out of control and I yelled back at Sam Balius. We were pushing each other. How did this thing get so out of hand?" He got up from behind his desk and walked out of his office and down the hall to the sanctuary. This time of day it would not have been uncommon to find someone at the altar praying. But not today! It seemed that the evil that was coming after Bill Thomas was bent on tearing everything he loved apart with him. Kneeling at the altar in the quietness of an empty church; Father Grissom poured out his soul to God. He knew Irina was not telling the truth. What he didn't know was the reason for it. "If only I could get her to see what harm she is doing to this town and the people living here. Maybe she would repent and tell the truth." Even as he prayed that prayer, something deep inside of him told him that Irina wasn't going to come forward on her own. There was a force using her, and until she could be freed from that power, she would never be able to tell the truth. "But what force, what power is using her, Lord? Surely you can show me more? If I knew just a little more of this puzzle, maybe I could figure out something that would bring this predicament to an end." Rising up from the altar, Father Grissom walked around the sanctuary praying. It was as if his heart was too heavy to be still. He had never before experienced anything like this situation. He had thought when he came here a few years back that he was through with the prison ministry. But now he found himself missing it with all its daily troubles.

* * * * *

Alissa Tidwell was sitting at her desk answering the phone. It seemed their phone sure rang a lot more lately. "Hey, Brad, are you going to go out there and check on Dr. Thomas' dog?"

"No! I can't help it if someone wanted to get even for all the trouble he has caused."

Alissa turned around in her chair. "Then you do believe he is guilty?"

"Brad threw up his hands. "I'm not saying that, but there wasn't anyone around to say that he didn't. In fact, outside of that foreign girl saying he did try something; there isn't one living soul who can testify to having seen anything. The more people I talk to at the school, including the kids attending classes there, no one, ever remembers at any time seeing them together outside of his classroom. Most didn't even know she was in one of his classes. Everyone saw her with Jonathan Wedgeworth, but never with Bill Thomas. That is what's driving me so crazy about this case. Nothing, and I mean nothing, makes any sense. Why, if it went to court today, the case would get thrown out for lack of evidence. And the judge would want my butt on a platter for not digging deep enough to turn up something. But how can you, when from all I can tell, nothing's there."

Floyd O'Neal walked in just about the time Brad was finishing his speech.

"Well, if you were to ask me…" "Well, I didn't." Brad barked back. "By the way what on earth are you doing in here at this time of day anyway?"

Floyd just grinned, "Came to eat my lunch. We still get a lunch break, don't we?"

Brad could feel his face turning red. "Just eat your lunch and shut up."

Les Tidwell walked in and said as he walked over to Alissa his wife, "Well, if you boys don't mind. I'm going to steal a kiss from my wife."

Alissa reached out and grabbed Les. "Steal nothing. Come here, you."

Brad walked outside and stood alone. It was cold and he didn't have a clue about what he was going to do. But he was also way too proud to ever admit that he didn't know what to do. No, in his mind everything would work itself out one way or the other. All he had to do was hold this town together until then.

Back in the office Les took a chair and sat down beside Alissa. "Hey, did you hear the latest?"

"No," she said leaning forward to catch every word.

"Well, I heard that the school board in wanting this whole mess settled before classes start again next week."

"Good luck with that one." Floyd said. "Why, they might as well ask us to make the sun start coming up in the west; no sir, this thing isn't going away no time soon."

Alissa put her head over on Les' shoulder. "Honey, when you drive pass the school, you don't ever slow down to look at all those girls, do you?"

Les rubbed Alissa' long black hair. "Now, you know I wouldn't ever. Besides, I already have to best looking woman in town."

Reaching up, she kissed him and lightly pushed away smiling. "Just remember, I know how to shoot a gun."

Floyd broke out to laughing so hard that he turned over in his chair. Brad walked back in. "Now, what's going on in here?"

"Nothing," Floyd said. "But I don't think you'll ever have to worry about old Les going off and getting himself into a mess like this one."

Les was holding Alissa close to him as Brad looked over at them. "What is that old chowderhead going off about now?" Brad said as he threw his hands up in the air, "Hey, we still work around here. Get back out there," Brad barked.

* * * * *

Alma Smith and Christine Gully were walking down the sidewalk taking everything in. Alma spoke up as they passed by Bob's Easy Fixings. "I heard that the city council called a meeting last night and told everyone to pack it up. Said that the city wide flea market was closing early this year. Said they have never seen so much fighting and quarreling going on in this town before."

"That's true," said Christine. "It's just plumb disgraceful, that's what it is. And we can thank Dr. Thomas for all this."

There was one thing Alma and Christine were both so good at, and that was judging everyone else, but never taking time to examine their own hearts. And too, while they were talking, they never seemed to notice who was walking up behind them. Mable King was out making some deliveries. "Why if it ain't diddly-squat and dimwit, and they still don't know how to keep their big mouths shut."

Christine turned and took one look at Mable and said to Alma. "Come on, let's cross the street here and head back home."

Mable stood there wondering if they were ever going to outgrow their sour outlook on life. Then she remembered what Fay said the day before. She said that she was outside when they walked by and she could have sworn the temperature dropped twenty degrees when they passed by."

* * * * *

Dorothy Eldridge was sitting behind her desk at Whitworth Antiques trying to get her books to line up as she called it. She was feeling a little better about herself though. Ever since she stopped going into Roy and Ruth Bailey's bakery, why she had lost ten pounds! "See," she thought to herself. "I didn't need to be going in there anyway. Pushing her glasses back up her nose, she went back to work on her books. The bell over the door rang as she looked up.

"Mother," Vickie Eldridge called out.

"Back here, dear. Where's your sister?"

"Oh, Kim had to work today, seems everyone is sick nowadays."

Dorothy looked over at her daughter. She knew about Dr. Travis and how her daughter felt about him. "You know I was thinking," she said without looking up, "why don't we have a big family dinner one night, you know like we used too, and you can ask that young Dr. Travis to come too."

"Mama," Vickie said. "I don't want to scare him off."

Dorothy took her glasses off and looked very intently at Vickie. "Well, if he has been able to stand up to all the hits you've been giving him, I think he can survive one night with all of us. Besides young lady, what's this I hear about you kissing Dr. Travis in the hallway?" Before Vickie could say anything, she saw her mother smiling. "I mean, I guess I should be thanking the Lord you weren't hog tieing him."

Dorothy was laughing as she looked over at Vickie. Her light blue eyes were laughing along with her as she saw in the look on Vickie's face. Vickie was waiting to get blown out, and here her mother was laughing. "Mama, you mean to say that you're not mad at me?"

"Why, child, heavens no. I'm just glad he stayed around long enough to find out you would kiss him and not just hit him every time you saw him. I swear; I used to tell your father that I didn't think you would ever get over your fear of boys. But I guess you finally have." Dorothy's eyes were overflowing with tears as she spoke.

"I miss daddy too, Mama. I guess that's why I could never find a boy I liked. None of them measure up to him."

Dorothy asked smiling, "So then, what about this Dr. Travis of yours?"

"Oh Mama, let me tell you what he did for Jerome and Annie Reinhart." With that, they spent the rest of the day talking. Not a soul came into the store. Vickie couldn't remember when she had spent such a day with her mother. It had been far too long she knew, but now she found that her mother could also be her friend to talk with about the new love in her life. A town outside was tearing itself apart, but in the backroom of an Antiques store a mother and daughter had reconnected.

As Vickie started to get up once to leave, Dorothy reached over and took her hand. "No one's coming in today, dear. You don't have to rush off." So, on she stayed. Not realizing that one day this day would be the most memorable day of her life.

* * * * *

Dr. Pittman was sitting in his office at his house working as hard as he could to try to buy some more time. He had heard about the board's meeting and how they wanted to go on and terminate Bill Thomas. In their minds, he had caused entirely too much trouble to ever teach in that school again. Dr. Pittman sat there seething as he thought about how some were already talking about putting Robert Lee Locklear in Bill's place as department head, and then when Dr. Pittman retired, making him the new University President. "Why I would rather see this school burn down to the ground. All that man cares about is power. He wants Bill's job and then mine so he can look down his nose at everyone. He can never see the worth of a soul, only how much he thinks he is better than they are. No sir, I have to find some way to stop this from happening."

Dr. Pittman didn't realize that his voice was being heard by his wife. He didn't know how loud he was talking back in his office. Clara sat there in a chair in the living room praying. She knew his heart could not take much more of this stress. Never had she felt so helpless in her life. It was as if all she could do was sit back and watch the man she loved and their beloved town being torn apart. Clara looked up toward heaven, "When, God, are you going to bring this nightmare to an end? I can't take much more and I know Harry's heart isn't going to hold out if this thing keeps on." Clara sat there silently crying. The last thing she wanted to do was to cause Harry to worry over her. But her fear just wouldn't leave; it hung on like an unwanted guest.

* * * * *

Jane stood there looking at DJ. He wondered if she was thinking about killing him now, or if she was going to wait until later.

"What are you looking at, dog?" Jane spit out as she yelled at DJ. "I hate dogs. Why, if I could have, I would have gotten rid of you two back when I was trying to get Bill's money. If I ever find out who sold me out, I'll kill them."

DJ knew he had to play it safe. This wasn't the time to lose one's head and do something foolish. He knew she meant to kill him before this thing was over, and if he saw even one chance of getting out alive, he was going to take it. So he sat there just watching Jane's every move. He listened to everything she said, and he prayed within his heart, asking the Creator to guide him and to watch over Maggie. He knew she was at home crying herself sick thinking that he was dead. He hated the fact that there wasn't any way he could get a message to her. His own heart was so heavy due to this fact. But he knew he couldn't dwell upon this very long. He had to keep a clear head if he was going to see an opportunity and be at his wits to take it. He knew Maggie was upset, but he also knew she wasn't alone during this time, and for that he was thankful.

* * * * *

It was getting late and even though no one was at the school, Robert Lee Locklear was sitting behind his desk working on some papers. If he hadn't been so busy the last day of school trying to find out what he could about Bill and his situation, he would have finished his work. Now that Robert had heard rumors that the board was thinking about getting rid of Bill and giving Bill's position to him, why he was just about beside himself. "I knew this day was going to arrive, it's my turn to get what I want. If the board would have given me that position in the first place, I would never have tried to get rid of Bill and maybe his wife and daughter would still be alive." Robert got up from behind his desk and walked toward the window. As he looked out, he could see the wind blowing and knew that it wouldn't be long before spring would arrive. "Hmm, with the departing of the cold weather in the next few weeks, it will signal my new day arriving. Yes, it's about time things turned out the way it should have been all along."

Robert Lee Locklear was one of those men who always forgot the help someone gave them in their hour of need. He had forgotten how Bill went to Dr. Pittman years ago when he had only been teaching for a little over a year at the school, and asked Dr. Pittman to give him another chance. Even though Bill knew Robert Lee wasn't going to make the best teacher, he still had compassion on him. And this was how he had been repaid. His wife and daughter were murdered, and now when he needed a friend, Robert Lee was going to a few board members telling them stories about Bill that weren't true. He knew that the board wasn't going to say anything to Dr. Pittman about what he said. They all knew how Dr. Pittman liked Bill, so they would keep that to themselves. But it had worked, Bill was out and he was in, and that was all that mattered to him.

* * * * *

Annie Reinhart woke up from her nap. She was still having some sickness due to her first treatment. "Honey, have you called and checked on Josh? I know he is worried and he wants to know what is happening to his Mama."

Jerome walked over and placed a cool wet rag upon her head. "Yes, I called my Mother and she said that Josh was doing just fine. She took him out to John and Janet's today. He played out there until he was just about frozen, but he is alright, dear."

"When do I go back for another treatment?"

"This coming Monday, dear remember the doctor said that they were going to have to give you your treatments close together to kill all the cancer."

Annie sat up in bed. "But they make me so sick."

"I know dear, but they are also killing the cancer, so we can put up with the sickness, and we are going to win this fight. Remember, we have a son and a family back home pulling for us. Not to mention an entire town. There isn't any place like Whitworth. It's the friendliest place in the world."

Annie looked over at Jerome, and she wondered if she was going to live to make it back to their friendly little mountain town, or if she was going to lose this battle just as her Mother had done. Jerome could tell what she was thinking by the look upon her face. He sat down beside her and held her close to him. "Now, stop thinking that way."

"What way?" She asked.

"You know what I'm saying. It's written all over your face. We are going to beat this thing, and we are going to do it together." Jerome kissed Annie lightly upon the forehead and held her close. He knew the weeks and months ahead of them were going to be rough for Annie. But he wasn't going to leave her side, no, not for a moment.

"Jerome?" Annie asked.

"Yes dear, what is it?"

"What did I ever do to deserve you?"

Jerome chuckled, "Mother has asked me time and again what did I ever do to deserve you. And you know, after all these years. I can't think of one thing. I'm just the luckiest man alive."

He was holding Annie close to him so that she couldn't see the tears that were filling his eyes, but she knew it. She could tell it by the way he spoke. She knew him better than he knew himself.

"O God," she prayed within her own heart. "I need Jerome, and he needs me. Please let these treatments work for me."

* * * * *

Frank Robbins, the pastor of University Baptist Church, was at the hospital visiting a few of his church members. "This flu is something else going around" he told Christa, his wife.

Christa worked in the business office at the hospital. "No, it isn't. Why I heard that there were seven fights today alone. It seems this whole town has lost its mind. Everyone is taking sides in this thing. Frank, I'm afraid this town isn't going to survive, everyone is mad at someone."

A dark look came over Frank's face as he spoke, "I know dear. Just today, I was at Bob's Easy Fixings for lunch and Greg Vice, the pastor of Christ Community Church came in."

"I know who Greg is, and where he is pastor."

"Yes, but did you know that he too had some very strong feelings about this whole mess? I tried to talk with him about how we ministers needed to get together to pray and see how we could bring people together and to stop taking sides. Why before I could even finish what I was saying, he went off on me. Told me that was the problem with the world today. Nobody wanted to stand up for anything. All people wanted to do was to stick their heads in the sand."

Frank looked at Christa with such sadness in his eyes. "Honey, before it was over, why we were yelling at each other and it took five men to pull us apart. I don't know what came over me, but I just lost it and before I knew it. I pushed Greg and he pushed back and then I hit him and he hit me."

"Oh, Frank, you didn't?"

"I hate to admit it, but yes I did."

"But you two have been friends for years. What are you going to do now?"

"Beg the church to forgive me for acting like such a fool, and pray that God will help us out of this mess."

* * * * *

Greg was driving home with his wife Tiffany. "I tell you that Frank Robbins is out of his mind." All I said was that we should make a stand for something and he went off on me."

Tiffany looked at her husband, "But dear, maybe this is one of those situations when it would be better if the ministers did stand together."

Greg, shouted, "What, how could you even say that after the man hit me? No, I'm taking a stand for what is right."

Shaking her head Tiffany knew that no one really knew what was right or wrong in this affair. "So then, you're saying that you believe Bill is right."

"Why of course not, I mean everyone knows he is guilty."

Tiffany sat in her seat where she couldn't look right at her husband. "Honey, you know that I never cross you and that I am always behind you. But this time I think you're wrong. No one knows anything about this situation, and everyone is getting mad over nothing."

"Nothing, how can you, a woman, say that a man attacking a woman is nothing?"

Tiffany very calmly looked at Greg. "Then please tell me where are the witnesses? From what I have heard, and this comes straight from the police office, they can't find one person who has ever seen Bill or that woman together, or even seen him talking to her. Honey, she spent all her time with Jonathan, not Bill."

Greg's pride wasn't going to let him admit right then the sick feeling that came over him. But for the first time he thought that maybe he was wrong after all and that maybe Frank was right. Were they just being used by the enemy here? Had they become so blind, that they couldn't see the working of the enemy right in their midst? The more he thought about it the sicker he got. Greg knew that somewhere, when the truth came out, everyone was going to feel like a fool over this.

* * * * *

Irina had worked all day at the cleaners. She was trying to help out since Wayne and Cindy Hawkins had to let their last worker go. Business was way down and if something didn't happen soon, they might lose everything they had. She sat there looking out the window, and wished for the day she had never met Jane. Never had she seen anyone filled with such hatred. She knew though, that if she told the truth now, her daughter was dead. Tears were flowing down her cheeks, how did she end up here? Irina forgot that she made a deal with an evil person to get her daughter back. Only now was she leaning that you can't make a deal with evil. For evil never keeps its promises. "What can I do, God?" Irina spoke out into an empty room. "What can I do, to undo all this pain and misery that I have caused these people? They don't deserve all of this; it's all my fault, God. Please don't let this town fall apart because of me." Irina was crying almost uncontrollably now. "I've hurt the only man who truly loved me, now he would never want to have anything to do with me. I've lost everything, I've gained nothing. Everything I did trying to get something back has only cost me more. O' God, I would be better off dead."

* * * * *

Moses' was finishing packing the car. "Hey dad, now don't forget anything you might need. We can't just drive back and pick it up you know."

Benny stuck his head around the door. "Boy, don't make me take my belt off to you now."

Moses laughed as his dad went back inside. He felt good; it was great having his dad back in his life again. He had DJ and Maggie to thank for that, and now they needed his help. He owed those two everything. He had his family back together, not to mention that Maggie had saved his life. No, this wasn't just a mission of mercy, it was a debt being paid. Smokey walked out to where Moses was packing the car. "What time are we leaving in the morning?"

Moses looked at Smokey and thought how glad he was that he was going to be there with them. "I plan on leaving around sunup."

Nodding his head in agreement, Smokey said, "It will be good to see Maggie again. I hope we get there in time to save DJ. They are my best friends. They taught me what I didn't know and now I can teach little Sky all he needs to know to be a good guardian. I owe those two a lot, Moses."

Moses reached down and patted Smokey on the head. "We all do my friend, we all do."

CHAPTER EIGHTEEN

Maggie's Darkest Hour

It was four o'clock in the morning as Moses, Benny, and Smokey headed out of the city toward the mountains and Whitworth. Benny was sitting in his seat with his arms wrapped around him. "Hey, I thought we weren't going to leave until 6 a.m. who's bright idea was it to leave at 4!"

Smokey was sitting in the back seat of the car. "Hmm, well, I guess that would be mine."

Benny turned around and looked at Smokey. "Please, for the love of a warm bed, please tell me what on earth possessed you to want to leave so blessed early?"

Moses was chuckling as he said, "Go on, Smokey. Tell dad your reason for wanting to leave early." "Well you see sir, Sky kept coming in there where I was sleeping and waking me up every hour asking if he could come along. He would say how much he could learn and that it would make him a better guardian if he came along. So, when I finally got him back to bed and told his mother to lay down with him, I went and woke up Moses and told him I thought it would be a good idea if we got on our way."

Benny shook his head, "Good idea, my foot. I'll tell you what a good idea would be, and that is staying in bed until 6 this morning. And son, slow down. If you get stopped for speeding, I'm not going to fix your ticket."

"Ok Dad, I'll slow down. Just get a handle on it, will you."

Smokey sat up and spoke to Benny. "I can understand how you feel, sir. I know it's not easy getting up this early when you get older."

"Older," Benny snapped, "Why I'll have you know that I can still out do any man ten years younger than me; maybe even twenty."

"Oh, I didn't mean to upset you sir, nor was I calling you old. I just meant that you…."

Moses butted in, "Smokey, the more you say, the deeper you are going to dig the hole you are already in. It's best to stop while you're ahead."

"Funny," Smokey said. "I don't feel like I'm ahead."

With that, Benny broke out laughing. "Ok, so I'm not a spring chicken anymore. I'm still young enough to take the two of you on and win."

Smokey grinned, "No doubt about it, sir. I'll just go ahead and surrender right now." Moses was laughing as he spoke, "Ok, we're all in good shape for our age, how about that?"

"That's fine with me," Benny said.

"I'm cool with it too," Smokey chimed in. "I just hope we get there before it starts raining later today."

Benny turned around and looked at Smokey. "What did you say?"

"I said…"

"I know what you said," Benny remarked. "What I want to know is how do you know it is going to rain later today?"

"Oh, that's easy. I heard it on the weather channel this morning right before we left. Moses cut the TV on and then he got so busy that he wasn't in there to hear the report."

Benny looked toward Moses. "Step on it, son."

"But Dad, if I go too fast I'll get stopped and I'll get a ticket."

"Boy, I'll fix your ticket. If it starts raining before we get there it will wash away what evidence there might be around the outside of the house. Now, put your foot to the floor and let's get this car moving."

"All right," Moses replied, as he pressed the accelerator down and got their speed up to 75 miles an hour.

"Boy, didn't you hear me? I said step on it, and that means 90 and nothing less."

Moses shook his head. "Dad, if they stop us we could end up in jail for going that fast." "Nonsense," Benny said. "Now if you don't have the nerve to drive this car, pull over and let me drive."

Moses put his foot down and they were up to 95 miles an hour and traveling fast. Smokey was sitting in the backseat looking out the window grinning. "Boy isn't this exciting!"

Benny just glared back at Smokey.

* * * * *

Maggie was sitting in a dark room by herself. She had never felt so alone in her life. She wasn't eating much and was hardly sleeping. It seemed that every time she closed her eyes she could see DJ's broken body laying there in front of her. Maggie knew she should try to get hold of herself, but her heart was so crushed. She knew one day one of them would outlive the other. But this was different, she thought. Someone came and took my DJ away from me. Someone wanting to hurt Bill, but in reality all they did was hurt her. Maggie had so turned inward that she couldn't see how much Bill and Paula were also hurting over

DJ's disappearance. She knew DJ would be upset with her too, for she hadn't even one time, spent her time in worship. Her heart just wasn't in it any more. She knew she was going to die from a broken heart, but if only she could have just five minutes with that crazy little boy she loved so much. She would tell him of the love she felt for him, and how he had made her life so wonderful. Tears filled her eyes as she sat there looking out the window. If ever she had a dark hour this was it. It was her darkest hour for sure.

* * * * *

Bill got out of bed that Thursday morning and walked into the living room. He sat by the fireplace trying to warm himself as he wondered where on earth DJ could be and who would do such a thing. If Bill had only known that his old nemesis was out of prison, he would have known who was behind all his troubles. But that's what being human is all about. We feel like we are flying blind sometimes, which is why we are called to walk close to the Lord. For if we follow His leading, then even though we may not always have all the facts, we are at least walking down the right path. He got up and walked across the room. Looking out the window, he wondered when Moses and Benny were going to arrive. Kneeing down by a chair, Bill lifted his heart up to God for little DJ. "Oh God, please take care of him. I promised Sally that I would never let anything happen to them, and now look what has happened. And to beat it all, no one has a clue as to who took him. He and Maggie have done so much for me, but not just me. They helped Sally first, and then me. I'm with the most wonderful woman now because of them. I would hate to think where I might be if they had not come into my life. I had forgotten about your love. They reminded me of that fact. First, by showing it to me by the way they loved each other and watched out for each other. Then, by the way they stopped Jane from stealing me blind. I owe DJ more than I could ever hope to repay. Please show me where he is somehow."

"So, you still think he's alive?" Maggie asked.

Bill turned around quickly. "Why yes, I do." "Hmm, I never took you for being too bright." Bill grinned at Maggie. "Well, when you first met me, I wasn't acting as if I was bright, that's for sure. But Maggie, we can't give up hope. We owe DJ more than that."

Turning to walk back out of the room Maggie said as she left. "No, you owe him more than that; I should have listened to him when he wanted to run away."

Bill's heart was filled with grief as he watched her leave the room. He knew only too well the pain she was experiencing and he knew the danger of allowing that type of pain to take root in your heart. "But how can I reach her Lord," he prayed.

* * * * *

It was around 6:30 when Paula walked into the kitchen. "I smelled the coffee, so I thought I would get up and join you for a cup. How's Maggie this morning?"

Bill had his head down as Paula spoke. "She blames me for all this. She is shutting herself off from everyone. Paula, she is going down the same path that I took when my wife and daughter were killed in the accident."

Paula picked up her cup of coffee, "Let me go and have a little talk with her this morning."

"It won't do any good," Bill said. "She blames you too."

Paula looked back at Bill and smiled. "I know, she thinks that if I hadn't come into the picture she might have changed her mind and left with DJ."

Bill looked a little baffled, "How did you know?"

Paula just smiled at him again, "Drink your coffee, dear. Maggie and I need to have a little girl talk."

*	*	*	*	*

Curtis Knox was sitting in his office thinking that he had finally put an end to Angelia and George getting together. George had asked for some time off without giving any reason. Curtis gave him the time off because he thought George was going to find a job somewhere else and leave quietly. What Curtis didn't know nor understand was the power of true love. George had fallen in love with Angelia. Even though he tried ever so hard not to, but her patience and the way Angelia would not give up on him, that had won him over. It was the first time anyone had ever treated him like he was of value. No, he was going to do whatever he had to, to clear his name. Angelia was down washing a truck by herself. Curtis had asked her earlier if she wanted any help, but she told him that she needed to be alone right now and just think. Yes, his plan had worked. "Why did I react that way to George? But the report, how could he be such a monster? How could he do that to someone?" Angelia shook her head. "Maybe I am better off without him in my life after all, Lord. But then why do I still feel the way I do about him? I just can't seem to get my mind off him. If I talked to him, maybe then I could clear this up in my head." Angelia didn't know that Curtis was watching her from the window upstairs. She didn't know that he had always watched her. She didn't know that in all truthfulness, Curtis was the one she should watch out for.

*	*	*	*	*

Maggie was sitting with her back to the door when Paula walked in the room. "I don't want to talk to anyone," she said as Paula entered the room.

"That's too bad young lady, because you're going to talk with me, and we're going to talk now."

Paula pulled a chair over close to Maggie and sat down. She reached down and tried to turn Maggie to where she would have to look at her. "I don't want to look at you," Maggie said. "You have your mate and you are going to have a baby. You have everything you want, what do I have now?"

With that, Paula sat up straight in the chair. "How dare you talk like that? How dare you say such things like that to me? I'll have you know that I love DJ as much as you or Bill. And how dare you for giving up on him."

Maggie turned and yelled at Paula. "He's gone, can't you get that through your head. He isn't coming back and I have lost him forever."

Paula reached down and took Maggie's face in her hands. "I'll have you know that I believe he is still alive, and I can tell you what he would do right now if it were you out there. He wouldn't be sitting in here crying. He would be praying and worshipping and bugging the devil out of Bill to find you!!" Paula's voice was loud now as she spoke.

"Paula," Maggie said. "I don't care about the tone I used, I'm good and mad right now, and I'm mad at you. So, get it together. We need your help if we are going to find him." Maggie turned toward the wall and started crying.

Paula got up and walked out of the room. She was crying as she came out into the hallway. Bill was standing there listening to what she said. "What?" Paula asked as she looked at him.

Bill raised both hands up in the air. "Nothing, I was just wondering what was going on, that's all."

"Well, nothing is going on right now." With that, Paula walked into their bedroom and slammed the door shut.

"Well, it wasn't what I had hoped for, but at least Paula has Maggie crying and she isn't sitting in the bedroom mad at herself and everyone else. Maybe she will start to think about how much we love her and DJ. That's what it is all about anyway; the love that you share with someone."

Bill walked back to get another cup of coffee, he hoped Moses and Benny would get there soon.

* * * * *

Irina sat in the window looking out at a town that was tearing itself apart. She knew that she had caused it all, but what could she do now? If she told the truth, her daughter's life would be in danger. She had already lost the only man that she felt she could ever love again. She had nothing to live for but her daughter. No matter what happened to this town or the people in it, she had to save her. Maybe that would be the only thing she ever did right in her life. At least she would get that right. Irina thought about her walk the day before. She passed by the Morning Blend and saw Jonathan inside working. She wanted so much to run inside and tell him the truth. She wanted to tell him how much she loved him and that she knew she could never feel that way about any other man as long as she lived. She wanted to tell him about her daughter and how she felt trapped by Jane. There was so much that she wanted to say, and yet, there wasn't anything she could say. Her heart hurt as she sat there looking out the window. "How did I ever end up here?"

* * * * *

Wayne was opening up the cleaners as Cindy walked in. "Do you think we're going to have much business today?"

Wayne shook his head not knowing. "The college kids will be back next week, so our business should pick up again some then, but how we're going to make it through this summer I don't know."

Cindy walked over to where Wayne was standing. "I just want to thank you for not questioning Irina and bugging her about all of this. She has so much on her right now."

Wayne sat down in a chair, "You know, we both knew Bill and his wife and daughter before the accident. And not one time did Bill ever give you the impression that he was the kind of man who would do this kind of thing. He was always with his wife, and he loved his daughter. Honey, he loved his family too much to do something like this. I can't see him doing anything even now to hurt their memory."

Cindy had a faraway look in her eyes. "I know, and he loves Paula. Everyone knows that if they have been around them just five minutes." Cindy's voice was trembling as she spoke. "Honey, I love that girl up there as if she was my own. I can't turn my back on her now."

Wayne got up and kissed Cindy. "Never thought we would, we're going to stand by her. She needs love dear, and a lot of it. Something is pushing her to do this. I can feel it."

Wayne looked back at Cindy as he walked across the room; she could see the tears forming in his eyes. "I feel the same way as you do about her. If she was our own, she would need our understanding and help right about now. So, I figure that is what she is going to get from us; and a lot of love to boot." Cindy jumped up and ran into her husband's arms. "I'm so thankful I have you in my life. But what if we lose our business?"

Wayne smiled, "Dear, I've been saving for years, if these folks want to clean their own clothes, well, we'll let them and we will retire."

Irina stood outside by the side door. She heard everything they said, and for the first time she knew that someone really did love her. Even if she was in the wrong they loved her anyway. Quietly she walked back up the steps. Once she was back inside, Irina fell across the bed and cried her heart out. She cried so hard the bed was shaking and she felt like her heart would break. Not only had she lost the only man who would ever love her, but now she risked losing the only family she might ever have in this country. "I've lost everything; I have nothing to live for. The only thing I can do is to save my daughter's life. I have nothing else to live for." In the midst of her darkness, she saw no hope.

What Irina didn't realize was that, even in the darkness, there is always hope. All she had to do was to find her way to the path of God's wonderful love. Then, and only then, would she be able to see how and what she needed to do to help her daughter and this town.

* * * * *

By nine Moses, Benny, and Smokey were driving into Bill's driveway. Bill walked outside with Paula right behind him. Smokey got out of the car and just stood there for a moment. "Look at him, Bill. I forget how noble and majestic he looks as he stands so straight."

"Yeah, but it makes me miss my little man all the more. He stands like that when he is out in the backyard, as if he owns the whole place."

Paula smiled, "You mean he doesn't?"

They were both laughing when Smokey walked up. "Good morning to you, Dr. Thomas."

"Hey, we're on first names basis here."

Smokey nodded, "Good, because I wasn't sure what to call Paula. I mean, should I call her Mrs. Dr. Thomas, or what?"

Paula's mouth fell open, "Why no, just call me Paula."

Smokey winked at Bill. "She still hasn't caught on yet, has she?"

Bill was holding his hand over his mouth trying hard not to laugh, when it hit Paula that Smokey was pulling her leg. "Hey, that's not fair."

Moses walked up to where they were standing. "Well folks, my Dad is making his rounds around the house. So, why don't we go inside and get some coffee. I got up very early this morning."

Smokey pushed in by Bill and Paula when Moses said that, Bill stepped back. "Hey, what's the rush fellow?"

Moses laughed softly. "Oh, don't mind him. I was just teasing Smokey for getting us up so early, that's all."

They were all sitting around the table when Benny walked in the backdoor. "Look here what I found. Out by your window on the front of the house I found these cigarette butts. And they even have lipstick on them."

Paula stood up to take a better look. "Wait now. You can't touch them. If there is anything on these, we don't want anyone else touching them." Paula looked over at Bill. "Do you think that young woman was watching our house? Maybe she is after the money after all."

Bill rubbed his hand through his hair. "No, I don't think it's her. Jonathan hates smoking. He would never date anyone who smokes."

Moses sat up in his chair. "Why don't we call him up and ask him to be sure?"

"Oh, no," Paula said.

"It's better if we just leave Jonathan out of this altogether," Bill remarked.

Benny poured himself a cup of coffee and took a seat by Moses. "I'm just glad we got up here before the rain came in today."

Bill looked funny at Benny. "Rain today; who told you it was going to rain today? The weather channel said just this morning that we were not going to get any rain for about five days."

Benny and Moses looked at Smokey. Smokey sat there and said, "I heard this morning that it was going to rain this afternoon in the Ozark Mountains."

"Boy," Benny spouted. "That's hundreds of miles from here, and to the north west of us at that."

Smokey smiled, "You mean there are more than one set of mountains around here?"

Why, of course there is," Benny said with even more emphasis.

It was then that they heard Paula with her hand over her mouth laughing so hard she was shaking all over. "What's so funny about driving 95 miles for nothing?" Moses asked.

"It's not that at all, it's just that y'all expect Smokey to know all the mountain ranges in the country. I know they are very smart, but they don't know everything."

Bill joined in laughing as he thought about it. Smokey started laughing, because he felt like it might ease things up a bit. It then hit Benny and Moses, so they joined in on the laughing as well. "I guess it didn't hurt anything by our getting here an hour or so earlier." Moses said.

"Not at all," Bill piped in. "we're always glad to have good friends come for a visit."

Smokey stood suddenly and looked toward the door leading to the hallway. Maggie stood there without saying a word to anyone. Smokey walked over to her and spoke in a language that none of them have ever heard. Maggie broke when Smokey finished speaking. "I can't feel him anymore, Smokey. I can't feel my DJ's presence anymore."

"All that means is that he is far away somewhere, Maggie. You mustn't lose hope now."

She looked up into Smokey's eyes. He saw the pain and sadness that had filled her heart. "I don't know if I can go on without him."

Smokey stepped closer to Maggie. He sat down in front of her. "I don't believe he's gone, but you have to get on with your life, you can't stop now. You have to go and remember, Maggie. Have you done that yet? Have you remembered your life with DJ?"

"No," she said barely over a whisper. Maggie started to cry and she buried her face in Smokey's long hair. As she cried, Smokey laid his head on top of her and spoke very gently. Paula told Bill later that she had never in all her life heard a voice that spoke with such love and compassion for someone who was hurting. After Maggie finished crying, she spoke something to Smokey and walked back into the back room.

"What's going on," Benny asked.

Smokey looked at Benny and then he spoke, "DJ, isn't dead."

"How do you know that," Moses asked very curiously.

"When I was speaking to Maggie and I laid my head over on her, I felt it. It's strong too, so I know he is still alive. But if we don't hurry, he could run out of time."

"Well, where is he?" Bill said.

"I wish I knew, sir. All I know is that he is alive, and that Maggie's heart is so heavy with grief that she can't feel it or either she will not allow herself to believe it. You see, even we guardians go through our times of loss. We can forget who we are and to whom we belong, just like you can."

Paula reached out and lightly touched Smokey. "So, what does Maggie need to remember?"

Smokey bowed his head for a moment. "I wish I had DJ here now. I could use his wisdom right about now. You see there are many things about us that you will never fully understand, and I'm not sure you will be able to understand this either."

"Try me," Paula said.

Smokey took a deep breath, "Ok, here goes nothing. When we lose a mate, for whatever reason, we spend time remembering everything we can about our life with them. It's like reliving your life together with them. It's our way of keeping memories about them alive. It is how we are able to pass on our stories."

Bill tried to speak, but the tears flowing from his eyes wouldn't allow him to. Moses was crying as well, and so was Benny. Benny finally spoke, "No, my friend. We too have that custom. When we lose someone we love, we too remember everything about them. How they looked the very first time we met, the very first kiss."

"When we held our first child," Moses said.

"And the shame of when we turn so inward that we forget to remember what they meant to us and we go off and try to forget by drinking away our pain." Bill had his head down as he spoke. "It's a shame I'll carry with me for the rest of my life."

"No sir," Benny spoke. "You need not carry shame. I know what it's like to get filled up with hurt over the loss of the one you love. I turned inward, but God forgives us. He understands how the pain can sometimes overcome us. And he will lead us back to his love, if only we will open our heart just a little."

It was then that they all heard a sound coming from the back room. It was singing. It was Maggie's voice being carried throughout the house like a sweet aroma. It was a healing aroma of God's love filling her heart as she remembered her DJ. Paula sat there and just listened. "I have never heard her voice sound so pure, Bill, can't you hear it?" Bill shook his head in agreement. Not able to speak from the tears once again filling his eyes.

"Now," Smokey said. "We need to get busy finding DJ."

CHAPTER NINETEEN

The Search Begins

It was after lunch that Bill, Moses, and Benny arrived at the police station. When Bill walked in, he could feel everyone's eyes on him. Floyd O'Neal was at his desk working on a report, and Les was talking to his wife Alissa. Even though she was the dispatcher, when they were all there, she would help out with paperwork and even help keep the station clean. Moses was standing next to Bill as they walked in, "Boy, does it feel cold in here."

"Tell me about it," Bill remarked. "I think it's worse now than the last time I was in here."

"Nonsense," Benny replied. "These boys are out to find the truth. Bet you they have been putting a lot of overtime in on this one."

Brad opened the door of his office. "I thought I was clear, Mr. Thomas. I don't have the time or manpower to look for your dog."

Benny spoke up, "Yes, I understand sir. You see I am retired from the department myself. I know how busy things can get around a police station." As Benny looked around he thought, but here, all I see is a lot of nothing going on.

"Well, now that is just what I need right now; a retired police officer coming up here from the big city to tell me how to do my job."

Moses couldn't believe the attitude he was hearing coming from the police chief. "Sir, my Father was a very good detective and worked hard to solve his cases."

"Oh, I see," Brad said. "So what you are saying is that we're not working hard around here?"

"Now, sir, my son can get a little carried away sometimes. I'm sure he didn't mean anything like that. All I want is to ask you to do me a favor. I found these cigarette butts outside Bill's window and they even have some lipstick on them. If you could send them to the lab, we might not only find out who took Bill's dog, but maybe who is also behind all of these lies."

Brad's face turned red, "I'm so glad you came up here and solved this case just like that. I mean, what was I thinking, that a few country cops could do anyway? I should have called down there to Atlanta and asked them to send me all the old retired cops they had, right after they got through with their water aerobics."

"What did you say?" Benny asked. His face starting to show that his patience was wearing thin.

"What, too much water has gotten into your ears as well?" Brad barked back.

Moses stood in front of his dad. "We need to quiet down here, if we are going to get any help."

Brad had just about had all he could stand. "Here's what I think. If Bill ole boy had kept his hands to himself, none of this would have ever happened."

Moses turned; his face was now the one showing anger. "I'll have you know that Bill Thomas is one of the finest men I have ever met." Moses voice was getting louder as he spoke.

Bill walked up to his side. "Moses, let's go. We're not going to get any help from these men. We'll have to come up with something else. I can't give up hope on DJ."

Benny said, "Bill's right. I think we have troubled these men enough. If we stay any longer, they might miss their afternoon nap."

Brad yelled, "Get out of my station, or I'll have you thrown in jail."

"We're leaving," Benny replied. "But as to the throwing us in jail, we have broken no laws, and if you do that sir, I would be forced to take you to court." Benny turned and walked out with Moses and Bill. Brad was so mad that when he went into his office he slammed the door so hard that it broke the glass in his door. He just stood there with his face getting more red by the moment.

Les looked over at Floyd, "It's about time we get back out there, don't you think?" "Yeah, and I mean now."

* * * * *

There was a light knock on the apartment door. Irina opened the door, just wishing everyone would leave her alone. Darlene Chisolm stood there with the biggest smile on her face you have ever seen. "Hey girl, I was wondering what happened to you. You haven't been back to work."

Irina looked surprised. "You haven't heard about what happened?"

Darlene threw her hand up, "My Mama told me never to listen to rumors. She said that only a fool would listen to them, and only a bigger fool would believe them."

Irina smile. "I think I would like your Mother."

"Hey, I know what," Darlene said as if she just had the greatest idea. "We could leave today and go down and see my folks. They would just love you."

Irina shook her head. "I can't leave town, the police chief told me that if I did, I would go to jail."

"I don't understand that," Darlene said. "You didn't do anything wrong."

Irina eyes filled up with tears. "Oh now, don't cry. I'm sure everything is going to work out ok."

Irina kept on shaking her head. "Not for me. Every since I came to this country, I have had nothing but trouble. I have wished many times that I had stayed in my own country."

Darlene patted Irina on the shoulder. "My Daddy has always said that trouble is like bad weather. Given enough time, it's going to change."

"You're so lucky," Irina said. "You have your family and your home. I am a little envious of you. No, a lot," Irina spoke softly.

Darlene didn't know what to think, no one had ever been envious of her. Why her family didn't have anything. They were just honest, hard working folks. "No, you're wrong, Irina. You do have family here. I'm your family. I'm going to take you for my sister. With that, she went in the kitchen and came back out with a knife.

"What are you going to do?" Irina asked a little worried.

"Oh, I guess you never heard about the customs of the Indians."

Irina shook her head no, all the while keeping her eyes on the knife. "Here let me show you," with that, Darlene took the knife and poked the end of her finger. Blood flowed out of her finger. "See, this is what the Indians did when they wanted to make someone their blood-brother."

"They would make their finger bleed?" Irina asked.

210

"Yeah, but there's more," and with that Darlene took Irina's finger and poked it with the knife. Blood flowed out of it, and before she could yell, Darlene placed their fingers together. "Now see, our blood is flowing together. That makes us blood-sisters. So you are not alone anymore. Whatever you are going through, I'm here for you. We're sisters now, and nothing can break this bond. It's a blood bond."

Tears were flowing freely down Irina's face. No one had ever cared that much for her. No one had ever said no matter what, I'm here for you. Struggling to get the words to come out, Irina said. "I don't know what to say."

"You don't have to say anything. You don't have to tell me anything. But just know that if you ever need someone, I'm here for you. And don't you go and sneak out of town. We're sisters now, and we have to stay in touch forever." Darlene reached over and kissed Irina on the cheek. "Sis, get some rest. I'll check on you later."

With that, Darlene left. Irina sat down in the middle of her apartment floor and cried. She was so confused. She was so hurt. How could anyone think enough of her to want to be her sister? How would Darlene feel if she knew the whole ugly truth? Would she still want to be her sister then? The pain just went deeper and deeper. Irina felt like she couldn't breathe sometimes. If only she had never met Jane, none of this would be happening to her. Why couldn't she have just accepted the fact that her daughter was lost to her, then maybe she could have met Jonathan and they would have fallen in love and everything would be right in her world. But now she was at the point of losing everything.

* * * * *

Jonathan watched Darlene leave Irina's apartment. He knew that when she asked about Irina and he told her how she needed a friend that Darlene would come to see about her. There were still some left in the south, Jonathan thought, that live by those old southern customs. He knew Darlene was one of those. "I only hope Irina didn't shut her out like she has me." Jonathan would give anything to just talk with her. Even with all the pain his heart was going through, he couldn't help himself. He still loved her more than he had let her know, and now he was kicking himself for that mistake. He turned and walked toward the Morning Blend. The thoughts of leaving town were ever with him now. It seemed that he had lost everything once again; a best friend, and the woman that he loved.

* * * * *

When Moses, Benny, and Bill arrived back at his house, Moses was just about fit to be tied. "I can't believe the way they treated us! They acted as if we were trying to come in there and take over things. All Dad wanted was a little help. Now tell me, was that so much?"

Benny patted Moses on the shoulder, "Let it go son, I'm alright. They didn't hurt my feelings, but they did slow us down a bit. But then again, maybe not," he said with a grin.

"What do you mean, Benny?" Paula asked, as she entered the room.

"I'll tell you in just a moment if Bill will allow me to use his phone?"

"You can call anyone you want to, sir. If it will help us find DJ, I don't care where they live."

Benny picked up the receiver and dialed the number he had in a little black book he pulled out of his pocket. He stood there as the phone rang, "Hello, yes, it's good to hear your voice again, sir. Tell me. Does that Mr. White still work for you? Good, may I speak with him please, sir? I need some help with a small problem I am having with the local police here. Yes, I'll hold."

Paula looked over at Bill. He was standing there listening to every word that Benny spoke to Mr. White. Benny talked only a few minutes and then hung up the phone. "The FBI will be here this afternoon to pick up the cigarette butts. It seems that Mrs. Sadie Lynn Hackwood was there for a visit, and she called on her cell phone while I talked to Mr. White. One call from her was all it took."

"Thank God, for Sadie Hackwood," Paula said in a loud voice.

"Amen," Bill added.

Smokey bowed his head and started a song. It was very moving and within the song there seemed to carry a spirit of hope, something Paula hasn't felt in weeks. What happened next surprised everyone. Maggie was standing in the doorway, and she joined in with the song that Smokey sang. Together their voices carried throughout the house. It was as if the very presence of peace itself had settled upon the house. When they finished singing, no one moved, no one made a sound. With that peace came such calm and hope no one wanted to do anything to disturb it.

* * * * *

Teresa Eldridge was standing in the bathroom putting on her makeup. Rusty walked to the door and looked at her. "Why don't you stay home tonight? Why can't we just go back to the way things were?" Teresa didn't look at him; she was trying to keep a stone face so that maybe he would walk away from her. Rusty wasn't going to walk away. He was going to have his say and he was going to have it now. "Teresa, I love you, and I don't care if we never have kids. Can't you get it through your head that I want you?"

She looked at him with her eyes filled with fire. "Well maybe I want them. Have you ever thought about that? Have you ever stopped to think how I feel knowing that I can never have kids?" Her voice was starting to shake as she spoke. Teresa stopped speaking. She didn't want to break down and cry. Crying didn't do any good anyway.

"Please stay home," Rusty begged.

"I want to go out and I am going." Rusty couldn't believe he was saying this but it just came out. "Are you sleeping with anyone?" he asked. Teresa was mad now and she wanted to hurt Rusty. "If I am, you can bet they don't care that I can't have kids."

It was then that she realized how much she had been hurting Rusty. The look of pain that shot across his face was one she would never forget. Rusty turned and walked away. By the time he was at the backdoor he was running. Teresa ran after him, yelling for him to come back, but it was no use. When she got to the backdoor she saw Rusty pulling out of the driveway. He was crying so hard he could hardly see which way he was going, but he sped off in a hurry. Teresa was yelling for him to come back, she was crying as she called out. But it was all to no avail, Rusty was gone. Teresa walked back into the house. She felt sick inside. Why had she done that? What made her tell a lie to her husband? She knew she had gone too far now. Now she was out on her own without anyone to care for her. Teresa sat in the middle of the floor and cried for the longest time. Hopelessness had set into her heart. Before now it was just anger, but now something far worse. Fear, the fear of being alone, was settling over her now. She got up and packed as many of her clothes as she could carry. As she walked out of the house it was as if something inside of her died. "How could I ever go this far?" she thought. "How could I ever hurt the man I love the way I have." Teresa drove off not knowing what would happen next. All she knew was what she had lost. Teresa thought Rusty's love for her was dead, what she had failed to see was just how deep his love for her had been.

* * * * *

Fay and May were getting ready for the supper crowd when Fay stopped and asked May, "Do you think our sweet little town is ever going to get back to normal?" May shook her head not knowing what to say. "I wish I knew. But, I have to believe that even with what all has happened here, things will one day get back to where they ought to be. I'm not saying it is going to be tomorrow, mind you. But I do believe it will happen."

Fay smiled, "Mama always said you looked on the bright side of things. And I'm glad you do." Even though their business had been down, they decided not to let things get them down. "Why heck, we've seen hard times before," Fay said. "And we're going to get through this time as well."

May finished wiping off the last table. "Ok, let's go in there and get to work then."

* * * * *

Chip Corey is sitting in the Morning Blend waiting for Nita Cotton to show up. He looked at his watch with his mind a thousand miles away; which is why he didn't see his Mother walk in and walk up to his table. Rebekah asked, "May I join you?"

Chip looked up in total surprise. "Why of course, I mean, sure."

Rebekah laughed, "So when is Nita supposed to show up?"

"Any minute now Mom, but you can stay and join us."

Rebekah smiled at her son, "No dear, I wouldn't want to spoil your time together."

"And who said you would spoil it," asked Nita as she walked up behind Rebekah.

"Why dear, I know you two want to be alone, and not bother with an old woman."

Nita reached over and lightly kissed Rebekah on the cheek. "You're not an old woman, and besides, we would love for you to stay. Wouldn't we, Chip?" "Mom, you know we would, please stay."

Rebekah sat down beside Nita allowing her to sit by Chip. "Ok, but the moment I start acting like an old busybody, send me home."

"Deal," Chip said laughing.

* * * * *

Vickie walked behind Dr. Travis Null and grabbed him. She put both of her hands over his eyes and said, "Guess who?"

"Let's see, what's the name of that new nurse down in ER?"

Travis felt a sharp blow to his back. "I'll show you a new nurse," Vickie said.

Travis turned around and grabbed Vickie and pulled her close. "Now you know I was only teasing you."

Vickie smiled at him with her lips pouted out in a kind of half smile, "So, who is this new nurse you're so taken with?"

Travis hugged Vickie closer to him. "Honey, if there is one here, I don't know it nor do I want to, all I want is you."

"Good answer," Vickie said. "Especially since my Mother is planning on having everyone over to the house for a meal one night soon. I would hate to tell her that you were in the hospital."

"Man, so would I. I have heard how good your Mom can cook."

Vickie jabbed Travis in the rib. "Are you saying that I can't cook?"

"No, I mean, I don't know." He stepped back before he got another jab in the ribs.

"I can't believe my ears; you are saying you don't believe I can cook."

Travis slowly reached out and took Vickie by the arms and pulled her back close to him. "No, I'm not. But let's face it. We only eat together up here at the hospital, so, you see, I have never tasted anything you cooked."

Vickie smiled, "Well, I can fix that."

Travis got a worried look on his face. "What do you mean?"

"I'm going to fix your supper tonight, that's all."

"But won't your Mom get upset if I come over there now and you do the cooking when she is planning to cook for us?"

Vickie placed her head on Travis' shoulder. "Not if I go over to your place and cook she won't."

"Ok, but tell me just one thing? When are you going to stop hitting me?"

Vickie stepped back, "On our wedding night."

Travis laughed, "And just how do you know we're going to get married?" "Simple," Vickie said. "I'll beat you up every day if we don't. Besides," she said as she started walking away. "You have thought more about that than anything else lately and you know it. I'll see you later at your place."

Travis ran his fingers through his hair. "Man, how did she know that?" He wondered.

* * * * *

Mable was walking down the sidewalk when Officer Floyd O' Neal pulled up beside her. "Now just what are you up to tonight?"

"Floyd, you could give someone heart failure sneaking up on them like that."

Floyd chuckled, "Well, next time I'll turn on my lights."

"Yeah, wouldn't that be great, I can just hear the whole town now. I wonder why they are hauling Mable in again."

Floyd laughed out loud. "Well, tell me one thing, how did you manage to hit Les so hard that you knocked him down?"

Mable said, "Promise you won't tell?"

"Ok, sure, I promise."

Mable pulled out a roll of dimes. "I keep a roll in my pocket, that way if anyone should ever get any ideas, I'll take him off his feet with one blow."

Floyd laughed again, "I knew I didn't need to try to grab you that night."

"Good thing too, because I would have put your lights out as well. I was mad as a hornet that night." "Well, get in and I'll give you ride home, no need to have some poor soul end up in the ER tonight." What Floyd wanted to say was that he wanted to give Mable a ride home because he wanted to make sure she was safe, but he just lost his nerve. He couldn't remember when he started feeling this way toward Mable, but he cared for her. He just wasn't sure she would ever care for him that way.

*　*　*　*　*

Irina was hiding in the shadows as Floyd and Mable pulled away in the police car. She didn't know why she was afraid, but lately it seemed every time she saw a police car her heart would just about stop. "Maybe," she thought, "it's because I know I'm lying, and I am afraid they will find out too." Irina walked the streets after it was dark. She didn't want anyone to see her or to speak to her, "all I want is to finish this thing and go back to jail." Her thoughts were so troubling to her that she felt she couldn't even voice them. And no matter how hard she tried, she couldn't silence them either. She was on the other side of the street when she passed by the Morning Blend. There sat Chip, Nita and Rebekah. She stopped and looked. Irina was hoping to see Jonathan. Then she saw him walking over to the table where Chip and his group were sitting. She backed up more into the shadows. She didn't want him to look out and see her standing there. Tears filled her eyes as she watched from across the street. How her heart was hurting so. She knew Jonathan was hurt because of all of this, but she also knew that if Jonathan ever found out the truth, he would hate her. Once she carried a gun, but not anymore. Even if she did end her pain, it would only seal her daughter's death. No, her lot was one of suffering. It seemed she would never know what true happiness was. All she had ever known was sorrow. Irina walked away. She couldn't bear to watch anymore. It was too painful for her. She knew that Father Grissom thought she was lying and that even Rebekah had told her as much, but did Jonathan know? She wanted to run in there and tell him the truth, but to do so would kill her daughter. She had no hope left in anyone. Little did Irina realize, she was now at the point in her life where God could start making her into the person he wanted her to be. She had to hit the bottom before she would be willing to turn her life over completely to him, and now she was there.

* * * * *

DJ lay in his cage. He looked and watched for any opening he might use to free himself, but there was none. Jane walked back into the building. She was upset that Bill was still out of jail. "Those dimwits are going to let him off, I can just see it. What is it going to take to put him in jail? I want him to suffer as he made me suffer."

DJ had to bite his tongue. He wanted to stand up and tell her that she went to jail for her own crimes, but he knew he had to keep his head about him. He did want to see his Maggie though. He thought the nights were the worst. Yes, he missed her the most at night. Their time of singing together was something he was missing so deeply. Oh, how he would love to hear her sweet voice again. He was beginning to wonder if he ever would hear her voice again. All he ever heard was the cursing and ranting of Jane. Boy, if that didn't give someone indigestion he didn't know what would. The only trouble was; Jane wasn't feeding him every day. She had pointed her gun at him and told him that if he cried for food, she would put an end to his crying. She had the man that was working for her feed him a time or two. He was so hungry, but that would have to wait. He had to find some way to free himself.

* * * * *

There was a knock on the door. Dr. Pittman opened the door to see Rusty standing there crying. "My boy, what on earth is the matter?"

"Dr. Pittman, I know it's late, but sir, could I have a moment of your time?"

Rusty entered the house and went back to the office. It was there that he poured out his heart to his friend and boss. "Come now boy, surely she isn't doing that."

"I think she is going out on me, sir. I don't know what to do."

"Hmm, ok now, let's look at this thing together. We know Teresa has been going to this one bar and dancing with other men, which I don't agree with, mind you. But you have no proof she has been sleeping with anyone, son."

Rusty stared at Dr. Pittman, "Sir, how did you know she was going to a bar to dance? All I told you was that I thought she was going out on me."

"Hmm, opened my mouth too soon again I see. You know Clara and I love you both. I knew about your problem before tonight, and I have been keeping a watch on things. Let's say, I have been making sure what you're afraid of hasn't happened."

"But how?" Rusty asked.

"Don't worry about the fine details, just know I care about you both and I care what happens to you. Now what I need to know is, do you still love her?"

Rusty was silent for a time, then he looked up. "Yes sir, with all my heart." "I knew you did, but I wanted you to hear yourself saying it. Now, I have a plan and if you will listen to me, I think we can bring this thing to an end by tomorrow night." Dr. Pittman sat in his office and told Rusty how he had been keeping an eye on things and that he had been working on a plan to help bring Teresa to her senses. "But it all depends on timing my boy, and that is where you come in. I need you to walk into the lion's mouth tomorrow night, but in the end, you'll have your wife back."

CHAPTER TWENTY

It was a clear Friday morning as Bill walked across the campus. He had just finished cleaning out his office. The board had given him 'til Monday morning, but he didn't want to face all the students and the other teachers. All he wanted right now was to find DJ. At this point, he wasn't sure he cared if he ever set foot back into a classroom again. His heart felt as heavy as a stone as he walked across the campus carrying the last box of books to his car. The box itself even felt heavier as he walked. When he placed the box in the trunk of his car and shut it, he turned to see Jonathan standing off to his right about 75 feet away. He just stood there watching Bill. "What should I do, Lord?" he prayed within his heart. Bill started toward Jonathan, but he turned and walked away. "Hmm, guess that answers my question. I had hoped I wouldn't see anyone today, but of all people, Lord, why Jonathan? He hates me, and he isn't willing to even listen to my side of the story."

* * * * *

Bob and Mary Ann were cleaning and getting ready for the lunch crowd. "Honey," Mary Ann said as Bob walked by her with a mop in his hand.

"Yeah sweetie, what do you need?"

Mary Ann's eyes looked like the picture of beauty to him with her red hair falling across her shoulders.

Bob put the mop down and walked back to where she was and kissed her. "See, you can read my mind," she said with a smile.

"Or you just knew what I wanted to do when I saw you leaning over that table wiping it off."

"Either way," Mary Ann said, "Just so long as you never stop."

Bob held her close to him. "Not as long as there is breath in my body will I ever stop loving you and holding you close."

Mary Ann put her head down on Bob's head. "You know, most people thought we wouldn't make it, with me being taller than you. But I think it has worked out just right."

"And why is that?" Bob asked.

"Because, this way you always know who's in charge." Mary Ann was chuckling as she spoke.

Bob moved his hands to where he could tickle Mary Ann. "Ah ha ha, stop tickling me," Mary Ann laughed as she tried to move away.

But Bob had her in his grasp, and even though he was only five feet two inches tall, he was very strong. He stopped and pulled her close again. "Now, tell me who's in charge?"

"Ok, ok," Mary Ann smiled. Then she said it real fast so she could get away. "I am."

As she turned Bob reached out and took her again into his arms. "Oh, are you going to get it now."

To most folks who might have passed by, this would have been normal for Bob and Mary Ann. They were always playing and carrying on like that, which is why everyone in town liked them. Even now, they had stayed out of the trouble and tried to be friendly to everyone.

* * * * *

Roy and Ruth were both working in the bakery when Sandy Philips came in. "Hello you two, I just popped in to see what y'all have today."

Roy laughed, "It all depends on how much weight you want to gain."

Ruth looked at Roy just a little put out with him. "Roy, you know not to ever mention women's weight. That isn't something we like to talk about anyway."

Sandy smiled, "Oh, that's alright, I have been able to keep my weight fairly under control. So, I told Leander, 'Honey, today we are going to get something from the bakery. I don't care how fattening it is, we are going to treat ourselves to something delicious.'

"That's what I like to hear," Roy said, "A woman with a good head on her shoulders."

Ruth placed her hands on her hips, "You mean you just like to make a sale, don't you?"

"Why sure, but can't they both come at the same time?"

Sandy laughed, "Well before I start something, let's see what I want, and then I'll try to figure out what Leander might want." Ruth reached for the chocolate doughnuts. "Oh no," Sandy said, I don't want chocolate," Before she could finish, Ruth raised her hand. "Dear, they're for Leander. I have waited on him enough over the years to know what he likes the best, and these just came out an hour ago."

"Well, on second thought," Sandy said smiling. "I'll take six of them. No use him eating them all by himself."

They all three looked at each other and howled with laughter. It was something that wasn't happening much these days. It seemed as if everyone was all tied up over what happened at the college.

* * * * *

Bill pulled into the driveway; his heart was so heavy that he didn't notice the black car following him. When he pulled in, the black car stopped far enough down the street that the driver could watch without being seen. Jane was loving every minute of it. "Now, how do you like your little world, Bill? Not so nice, is it?" She lit a cigarette and slowly took a deep drag on it. As she blew the smoke out into the car her smile got bigger and bigger. "Wouldn't it be wonderful if he got so down and out that he just blew his brains out?" She took another drag on the cigarette and held it in while she let her mind wander and daydream about how it would look to see Paula walking into a room finding Bill dead. "Hmm, makes me feel warm all over just thinking about it."

One thing DJ realized about Jane while he was locked up in the cage; she was totally evil, just like Maggie said. Even though he was still praying for her, the thoughts were already forcing their way into his mind that just maybe Jane was beyond help. Jane drove by real slowly after Bill had walked in the house. "If I could get the other dog, then I could go on and kill them both now and dump their bodies in his yard one night." She laughed as she drove away, a laugh that would make even a hard-hearted man shudder.

* * * * *

Bill walked in the backdoor to look at him you would have thought that he had just lost his best friend. In his mind he did just that, seeing Jonathan again brought home to him just what this had cost him. Paula looked worried, "Is everything alright, dear?"

"Yeah; no it isn't, and I don't think it ever will be again. I wish now we had never come back here." He sat down in a chair and put his head in his hands. "There are times when I feel like I have been kicked more than my fair share. I just wish it would all go away."

Maggie walked over to Bill and touched him with her nose. "I know how you feel, Bill, but believe me when I say that you need to get up and not allow that frame of mind take hold. Look what it almost did to me, and you loved me enough to show me where I was wrong, so," Maggie smiled. "Get off your dead rear end and stop feeling sorry for yourself!"

Bill jerked his head up with a shocked look upon his face.

Moses just lost it and laughed so hard he had to sit on the floor. Benny grabbed his cup of coffee and headed toward Bill's office laughing so loud you could have heard him outside. Smokey just sat over against the wall smiling. He knew DJ would be so proud of Maggie right now. "Hmm, I'll have to remember to tell him about this when we get him back home." Paula walked over to where Maggie was and pulled a chair up beside her. "I wish I wasn't so big now, I would sit down on the floor with you and give you the biggest hug."

Maggie put her head over on Paula, "Can you ever forgive me for the way I talked to you?"

"Oh Maggie," Paula said with her eyes filling up with tears, "You know I love you and that you were forgiven the moment it happened."

"This is good," Smokey said. "I like to see families pulling together in love. It makes me thankful Lady and I have found our family."

Moses, still on the floor, reached over and pulled Smokey close to him. "Well my friend, I'm sure glad you found us. Life would have been very lonely without you around."

"Yes," Maggie said. "Every guardian needs a home and a charge to watch over, but also to be a part of. There isn't anything more important than family. I'm so sorry I almost forgot that."

Bill reached down and rubbed Maggie on the back. "As long as I am alive young lady, you will always have a home. Now, let's start making plans for lunch, and then we are going to talk about what to do when the FBI report arrives on Monday."

Paula looked startled, "You mean the report is arriving on Monday?"

Bill looked up, "I believe it is."

* * * * *

It was already getting late and Dr. Pittman had not arrived yet with the help he had promised. Rusty sat there waiting, but his patience was starting to wear thin. He was beginning to let his mind run away with him, and the longer he sat there the more uneasy he became. Rusty looked at his watch, it was 9:30. Teresa had been in the bar for over two hours now. Only God knows what she is doing in there. Should I even care, Rusty thought to himself, then he remembered the first time he saw her and how he fell in love with her at first sight. That was it, he got out of the car and headed in the bar, this time she was coming home. Teresa had been drinking but she wasn't drunk yet, although she was out on the dance floor making quite a show. Her long chestnut hair was flying all over the place as she moved over the dance floor. Her green eyes were already starting to show signs of her drinking; they were starting to look a little red in color as well. Teresa was trying to kill the pain in her own heart. She knew she had lost Rusty for good, and there just wasn't that much to live for now.

There was a young man over in the corner watching her intently. Everyone knew him as Bubba. He was tall and just about the worst student that had ever stepped foot on any college campus. After all, he was there only to meet girls, but it seemed even they had better taste than to fool with the likes of him. "Hey," he said to the group of guys with him. "I'm going to dance with that history teacher and take her back to my place. Yeah, I think she needs a man in her life." The other guys were all about as drunk as Bubba, and they all thought it was a good idea. "Tell you boys what, when I'm through with her, y'all can have her." They looked at each other in a drunken glare, and laughed while they all took another drink and edged Bubba on. Bubba walked out on the dance floor and started to dance with Teresa. She felt uneasy about it because of the way he was looking at her. "Hey," he said. "Don't you teach history at the school?"

"Yes, I do. But I'm not here to dance with anyone; I just come here to dance and forget about things."

"Well yeah, I can help you forget." With that, he reached out and grabbed her. Teresa tried to push away, but he was too strong for her.

"Let me go," she yelled at him.

But Bubba had been drinking too much, he held on and then he grabbed her face and tried to kiss her. Teresa turned her head and yelled for help. It was then that Rusty came charging in like a wild bull. He pulled Teresa away from Bubba and knocked him to the floor. What Rusty didn't count on was Bubba's friends coming to his aid. One of them came up behind Rusty and grabbed him, holding his arms behind his back. Another one hit him in the stomach. Rusty would have hit the floor but they held him up, while yet another one hit him again. Teresa saw what was happening and she came in and jumped on Bubba's back as he took his turn hitting Rusty. "Let him go," she yelled.

Bubba threw her off his back and hit Teresa across the face. "I'm going to teach your boyfriend here a lesson, and then I'm going to take you back to my place where me and my friends are going to treat you like the tramp you are.

"She's my wife, let her go," Rusty said.

Bubba smiled, "Well, it seems, teacher you can't get it done, so I'll have to do it for you." About that time a voice spoke up from across the room. "I think it would be in your best interest to listen to him." Bubba looked toward the door and saw Dr. Pittman standing there by himself.

"Great" Rusty thought to himself, "He came alone."

"Hey old man," Bubba spouted off. "You had better leave while you can. This ain't school, and I don't have to listen to an old fool like you here."

Dr. Pittman shook his head. "Now that's the trouble with the youth these days. No respect for their elders, and I swear, this group has to be the dullest group I have seen in years. I don't know how you ever made it in, but believe me when I tell you now that your college days are over here. So, why not do yourselves a favor and let them go."

Bubba and his friends laughed. Bubba took a step toward Dr. Pittman thinking he would run, but he stood his ground. "Old man, you had better leave now, or you will suffer with this old fool here, and she is going with us! Do you hear me, old man?"

"Yes, and I'm sorry you can't be reasoned with." With that Dr. Pittman whistled. In came five of the biggest football players that college had ever had on their team. "Now," Dr. Pittman said. "Let them go."

The other fellows were already letting Rusty go, and Bubba took his hand off Teresa's arm. Teresa ran to Rusty and grabbed him. "I'm so sorry," she whispered. "There hasn't been anyone else, I promise."

"I know," Rusty said as he brushed her hair back away from her face. "Let's go home." Teresa put her arms around his neck. "I want to, please forgive me." With that, they held each other and walked past Dr. Pittman and his bodyguards. "Thank you sir," Rusty said.

"Don't mention it my boy, glad to help." After they walked out, Bubba and his friends looked around, wondering what was going to happen next. "Now," Dr. Pittman said. "It's time for you boys to pack up and leave our fair town." With that he turned to walk out, but as he did, he looked at the ballplayers. "You boys know what to do now."

Rumor had it the bar was shut down for three weeks. Seemed there was a big fight in there, if you can call it that. Anyway, when the police got there the ball players had left and Bubba and his friends weren't in the best of shape.

When Rusty and Teresa got home that night, Teresa was crying over the way she had been acting. "Will you ever be able to forgive me," she said with her voice shaking.

Rusty brushed her hair back. "Honey, I never stopped loving you, and I don't have any plans on stopping now. I forgave you long before tonight. Let's put it behind us, please?"

Teresa smiled, "But I still can't give you any kids."

"I don't care; it's you I want more than anything else in the world. As long as we have each other, nothing else matters to me." Teresa learned that night the strength of true love, and its ability to forgive.

Dr. Pittman walked in his backdoor, Clara was waiting for him. "Well, how did it go?" Smiling he said, "We have two fine teachers again." "You ole goat, next time you had better let me know beforehand what you're up to." With that, she reached over and kissed him lightly.

CHAPTER TWENTY ONE

A Boiling Pot

It was 7:45 on a clear Monday morning as Dr. Pittman walked up to the door. He kept thinking to himself that somehow things were going to turn around for the better. As he unlocked the door to the administration building, he felt someone grab his arm from behind. "Just a minute, you old goat; I want to have a word with you." Robert Lee Locklear was red face and as mad as he could be. "I heard how you stopped my getting the department chair, now I want to know why?"

Dr. Pittman very coolly looked down at his arm that Robert Lee had grasped. He didn't speak, he just stared quietly. Slowly Robert released his grip on Dr. Pittman's arm. "Now, that's better," Dr. Pittman said. "First, let me state that I don't owe you any explanation, and you should be one of Bill Thomas' best supporters, for it was Bill Thomas who kept you from being terminated years ago. The board wanted to let you go and so did I, but Bill came to me and asked that I give you another chance. And if my memory serves me, he worked with you and helped you get your feet under you so that you became a better teacher. But, you are no Bill Thomas, sir. So, why did I stop the board from giving you that position? Because in my estimation of you; you are still not a very good teacher." Robert Lee Locklear's face was as red as any Christmas lights you might see on a holiday tree. He pushed Dr. Pittman back against the door and yelled, "I don't care about your opinion of me, or anyone else's opinion either as a matter of fact, but I do want that chair and you are going to give it to me. Dr. Pittman could see that Robert was just about out of control. "Sir, you had better rethink your behavior right now. For you are standing on very thin ice."

Robert backed up, realizing that he had gone too far. "I'm sorry, Dr. Pittman, It's just I was hoping to get that position. I guess I let things get out of hand."

"This is something Bill Thomas would never have done. Robert I'm not against you, you're just not cut out for that position, that's all."

Robert's eyes were flaming with anger, but he knew he couldn't do anything about it right now. He turned and walked away quickly, trying to figure out how he could undo his mistake.

Dr. Pittman was shaken by Robert's attack. He was fearful that things were going to get out of hand. In his heart he knew there wasn't anything he could do to protect himself. He opened the door and walked into the outer office. He sat down in the first chair he came to. He reached up and placed his hand over his heart. The pain was almost unbearable. He was afraid he wasn't going to be able to help Bill out of the mess he was in. "Please Lord, not now. Surely there is something more for me to do?"

Judy Whitsey was the secretary who worked in the outer office. She had seen Robert Lee Locklear pushing Dr. Pittman up against the door and was able to call the police when he walked away. As she entered the building, she saw Dr. Pittman sitting in the chair. Just one look at Dr. Pittman was all that was needed. Judy picked up the phone and called the hospital. "Give me Dr. Adcock now!" When Dr. Adcock picked up the phone all he heard was, "It's Dr. Pittman's heart. You had better get over here now." Judy turned back to Dr. Pittman who looked an ashen white color. "Please hold on, sir. Help is coming."

* * * * *

Paula was making coffee when the phone rang, "Hello," as she listened to what Clara was saying, she dropped the coffee pot, shattering glass went all over the floor.

"Bill, get in here now." Bill, Moses, and Benny came running into the kitchen along with Maggie and Smokey. "It's Dr. Pittman honey, it's his heart. Clara said they're not sure he will make it."

Benny spoke up, "Y'all go on and I'll stay here, clean up the broken pot, and wait for the FBI."

"Thanks Dad," Moses said. Bill just looked at Benny and nodded, as he ran to the bedroom to get dressed. It only took minutes before they were all heading out in a hurry.

Jane was down the street watching as they left. "Hmm, I wonder why they left in such a hurry? No, they can't know anything about me. That little tramp knows better than to rat me out."

* * * * *

Clara was in the waiting room as Bill and Paula walked in. "Moses will be here in a minute," Bill said. "He is parking the car for us."

Clara smiled weakly, "What am I going to do if I lose him, Bill?"

Bill sat down by Clara, "First we're going to stop talking as if things aren't going to go alright. I know Dr. Pittman, and he's a fighter."

Paula sat down on the other side of Clara. "We can't give up hope. That's the one thing you taught me, remember?"

235

Clara smiled with tears running down her cheeks, "I'm trying, I really am."

With that she put her head over on Paula's shoulder and cried. Paula held her in her arms while Bill patted her on the back. "It's going to be ok," Paula kept saying to her. "I don't know how I know, but I just know."

Moses walked in the room and saw what was happening; he bowed his head and quietly prayed. As he prayed he also prayed about the FBI report, asking that it would indeed arrive that day.

Vickie Eldridge walked into the room. Clara looked up at her and held out her hand to her. Vickie took her hand and knelt down in front of her. "You know He is in the best hands. I hate to say this, and if Dr. Adcock heard me say this he would never let me live it down. But he is one of the best heart doctors in the state. If anyone can pull Dr. Pittman through this, Howard can."

"Well, I'll tell him you spoke so highly of him," Kim Adcock said. "Rat's," Vickie said. "Just my luck my sister would walk in." Moses laughed, "Well, I'm glad to hear he is in such good hands, but I think we shouldn't forget about the true healer, and ask Him to touch Dr. Pittman and be with Dr. Adcock as well."

"Yes, Bill said, "Let's do that now." With that, they all took hands and bowed their heads. "More things are done through prayer," Moses thought to himself, "than this old world could ever imagine."

* * * * *

Jane was sitting down the street in her car waiting, hoping Maggie would come outside by herself. Maggie went to the backdoor, and was going through the doggie door when Smokey stopped her. "Where are you going, Maggie?"

Maggie looked back at him just a little agitated, "Well if you must know, I'm going outside to do my business."

"Ok, I'm coming with you."

"You're what?" Maggie said. "I have you know, I am old enough to take care of that without anyone's help."

Smokey laughed lightly as he shook his head. "No, it's not that. If the person who grabbed DJ is hanging around they might try to take you as well. I just thought my presence outside would make them think twice about trying anything like that. Maggie, if they got you, then what would keep them from killing you and DJ? Your staying safe might be the only thing keeping him alive."

Maggie put her head down, "You're right of course. It's just, well, DJ is the only one who ever went with me." "I'll stay on the other side of the yard, but at least that way you'll be safe." "Thank you Smokey," Maggie said. "I should have thought about that, it just never crossed my mind."

As they walked outside, Benny thought to himself. "That Smokey has one good head on him."

As Maggie walked outside, Jane saw her and started to get out of her car, when she saw Smokey walking around the backyard. "That's dog is too big. I'll have to wait and try to grab her later."

Jane drove off cursing because she wasn't able to snatch Maggie as well. "I could have thrown their dead bodies out tonight if I could have gotten my hands on her."

* * * * *

It was after lunch when Bill, Paula, and Moses arrived back at Bill's house. Benny sat in the living room reading. "What did you find to read Dad," Moses asked.

"Oh, nothing, just this FBI file, that's all."

"What!" Paula said. "What does it say? Who was standing outside our window?"

Benny laughed, "Hey, wait a minute, you're asking way too many questions at once." Benny looked at Bill. "Maybe we should talk outside."

"No," Bill said. "We're in this thing together; I have nothing to hide from my wife."

"Ok," he said as he blew air out between his lips. "Who is Jane Hendricks?"

She's five feet nine inches tall with dark brown hair." "I know what she looks like," Bill said. "But she's in prison. Why are you asking about her?" Benny put the file down, "She's not in prison anymore my friend, she got out, because they never finished reading her rights, it seems, when she was arrested. She tried to get away from the officers and they had to struggle with her, and they forgot to finish reading them to her. But while in prison, she remembered and called for a mistrial. Well, when they got the film from the police car and watched it in court, there it was for the whole world to see. So, the judge threw it out and let her go. But it seems she has not forgotten you, my friend. So, why is she after you?"

Moses spoke up, "Oh Dad, I never told you what DJ and Maggie told me. I guess I let it slip my mind."

Paula stood there with her mouth wide open. "You mean to tell me they let her out of prison, just because they never finished reading to her, her rights?"

"Yes," said Benny. "That's the law."

Paula turned around and looked at Bill, he could tell she was about to blow, when Maggie walked up to her. "Paula, remember, she has DJ, we have to keep a cool head about us if you're going to help him."

Paula's eyes were filling up with tears. "When is that she-devil going to leave us alone?" Paula walked to the bedroom. Bill looked at Maggie as if to say, would you follow her? "No, Bill. I'm staying to hear what the report has to say. It's my DJ out there and I have a right to know everything as it is read."

"Ok girl, you're right. You do have a right to hear it firsthand." Benny was reading as they were all talking, then he looked up, "Now this is very interesting." "What Dad? For Pete's sake, tell us what you are reading." "Hmm, it says here that Jane was placed in the cell with one Irina Holton, who took her maiden name back after she got out of prison. She was in there for killing her husband."

"Bill's face turned ashen white, "Then she is in this thing with Jane."

"Wait there's more; Irina has a daughter she lost when she went to prison. It seems she was trying to get help while in prison to find her child, but with the murder charge against her, no one would help her."

"Then that's where Jane comes into this picture." Paula said as she stood in the doorway. I knew Irina went to prison for killing her husband, but he was a drug runner and was abusive as well. Irina stated in court that he beat her."

"Bill looked shocked, "How did you know all of this, and when did you find it out?"

"I promised I would never tell anyone, but it came from her own confession."

"Dr. Pittman," Bill said. "He's friends with Father Grissom."

"Bill Thomas, I didn't tell you that."

"I know, but think about it. Irina goes to Father Grissom's church, and he is still working part time as a parole officer. It stands to reason that he is her parole officer now doesn't it?"

"So, what do we do now?" Smokey asked.

"What do you mean, what do we do?" Moses said. "We are going to the police right now." "No we're not." Maggie said, as she walked to the middle of the room. "It's my DJ out there, but I know him well enough to know that the first thing he would say is, how can we help Irina?"

Everyone sat in silence for a while, thinking. Bill's eyes lit up, "I think I know how, and also who will help us."

* * * * *

Irina was sitting on a bench in the park, trying to forget what she knew she would never be able to forget, her daughter and how much she was hurting this town and Jonathan. "I thought I might find you here," Rebekah Corey said.

Irina turned and looked surprised at first. "What do you want?" She said it in a very cold manner.

"If you would allow me, I would like to talk with you for just a moment."

"Why should I talk to you? You hate me just like everyone else in this town."

Rebekah sat down beside Irina. "First, let me say that I don't hate you, and I am sure everyone in this town doesn't hate you either. It must be easy to hide behind that kind of excuse. 'Everyone hates me has been the biggest wall for people to hide behind for years. Child, no one hates you. And this might surprise you, but Bill Thomas doesn't hate you either. In fact, he is the one who asked me to come and talk with you."

Irina didn't know what to do. Should she run, did Bill know something about her past? Why did he want Rebekah to talk to her? "So, why should I care if he asked you to talk to me? I'm not going to lie for him." "No, but you would lie for Jane Hendricks, wouldn't you?"

Irina turned suddenly; it was as if she had been slapped in the face. "Who? I don't know anyone by that name."

Rebekah smiled, she saw by the way Irina reacted, she knew she had her right where she wanted her. "Sure you do, my dear. She was the one you shared a cell with in prison."

Irina's face turned white with fear. This could only mean that Father Grissom had been checking out who she knew in prison and he had told Bill Thomas everything.

"I.., I'm not sure what you are getting at?" Irina bit her bottom lip; her nerves were already on edge, she didn't know if she could take much more.

"Well, let me help you connect the dots. You went to prison for killing your husband, but from what I am told, you were only defending yourself. Ok, I can understand that. His family took your daughter and they are hiding her from you. Jane asked you to help her with something; in return she was going to help you find your daughter. So, how am I doing so far?"

Everything in Irina told her to run, but she felt like there was a ton sitting on her heart, instead she broke down and cried. "If you tell anyone she is going to have my daughter hurt and then they are going to kill her. Please, you can't tell the police. I am begging you."

Rebekah had spent her life looking in the face of students who told one lie after another as to why they didn't turn their papers in on time, but as she looked into Irina's face she knew she was telling the truth. "I never said I was going to tell anyone, now did I? But you need to know that the information I have is going to be told to the police. And you should know that Jane will most likely have your daughter killed anyway. She isn't known for caring about anyone but herself."

Irina was shaking so hard she could hardly sit still. She started to jump up, but Rebekah grabbed her arm and pulled her back down.

"This isn't something you can run from child; there are times when we have to face what we have done. You need to tell the truth."

"If Father Grissom hadn't lied to me, you wouldn't know any of this. He promised me he would never tell anyone I was in prison."

"He didn't tell anyone," Rebekah said. The FBI found evidence outside Bill's house which led them to Jane, which in turn, led them to you."

"The FBI," Irina said softly. Now her worse fears had come to pass. Now Jane would kill her daughter for sure. Irina started crying as she jumped up and took off running. Rebekah called after her, but it was no use. Her heart was so heavy and filled with fear that she wasn't able to hear. So, she ran and ran, until she found herself at St. Paul's Catholic Church.

* * * * *

The Church was dimly lit when Irina went inside. She fell at the altar and cried. There wasn't anyone else in the church so she thought she was all alone. All she had left was her grief. She had now finally lost everything in this world that mattered to her. She had now reached her end. Finally, Irina was exactly where she needed to be. Father Grissom was in his office working on his sermon, but his heart wasn't in it. There was just too much going on in this town and he wanted to do something to help make things right. But to do that, he knew he would have to break his word, and that he couldn't do. He talked to Dr. Pittman to help Paula, but he was given Dr. Pittman's word that no one else would ever be told. He knew Dr. Pittman was a man of honor, but his heart wasn't happy watching this peaceful little town come apart. He heard someone crying out in the church; quietly he opened his office door and listened. He could tell it was Irina, mainly because she was his only member who spoke Russian. As he walked up behind her, he could tell that something was troubling her very deeply. He sat down on the altar beside her. "What can I help you with, my child?"

Irina looked up at Father Grissom, "My daughter is dead."

With that, she wailed and placed her head on his knees. Father Grissom got down beside Irina as she fell over on him and cried until her whole body was shaking. He didn't know what had happened, but he sensed that right now all he needed to do was to hold her and pray. "Heavenly Father, I lift this poor lost soul up to you, please come and speak peace to her heart."

* * * * *

Bill hung up the phone. "That was Rebekah, she said that after she told Irina that the FBI knew everything she got up and ran away."

Benny stood up, "Then we have to go and find her. She has to tell the truth." Moses looked over at Bill, "We have enough evidence to clear you, you know that, but without Irina telling the truth there will always be some who will doubt." Paula walked over to the sink, "Then we failed."

"I wouldn't say that," Bill said smiling.

"And just why not?" Paula asked holding her stomach after the baby kicked her.

"Because I know what direction she was headed."

"Well, speak up man," Moses said.

Bill picked up his cup of coffee and took a sip, "She was headed toward Father Grissom's church."

Benny's eyes were wet with tears as he spoke. "Then it is out of our hands all together now."

Moses bowed his head and started singing a song he learned from DJ and Maggie when they were staying with him. Maggie joined in as well as Smokey. It was an ancient tongue they were singing, long lost to modern man. But as they sang the presence of peace filled the house, thicker than a morning fog, so thick that it could be felt. Everyone just sat there not saying a word as Moses, Maggie, and Smokey finished singing. Something was going to happen that day; they all knew that, but just what, no one was sure. But they knew whatever happened; it would all work out for the good of everyone.

* * * * *

Irina was still sitting at the altar when Father Grissom got back with a cup of hot tea. "Now, my Mother always told me that hot tea was the best thing to drink when you were feeling down and out. So child, why do you say your daughter is dead?" Irina didn't know how or where to start. "My daughter was taken from me by my husband's family and when I got out of prison they hid her from me. Since I had been in prison, no one would help me. I met this woman in prison who promised to help me if I helped her. Father Grissom, she told me that Bill Thomas was a very bad man and that he had hurt a lot of people, so all I would be doing was helping him get what he deserved."

"You see that's the problem with trying to help someone get even. You're never really sure who you are helping, are you?"

Irina nodded her head, "I see that now, but what can I do? When I pray, I feel like heaven is a million miles away."

"Hmm, well maybe it's not that heaven is so far as you're not on speaking grounds."

Irina looked bewildered, "I don't understand father, I was baptized as a child."

"A grin came across Father Grissom's face. "So was I, child. But that doesn't make one a Christian, any more than standing out in the middle of a field will make you a cow. You have to be born again, Irina. I was in the ministry five years before I found this out."

He could tell by the way she looked at him she was without a clue as to what he was saying. "Well, how did you find out that you were not, hmm, born again you called it?"

Father Grissom walked over and took a seat on the pew, "Well, it happened when I made the biggest mistake of my life, and one that almost cost me being a priest. I was at my first parish when I was a young priest. There was a young woman in the congregation who needed someone to talk to and of course as the priest, I took it upon myself to try to help her. What I didn't know was that she was suffering from a very low self-esteem and was looking more for love than she was for help. Well, one thing led to another and before I knew it, I was in a full blown affair. Now, I didn't start out to end up in an affair, and I still look back some times and wonder just how it all happened. But after a few months, she came to me one day and told me that she was going to have my child. It hit me like a ton of bricks. I think it was then that the magnitude of my sin really hit me. I knew what this was going to do to the church and how it would hurt so many lives. But before I could go and confess it to my bishop, she lost the baby. This sent her into a deep dark depression; one that turned what she thought was love for me into pure hatred. She called the bishop and told him how I had seduced her. I was sent away from my parish and placed into a monastery to wait to see what was going to become of me. Irina, I couldn't go back home. I had shamed my family so."

She nodded her head, fully understanding. "So, I waited. I was there five months before anyone said anything to me. I was told that I needed to pray to see if I was truly wanting to be a priest or not. An old priest that I had met a few years before came to see me. He was very kind to me and asked me if I had ever received Christ into my heart. He read John chapter 3 to me and said that I was like Nicodemus. While I had studied about the Bible and church history, I had never met the One behind the story. I had never come face to face with Christ. After we talked for over five hours, he prayed with me to receive Christ and then prayed that the Lord would fill me with His Holy Spirit. All I can tell you is that from that moment on, nothing in my life has been the same. I stayed in the monastery for three years and when I left there I when to work in the prison. I felt like I had been set free by Christ, and I wanted to take His message of love and freedom to those behind bars. Until about five years ago, that is where I have been all of my life." "And do you think," Irina stopped for a moment. She was almost afraid to ask. "You believe God could forgive me for all that I have done?" "Oh child, yes, a thousand times yes," Father Grissom had tears in his eyes as he spoke. He could sense that something he had told Irina had rung true in her own heart. He could see that dim ray of light and hope beginning to shine through all her confusion.

"Father," Irina spoke.

"Yes my child."

"Could you pray with me the way your friend prayed with you?"

"It would be my honor, Irina." Father Grissom knelt down beside Irina and led her in a very simple prayer. After Irina prayed to receive Christ, Father Grissom prayed that she would be filled with His Holy Spirit as well. Irina had never felt so clean in all her life. It was as if the weight of the world was taken off of her shoulders. "Now," Father Grissom said. "Don't you think it's about time we went and spoke to the police?"

Shaking her head no, she looked up at him with a peace that surpassed anything she had ever known. "Not yet. I need to see one person first and ask him to forgive me."

Nodding in agreement Father Grissom said, "I'll get my car and drive you myself."

It was late Monday afternoon and Bill and Paula were getting ready to go back to the hospital when there was a knock at the backdoor. Moses answered it for them, and when he saw Father Grissom and Irina, he called out. "Bill, you have some company." Bill walked into the kitchen. When he saw Irina he stopped dead in his tracks. "Dr. Thomas," Father Grissom said. "Could we have just a moment of your time, please sir?" Paula walked in when she heard Father Grissom's voice. "What do you want?" She asked Irina.

"Please," Irina said softly. "If I could just say what I came to say, then I will leave."

"Alright, have a seat and tell us what's on your mind," Bill said.

"First, I want to ask you to forgive me for lying about you. I am sorry and there is nothing I can do to undo the hurt and pain I caused you. Please forgive me. I am going to go and tell the police everything today, and that way your name will be cleared. Then I guess I'll go back to prison." Irina tried to smile.

"No wait," Paula said. "Bill isn't going to press any charges against you. If you tell the truth, that's all we want. No one needs to go to prison do they, honey?" Paula looked at Bill searching, hoping he knew some way to keep that from happening.

"No, indeed not, I'll talk with the police myself and tell them that I am not going to press any charges. Father, can't you help us here as well?"

Father Grissom rubbed his face. "Now that you bring it up, I can't remember ever writing anything about this down. And with my busy church work, I'm sure I have forgotten many of the fine points of the matter. Why, I would be afraid to write a report about anything now. Just doesn't seem right to write down the wrong thing."

Irina stood there crying. "You mean you would do that for me?" Paula walked over to her and put her arm around her. "Yes, we will.

And anything else we can to help you." Benny jumped up, "Good, now let's go see the police." "Wait," Irina said. "Jane has a man working for her. He drives a black car around town and he even gets out and walks through town listening to what people are saying. That way she knows everything that is happening. If she finds out before they can pick her up, my little girl will be dead."

"That's not going to happen," a voice said coming from the back. Maggie walked out where everyone could see her. "We're going to help you save your little girl."

Irina looked shocked, "What is this?" she exclaimed and Father Grissom crossed himself, "May the Lord watch over us all."

"Ok, ok," Bill said, looking at Maggie. "Now you know a very old secret which we all know, but you have to promise that you will never tell a living soul." Maggie can and will help us, and believe me, you want her help."

Irina looked at Maggie. Maggie walked over to her. "Look, Jane has my DJ, and if we don't find him soon, she will kill him. I need your help as much as you need ours."

"So," Paula said. "What is it? Will you help us?"

"Yes," Irina said. "And I will never tell anyone about Maggie."

Father Grissom stood there looking bewildered. "But how can she talk?"

Moses poured a cup of coffee, "Sit down for the most wonderful story." They sat there for an hour while Moses told them about guardians.

When Moses had finished, Maggie walked up and said. "What you need to do is talk with the police. Tell them about the man in the black car. Tell them to grab him first and then they will be able to find out where Jane is." "I know where she is," Irina said. "But without the police, you would be killed. She has a gun and she will use it. She is crazy with hatred. I know, my husband was that way. He hated everyone and it drove him to beat me for nothing. Sometimes He said he was doing it just so I wouldn't forget what he would do to me. She would kill DJ and anyone else who tries to stop her."

"Then what can we do?" Paula asked.

"Get the man picked up first, and then go out there with everything this police department has. If we catch her off guard, we might be able to get in there before she can do anything." Benny said.

"And if you can't?" Maggie said.

Benny knelt down before her. "Even if I have to give my life for his, Maggie; I promise you I will do everything in my power to bring him home safe and sound."

"That's all I can ask for." With that, she walked out of the room to go back to the back bedroom to wait and pray.

Smokey got up and said, "I'm in, let's bring him home." "Father Grissom looked at Smokey, "May the Lord preserve us."

CHAPTER TWENTY TWO

A Race against Time

It was late that Monday afternoon when Bill, Moses, Benny, Father Grissom, and Irina arrived at the police station. Brad looked plum bewildered when he saw all of them walking in together. "Just what in the name of heaven is going on now?" he asked.

Bill spoke up, "First Brad, I want you to listen to this young lady here, and then we need to talk very seriously about how we are going to go about this."

Brad looked at Irina, "Ok then, let's hear it."

Irina took a seat and started talking, after 30 minutes, she sighed, "So you see officer. That is the truth. I lied to save my daughter."

Brad's face turned red with anger, "You mean that no good floozie threatened to have your daughter murdered if you didn't help her get even with Dr. Thomas?"

"Yes sir," Irina said sheepishly.

"No mam, it ain't going to happen on my watch. Where's my gun. Why we'll go out there right now and pick her sorry carcass up."

Benny stepped forward, "No, we can't yet. I'm not trying to mind your business Brad, but if we don't grab the man working for her first, Irina's daughter and Bill's dog will both be dead." "Ok, ok, you're right, I just can't believe something like this is happening right here in our lazy little town." "Les, skedaddle now and keep an eye on that fellow. If he isn't in town call back and just say that the Heartland Grill isn't having fries tonight. That way if he has any means of listening in on our calls he wouldn't suspect a thing. Alissa go in my office and call the state police, when you get them on the phone tell me. I'm going to get us some back up for this job. That Jane lady might have even more men working for her than Irina saw. No use walking into a trap."

"Good thinking," Benny said. Thinking to himself, this man isn't a bad cop after all. I guess I misjudged him.

Father Grissom, take Irina back to her apartment, and young lady, stay there until this thing is over, do you hear me?"

Nodding her head, Irina slowly turned to walk out with Father Grissom.

"Wait," Bill said as Irina turned to walk away. "I'm not going to press any charges against her and Father Grissom isn't going to report anything. I guess what I am trying to ask is, Irina isn't going to be in any trouble is she?"

Brad smiled. "Normally, I would throw the book at her, but under the circumstances, not on my end. No, she came in of her own free will and helped us out here. I'll talk with the D A. We will just say that we worked out a deal where no charges would be pressed against her for her help."

"The District Attorney will do that?" Moses asked.

"He better, I'm married to his sister," Brad said. "And you haven't seen nothing until you've seen that little woman get fired up." "Thank God, for brothers-in-law," Benny said.

"Amen," Said Father Grissom.

*　*　*　*　*

Angelia was on duty and she was sitting down watching TV. Curtis walked in the room where the TV was. "You know, I think you're wasting a lot of time worrying about George Lackey. He's gone and it is probably for the best. Besides, there are a lot better men around here than George."

Angelia got up, "I'm not in the mood to talk right now, Curtis. Just drop it, ok?"

Curtis was getting tired of waiting for Angelia to come around. "I have cared about you for a long time, why can't you see that?"

"I have, but why can't you see that I don't feel the same way and never will."

"You're wasting your time on that sleazebag. He's no good and never will be." With that, Curtis grabbed Angelia by the arms and tried to pull her close to him. But before he could get a grip on her, Angelia placed her knee in just the right place. Curtis backed up and bent over grasping for air. Angelia backed away from him and ran out of the room. She was walking down around the trucks when Curtis came up behind her and grabbed her. He pinned her arms so that she couldn't move. "I'm going to show you what it's like to have a real man, then you'll forget all about George Lackey."

"You better let me go. Curtis I swear, I'll tell on you if you harm me." Angelia was afraid. She wasn't strong enough to break his hold, and there wasn't anyone else around. She knew that if she couldn't talk some sense into Curtis, he was going to rape her. She was crying as she yelled at him. "Let me go." Her voice rang through the station.

"No one is here, it's just you and me honey, and I'll tell them you begged me to sleep with you and when I said I wouldn't marry you, you made up the lie that I raped you. It worked before." Curtis was laughing as he held her even tighter.

"But you forgot about one thing Curtis," George said as he walked up. "The lady ain't alone now." When Curtis turned to see where George was, he was hit right between the eyes. Curtis went down, but George grabbed Angelia before she fell. "Run for help," he said as she looked into his eyes.

Angelia ran into the office to call Brad, Curtis came up with a knife in his hand. "Well, it won't save you." Curtis lunged at George with the knife. He barely cut George on the arm, but George moved out of the way before he could do any major damage. Curtis grinned, I know how to use a knife, and I am going to cut you up into a thousand little pieces."

"I don't think so," Angelia said. With that, she turned on the hose and the force of the water knocked Curtis off his feet and into the side of the truck. He hit the truck so hard that he was out like a light. Angelia ran over to George and threw her arms around him. "Where have you been?"

"I have a copy of the report you saw, but this is the real report, not one that Curtis tampered with to make me look worse than I am. I need to tell you what happened. But first let's get him ready for Brad."

Angelia put her head on George's chest, "Just promise me you'll never disappear like that again."

"You got it." George said.

* * * * *

Robert Lee Locklear was standing in the middle of the room before the entire school board. Everyone had heard how he attacked Dr. Pittman, and with Dr. Pittman in surgery, this only made matters worse for Robert Lee Locklear. The Chairman of the Board looked up at Robert

Lee, "Sir, everyone on this campus has heard how you attacked Dr. Pittman today. And to be frankly honest with you, I would rather press charges against you, but Clara asked that we just terminate you. She seems to think that is the best way to deal with you, sir. So, please understand, we are also going to have your teaching license revoked as well. You don't belong in a classroom anywhere."

Robert Lee stood there speechless. What was he going to do now? He had worked so hard all these years and now everything was blowing up in his face. "You can't do that. I won't let you." He said gritting his teeth.

"You are going to clear out your desk now, and if I see you anywhere around this campus again, I'll have you locked up for good." The chairman stood as he spoke. "Dr. Pittman is a good friend, and you sir.., I can't think of anything low enough to describe you. Just get out of my sight before I forget my promise to Clara Pittman."

Robert Lee walked out of the meeting an angry and wounded man. He had lost everything. He wasn't going to allow Bill Thomas to live long enough to enjoy what should be his. Even if he had to do it himself this time, Bill Thomas was going to die. No one was going to take everything away from him and give it to someone else.

* * * * *

Brad was driving away with Curtis in the backseat of his police car. George looked at Angelia. "Ok, now I guess I have to come clean with you."

"George, why didn't you just tell me the truth right from the start; then none of this would ever have happened."

"Because in a way, I am guilty, I teased a young girl when she came to work for the Fire Department. I told her how we didn't have time to wait for her to do her nails, or blow dry her hair. We save lives here, I told her. Yeah, some big liar I was."

"But I read the report, she was told to pull back just like everyone else, and she ran into the building anyway. George, that wasn't your fault."

George looked at Angelia, "Please, don't try to make it easy for me to forget what I did. If I hadn't pushed her by always picking at her and making fun of her she might have pulled back, but you see, I'll never know that for sure now. Angelia, that's what I have to live with. That is why I couldn't be nice to you when I first came here. My guilt was eating me alive, and every time you were nice to me, it only pushed the knife of my own guilt deeper into my own heart. Do you understand that?"

"Yes, I think I do. But, you didn't make her run into that building. Don't you think that I didn't get the same treatment from the men at the first station where I worked? Why they would leave dolls on my bed, and other things to remind me that I was a girl in a man's world. But I never wanted to run into a building that the chief told everyone to pull out of. And yes, I have seen those who are gung-ho, who would place not only themselves at risk, but others as well. And so have you, men as well as women. What happened to that girl, well, sometimes it just happens. Maybe we need better ways to detect if a person is an over achieving gung-ho type. I don't know. But I do know you can't keep carrying this thing around inside of you for the rest of your life."

George smiled at Angelia. "Boy, who made you so tough?"

Angelia stepped back and squared her shoulders. "I'm a firefighter, sir. We have to be tough to make it through the day."

Angelia stepped up to George and put her arms around him. "But I'm still a woman, who has fallen in love with a man who has been pushing me away from the very beginning."

"Well, I'll see if I can't do better." George said smiling. He reached down and kissed Angelia lightly on the lips.

"What was that?" She asked. "My Daddy use to kiss me like that when I was a little girl while he was tucking me in bed." With that she threw her arms around his neck and kissed George big time. "Now," she said. "That's how it's done."

"Yes mam," George said, as he kissed her again.

* * * * *

DJ was sitting in the cage, waiting for any mistake. If he got just one chance, he was going to take it. Jane was walking around the room yelling and kicking the trash can. "I went by Bill's house and there was your little friend outside, but as I got closer I saw this other big dog outside with her. Now why did that dimwit have to go and get another dog? Seems he has replaced you with a big bluish collie, so maybe you're not that special after all, maybe I should go ahead and shoot you now?" DJ wasn't listening to Jane any more. He knew that dog was Smokey, and if Smokey was there, then so were Moses and Benny. Help had arrived; he had hope for the first time since Jane had grabbed him. But he had to be careful so that she wouldn't realize that he understood what she was saying. So he just sat there as if he didn't know a word she was saying. Jane walked over and kicked the cage, "You stupid dog. You're so dumb. I can't see why Bill thought so much of you anyway. I'm going to get the other one and then, I'll kill you both together."

DJ lay down and just closed his eyes. Let her curse and fuss all she wants to. Smokey would never allow her to grab Maggie. At least now he had that much off his mind. He knew his love was safe.

Just then the door opened, and Jane's man walked in. "What the hell are you doing here?" she snapped. Before he could answer, Jane was cursing again. "Have they picked up Bill yet? Is the town still tearing itself apart?"

"No, they haven't picked him up yet, and things are quieting down in town."

"What!! Get back out there and find out what they are going to do with Bill. And start talking in town about how you have read reports about how more college teachers are having affairs with students these days. But don't just do nothing, I'm paying you good money, now get back to work!"

"Alright," the man snapped back. "But you said when we first came here to lay low and not speak to anyone." Jane's face was turning three shades of red. "Well, I've changed my mind." She yelled. The man turned and walked out the door, slamming it as he left. "One more time, and I am going to put a hole right through his head." Jane said coldly.

* * * * *

Bill, Moses, and Benny walked in the back-door. Paula was sitting there with Smokey waiting. "Well, what did they say? When are they going after Jane?"

"Hold on now," Benny said. "First, they have to pick up the man who's working with her, and then they are going after her. The state police will be here tomorrow and after the man is picked up, they are going to wait for it to get dark, and then go after her."

"Why wait until it's dark?" Paula was starting to get a little nervous as she spoke.

"Because," Maggie said as she walked in. "They can get closer before she knows they are there, right?"

"Yes, that's right. They don't want anything to go wrong when she is arrested this time. Jane is going to go back to prison for a very long time."

Paula bit her bottom lip. "But what about DJ, what's going to happen to him?"

Benny spoke up. "I already told Maggie that I would do whatever I had to, to save DJ. I owe her that much."

Smokey bowed his head and started a song, Maggie joined in with him. It was one Bill and the others had never heard. It was a song that was sung before a battle, when the chances were great that someone might die.

CHAPTER TWENTY THREE

The Reckoning

Chip was waiting for Jonathan to open the Morning Blend early that Tuesday morning. There was still a crisp bite in the air as Jonathan walked up to where Chip was waiting. "My, the coffee must be getting better. I don't think I ever had anyone waiting to get in before."

Chip's face turned a little red, "Please don't be mad, but I'm not here for the coffee. Nita is going to meet me here before we go to work. I have something I want to ask her."

"Hmm," Jonathan said. "Sounds like it's mighty important. I mean if it can't wait until after work."

Chip put his head down, "It is, sir."

Jonathan opened the door wide for Chip. "Then by all means my good fellow, come in and wait for the fair maiden." Chip laughed as he walked by Jonathan and took his seat at their favorite table. "I just hope your heart doesn't get broken like mine," Jonathan thought to himself.

Before Jonathan got around the counter to start the coffee Nita walked in. "Hello Dr. Wedgeworth," she said. "Now, what did I tell you two, here at the Morning Blend, I am just plain old Jonathan." "Oh, yes sir, I forgot," Nita said smiling, as she walked over to the table where Chip was sitting. Chip stood to greet her. "Hey, you look so beautiful this morning." Nita's face lit up, she loved the way Chip had finally found his nerve and would talk to her, telling her how he felt.

"And you, why you are so handsome. I'm going to have to keep an eye on you; you're just too good looking to leave alone." Nita was giggling as she spoke.

"Now that you bring it up, that is what I wanted to talk to you about this morning. I thought about waiting until after we were through with our classes, but I just couldn't put it off any longer." Nita looked a little nervous. She wasn't sure just where this was heading. Chip reached over and took her hand. "No, it's not what you're thinking." With that, he pulled out a small box and got down on one knee. "Nita Cotton, would you do me the greatest honor of being my wife for the rest of our lives?"

Nita threw her hands up over her mouth, and then she broke out crying. "Yes, oh yes I will marry you." She was in Chip's arms crying and kissing him. "I love you with all my heart; there isn't anyone else in this whole world I would rather marry. Oh, I can't believe this is happening."

Jonathan stood behind the counter with his eyes filled with tears. His heart was breaking, and yet at the same time it was overflowing. Never had he felt such an odd thing.

"Well," he said as he wiped his eyes. "Your lattes are on the house today."

* * * * *

Rebekah Corey was standing across the street just watching with tears running down her cheeks. "Hmm, that little tip I got over the phone about Chip buying a ring paid off. Now, I'm going to have a daughter, and that girl is going to make him one fine wife." Rebekah started walking toward the bakery. That's where his father asked me to marry him. I wonder if Chip remembered that today was our anniversary, oh well, even if he didn't, this is still a wonderful day for me. I have years of wonderful memories and now this. A cup of coffee and a chocolate doughnut, that's what his father bought me that day. I have the same thing every year. Yes, I have wonderful memories.

* * * * *

Jerome was sitting on the side of Annie's bed. He was holding a pail while she was so sick. "Oh, God, Jerome, please tell me that this is going to end soon."

Placing his hand on her shoulder, "It will, I promise."

Annie was so pale as she looked up into his eyes. Jerome looked deep into her green eyes. That was the most beautiful sight to him. "Now why are you smiling?"

"Because every time I look into your eyes, I remember the very first time I saw you, and how I was so smitten, you stole my heart back then and you know it."

Annie laid her head back on his arm. "All I want is to go home."

Jerome held her close, "And we will, just as soon as you finish the treatments. Then we're going home to grow old together, and don't you forget it, either." "But why did you shave your head?" Annie asked Jerome.

"I told you, we're in this thing together. I'm never going to leave your side. You are the love of my life, and only you. Since your hair is coming out, then so is mine. Together, always, I mean that." Jerome lightly kissed Annie.

She wrapped her arms around him. "You are the only man I have ever loved; I can't imagine ever loving anyone else."

Smiling Jerome said, "Does that mean I knocked your dad out of his place?"

"No, but you are next in line, you know that."

Jerome held Annie even closer. "Soon we're going to be home, dear."

* * * * *

Wayne was sweeping out the cleaners when Cindy walked in. "Not much business today?"

"Nope, but that's ok too, because I need to do a little repair work, so this way I will be able to do it without having to put it off until late at night. You see, if you look for it you can find something good in anything."

Cindy smiled at Wayne. She knew their business had been slow due to Irina living in their apartment upstairs, but she also knew they were the only ones who would help her during this time. "I think I saw Irina going upstairs a little while ago." Wayne said.

"Why don't you go and see if she is hungry."

Cindy smiled, "You always think about others before yourself. Why don't we go up together and ask her to go the Heartland Grill for a bite to eat."

Wayne dropped the broom, "Thank God, I was looking for a reason to stop sweeping." Together they walked up the stairs, but neither of them knew what was about to happen. Cindy knocked on the door. "Yes, who is it?" Irina asked.

"It's Cindy and Wayne, dear. We were wondering if you wanted to go and get a bite to eat?"

They heard the door unlock. Irina opened the door wide so that they could come in. "No, I can't go out today, but please come in. I have something I need to tell you both."

Wayne and Cindy both took a seat. "What is it, dear?" Cindy asked.

Irina's eyes were already red from crying. "Well," she shook as she started crying again. Cindy stood up to comfort her. Irina held out her hand to stop her. "No, please let me finish. You see, I have lied to you both about everything. I hate myself for doing it."

"Then why did you do it, dear?" Cindy asked with such compassion in her voice.

"Because, I was trying to find my daughter, you see, oh, there is so much to tell you and I don't know where to start."

Wayne said, "At the beginning is always the best place I have found." He stood and walked over to Irina, come on now dear, sit down here with us and tell us everything."

Irina took her seat and started telling Wayne and Cindy about how she came to America to go to school and that she fell in love with a man who she thought was a good man until she found out later that he was everything but a good man. She told them how he would get drunk and beat her, and how once she was even afraid that he was going to kill her while their baby daughter slept in the next room. She confessed to them about the night she fought back and took a knife and killed him. "I didn't mean to kill him," she said. "I was so afraid he was going to kill me that I wasn't thinking." Tears just kept running down Cindy's face. Never in her life had she seen such pain and anguish in one life. Irina told them about Jane and how Jane had lied to her about Bill Thomas. She went on to tell them about how she had run to the church the night before and how Father Grissom had prayed with her. "Now I know I have peace, and I believe we will be able to save my daughter, even though I may never find her. At least she will be safe, which at this point, is all that matters to me. So if you want me to leave now, I can understand, but please let me stay until they have arrested Jane."

"My dear," Wayne spoke as he got up. "You should have trusted the people of this town, but I can understand why you felt like you couldn't. But as for your leaving, Irina, we love you and feel as if you are our own child. Why, we could no more ask you to leave than we could ask our own flesh and blood."

Irina sat there crying. "You want me to stay?"

Cindy reached over and kissed her on the cheek. "Why, of course we do. We knew you weren't telling us everything, but we figured you would in your own good time."

Wayne said, "Well then, I'll go and pick us up something and bring it back here to eat. How does that sound to you two ladies?"

"Irina was wiping her eyes, "It sounds great to me."

Cindy stood up and kissed Wayne, "Me too."

* * * * *

Vickie Eldridge was making her rounds. She stopped in to check on Dr. Pittman in CCU, "How is Dr. Pittman doing today, Clara?" "Clara looked so tired, she hadn't slept much that night. She had stayed out in the waiting room all night. "Dr. Adcock said he went through the surgery ok and that if there weren't any complications he should be moved to a step down room by tomorrow. I have tried to reach Bill, but no one answered his phone."

Vickie held up her hands, "I don't know, but I'm sure there has to be an explanation or they would be here right now."

Clara smiled, "I know, I..., I just wanted to talk to Bill, that's all."

"Then by all means, let's talk." Bill said as he and Paula walked in the CCU waiting room. Clara stood up, before she could say anything, she started crying. "Now now," Bill said. "I know Dr. Pittman, and he is one tough old bird. He is going to pull through this with flying colors."

"I know," Clara said wiping her eyes. "But, his days at the university are over and your name hasn't been cleared yet, so who is going to take his place? He loves that school, you know that."

"I know," Bill said with deep feeling.

"But," Paula said. "Bill's name will be cleared by the end of the day."

"What?" Clara said.

"It's a long story," Bill chimed in.

"Well, I have plenty of time for long stories. So, tell me. What's going on?"

Paula leaned in, "Oh Clara, you just want believe what has happened. Irina came forward..,"

Bill held up his hand. "Not here, not yet, I'm sorry Clara. But we really can't say anything until after today."

Looking at Paula and Vickie, "So please Vickie, what you have heard so far needs to be kept quiet. And I mean that."

Vickie could tell by the look on Bill's face that this was very serious, "Yes sir, I won't say a word. Not even to my sister, who will just die when it all comes out and she finds out that I knew something before her."

Clara knew Bill Thomas, and she knew if he said it had to wait then there was a good reason for it. "I can wait. Besides, I think I would rather hear it with Harry for the first time."

"That's a deal," Bill said.

* * * * *

Dr. Sam Balius was walking down the sidewalk with his mind a thousand miles away. He was still thinking about how he had allowed himself to get irritated that day. Never in all his life had he allowed himself to get in such a state of mind. He was so caught up in his thoughts that he didn't see Father Grissom walking toward him. "I was just coming over to see you myself." Father Grissom said. "Sam, I feel just awful about what happened."

"It's not your place to say anything; I can't believe I let myself get so out of control. I need to ask you to forgive me." Father Grissom reached out and hugged Sam around the neck. "No, I should have come sooner. I could have, but I allowed my pride to get in and that held me back. Please Sam, forgive me."

Sam just held onto his good friend. "Let's never let anything like this ever happen again."

Nodding Father Grissom said. "If you can come over to my office, I might even let you beat me in a game of chess."

"Now, don't go and get my hopes up."

Father Grissom looked around at the town. What are we going to do about our town, Sam?"

"I think I have an idea, but things are going to have to change first. Nothing will happen until this thing with Bill gets resolved."

"Come on and let's drink coffee and play a game of chess. What I am going to tell you will make you want to shout, because, before this night is over, everything will be set right again."

Sam's face was beaming. "Thank God, He has answered prayer once more."

* * * * *

Benny was at the police station with Brad and Floyd. Floyd looked over at Benny, "You know Mr. Ellison, if it hadn't been for you, we could still be sitting around not knowing what to do next." Brad looked at Floyd a little agitated, "Ok, ok, I know when I'm wrong. And Floyd is right; I owe you a lot for this, sir. This is going to save our town a lot of heartache. Thank you Mr. Ellison for your fine police work, and forgive me for being too prideful to listen."

Benny held out his hand to Brad, "That's ok, Brad. If the shoe had been on the other foot, I might have acted, well, I would have acted the same way, there's no might to it. So, let's just put it behind us and bring this woman down."

"Boy, that sounds good to me," Floyd said.

Alissa said, "Les called in a little while ago and said he had spotted the man who is working with Jane Hendricks. He is following him, but not too close. Just as soon as the state police get there, they are going to take him into custody."

"Ok, then," Brad said. "After he is brought in, we will plan how we are going to move out on the old farm and take Jane as well."

*****

Les was following Jane's man, but he stayed far behind him. He did wonder why the man seemed to look a little distracted. Every time the man turned around to make sure he wasn't being followed, Les would duck into a building or into a doorway. In all truthfulness, if he had been at his wits, he would have seen Les, but he was still so upset over the way Jane had talked to him the night before that he wasn't watching very closely to what was going on around him. He never even noticed when the state police car rode by him, nor did he notice that they pulled into the side street ahead of him. By the time he got to the street, Les was right behind him, so when the state police stepped out to grab him, as he turned to run, Les grabbed him and took him down. "That was a good take down," commented a state police man.

"Ten years of kung-fu, I got into it watching old reruns on TV. There is always some kid here whose dad teaches it. So over the years I have studied about five different styles. I just love it."

The state police man smiled, "Well, let's read him his rights, and take him in for questioning."

"I ain't telling you nothing," he barked.

"Who said we wanted you to," Les snapped. He pushed the state police away and reached for his cell phone, but before he could hit a button Les kicked it out of his hand, causing it to hit the street and break into a hundred pieces.

"Ok, now we have to move," Les said. And with that they placed him into a car and were off.

* * * * *

By now Bill and Moses were at the police station. Bill was standing over in the corner trying to stay out of everyone's way. Moses stood with him, "It won't be long now. They are bringing the man in and then just as soon as it gets dark, we are going after DJ." Brad walked over to Bill. "Mr…I mean Dr. Thomas. I want to say how sorry I am for the way I talked to you the other day. I had no right to say those things to you and to treat your friends the way I did. Please accept my apology for acting the way I did." Bill just reached out and patted Brad on the shoulder. "You are a good cop, and you have always done what was right for this town. I know this has put a lot of stress on you as well. You were only looking out for your town; there is no fault in that."

Brad shook his head. "Thank you sir," Brad said as he turned and walked back over to where Benny was standing with the other state police.

Moses whispered to Bill, "Man, you let him off too light. Why I would have told him what was what. I would have given it to him."

Bill looked out of the corner of his eye at Moses. "Well, I would have wanted to," said Moses.

"Whoever said I didn't," Bill replied.

Together they both started laughing, Moses pushed Bill on the arm. "Man, it sure has been good to be up here with you folks."

"Yeah, I have enjoyed y'all being here, just wish it wasn't for this reason."

Benny walked over to them and whispered. "This is very serious business, now you two need to keep it down over here. Moses, you know better than to act that way."

Moses started to say something but Benny turned and walked away. Moses looked away from his Dad so he didn't see Benny look back and grin. Brad was standing over by the wall chuckling to himself. "Hmm," Bill thought, "it seems everyone is having their fun tonight. And why not, this nightmare is just about over."

About that time the door was thrown wide open with Les leading his man in the police station. "Hey, I want my phone call," the man demanded. Brad looked over at Alissa, "Are the phones still down?" "Yes sir, dead as a doornail." About that time the phone rang. "Well my goodness, looks like the phone company has it fixed."

Alissa answered the phone, while Les tried to move the man to his cell. "Hey, I want my phone call." Alissa hung up the receiver. Brad looked at her.

Alissa picked up the receiver again. "Darn, it's down again." Alissa put the receiver down. "Oh well, maybe they'll have it fixed up right nice tomorrow."

"Now, I know that woman is nothing but a no good liar."

Les pushed him toward the cells. "That's my wife you're talking about, and the person you are wanting to call will be here with you soon enough."

* * * * *

Paula was sitting at home with Maggie. She was worried about Bill, Moses, and Benny going with the police to take Jane into custody. "I sure hope no one is hurt tonight." Paula voice carried her nervousness. Maggie just sat there not saying a word. "I mean, I don't want anyone seriously hurt."

Maggie looked at Paula. "Benny isn't going to place himself in harm's way for DJ. I told Moses to stop him before he could do that."

"But why did you do that, Maggie?"

"Because as much as I love that silly boy, I know DJ would rather die than someone give up their life for his. So, you see, DJ isn't coming back home alive."

Maggie's voice carried with it such a seriousness to it that hit Paula hard. She placed her head down and cried. Maggie sat there, knowing that they had done all they could do. It was in the Creator's hands now.

* * * * *

At the police station plans were being made. Everyone was being given their place to be and orders were being given to make sure that Jane had her rights read to her in front of two or more witnesses. "I don't want any mistake this time. No judge is going to throw this arrest out because we didn't do our jobs." Brad was very serious when he said that. The life of this town was on the line here, and he wanted this thing ended tonight.

"Ok," said the State Police, "let's go." With that they all loaded up in their cars and headed toward the old farm. "She is using the old barn for her hideout so I want every door going into that place covered." Bill, Moses, and Benny rode with Les. No one said anything; it was just too stressful to talk. They all sat in silence while they headed toward the old farm house.

* * * * *

Jane was walking around trying to reach her man. "How many times have I told that fool to leave his cell phone on. I bet he let it run down, when I get my hands on him..." She looked over at DJ, "You know, just as soon as they arrest Bill, you're dead." Jane laughed with such a wicked laugh.

DJ had wondered how he had ever thought she might be reached. He had never seen such an evil person who was so completely given over to hatred. He was beginning to think that there wasn't going to be a way out for him. Deep sadness came over him and for the first time he was losing hope that he was ever going to see Maggie again. Jane saw it, she saw sadness in his eyes. "Oh, does the little dog feel sad?" Then she laughed again as she kicked his cage. "This is going to be more fun than I thought. Maybe I should film killing the dog. That way when Bill ole boy finally gets out of jail, I'll mail it to him to watch." Jane laughed even more. She reached over and pulled out a bottle. She took a drink and then took another. "I was going to wait until you were dead, but since that is going to happen really soon, why wait any longer."

DJ placed his head down and quietly prayed within his heart. He knew this was going to be his last night on this earth. He had always tried to be the very best guardian he could be, and to put others before himself. So if tonight was going to be his last, he was ready. He had finished his task. Jane was starting to get just a little bit tipsy. She was drinking too fast to have not eaten in the last few hours. She didn't hear the sounds of cars rushing toward the building, but her captor did. He listened, but tried not to show that he was listening to any noise. It was then that Jane heard the cars. She ran to the window and looked out.

There were police cars filling the yard outside. She ran and got the file on Irina's daughter. She opened it and read the address, and then she threw in into the fire. "Damn that fool, he turned over on me.

Well at least Bill isn't going to get his little dog back." With that, she pulled out her 38 and pointed it at DJ. It was right then that he knew what to do. "Ok go ahead and shoot the dog," DJ shouted with defiance.

Jane's mouth fell open. "What was this?" she thought. "That's right, shoot me if you've got the nerve. But before you do, let me tell you something. You think it was Bill who sent you up. "Wrong," it was me, and Maggie that is. We set you up. We were listening to everything you said on the phone. We even taped it, too. Yeah, that's right. You were outsmarted by Bill's dogs, lady. So how does that make you feel?" Jane stepped back even more, she couldn't believe what she was hearing and seeing. "And oh yeah, the lady at the bank, I was the one who gave her the idea of how to make your account attempt to transfer money out of Bill's account after the bank shut down for the day. She had to fool around with it, but she sure made it work. And you went up the river for it. Bill didn't do it, I did."

Jane's anger was just about to explode. "So it was you then. Well, I might not be able to get my hands on Bill, but it seems I got the one I really wanted anyway."

DJ shook his head. "Man overkill."

"I think that just about says it all," Jane spit out. With that, she raised the gun and pointed it at DJ. Just then the door burst open with Benny running in and Moses right behind him. Benny saw Jane's gun pointed at DJ, and as he tried to jump in front of the cage, Moses grabbed him from behind and held him fast. Les pushed by them and jumped at Jane. She looked at him for just a moment, which was just enough distraction. Before she could pull the trigger, Les hit her hard flying through the air. The gun went off, Boom, but her hand was pointed away from DJ's cage. When she hit the floor, Jane hit it so hard that the gun went flying out of her hand. Les had her arms behind her and cuffed her before you could say, Jack Robbins.

Benny looked at Moses, "Why did you stop me?"

"Because I promised Maggie I would Dad." "What! I promised her I would do whatever it took to save DJ." "She knew that dad, and Maggie knew you meant it too. But she said that she knew DJ, and that he wouldn't want you or anyone dying trying to save him. She made me promise, Dad."

Bill came running in and looked around. DJ started barking his head off. Les pulled Jane up to her feet. Jane looked wild in her eyes. "That dog can talk. I'm telling you that dog can talk. They are the ones, he and the other one, they are the ones who had me sent up. They can talk." Jane was trying as hard as she could to break free from Les.

"Yeah, I've seen this before," Benny said. "They just keep on feeding on all that hatred and it drives them out of their mind. Happened once, oh, I don't remember, it was years ago."

Brad looked at Jane and then at Benny. "Say you've seen this before?"

"Oh yeah, she's a goner for sure."

"Well then, what do you think I should do?" Brad asked.

"First, read her her rights and then lock her up where no one can talk to her. I would call in a shrink and have him check her out. You might even get a closed trial with her being out of her mind and all."

Jane was cursing now as loudly as she could. Brad walked over to her and yelled, "Hey you, shut up. Ok Les, do your thing."

Les read Jane her rights twice in English and once in Spanish. "That way I have covered all my bases," he said, proud of himself.

Bill reached down and picked up DJ out of the cage. "I know someone who can't wait to see you, young man." He held DJ close. DJ whispered in his ear when no one was looking. "Thank you for coming for me, Bill." Bill's eyes were full of tears, "I couldn't do anything else."

Looking around at Moses and Benny he said. "I don't know about you two but I'm hungry."

"Here, here," Moses said.

Benny was getting up from the floor. "I could eat a horse."

Jane was crying as they carried her out. "But I'm telling you the truth that dog can talk."

* * * * *

Paula was just about fit to be tied when she heard the car drive up. Maggie gasped, "I can't go in there, dear. Would you go in there and tell me what has happened?"

It was then that they heard Smokey's voice, "Oh Maggie, look what the cats dragged in."

Maggie's eyes lit up. "DJ, he's alive." With that, she flew in there as fast as she could. There he stood waiting for her. Maggie ran up to him and started smelling of him and then she pushed him with her body. "Do you know how worried I was about you? Next time someone tries to grab you, for goodness sakes, run away."

DJ smiled and put his head over on Maggie, "I missed you too, my Love."

Maggie stepped back, "You have lost some weight. Bill, could you get him something to eat?"

"Right on it girl, and you could use something too, you haven't been eating much here lately yourself." DJ looked at Maggie, "Don't say it, I know I shouldn't have worried, I know we are sometimes called upon to die for our charge, but that doesn't mean I can ever stop loving you."

DJ rubbed his face next to Maggie's. "After we eat, can we just get some rest and talk about this tomorrow? You can't imagine how much I have missed my bed."

Maggie pushed him again, "You old softy."

Paula walked up to Bill. "What about Jane?"

Bill laughed, "You'll have to ask DJ about that, he has her going to the state prison for the criminally insane."

Maggie picked her head up out of her bowl. "What, I want to hear about this." "Tomorrow, can't it wait until tomorrow?" DJ asked.

"No it can't," Paula said, taking a seat. "You can have a double portion to eat, but please tell me everything. I mean, she might never get out."

"Ok, ok, then I'll tell you what happened."

With that DJ finished his food and then he sat up for more than an hour telling them how at the last minute, he knew what to do to buy himself enough time. Everyone was listening, and Smokey was taking it all in as well. Never had one house been filled with such joy and happiness.

When DJ finished telling his story, he and Maggie laid down by the fireplace. Maggie got over real close to him. "I thought I wasn't ever going to see you again."

"I know, and I thought I wouldn't see you either. But it seems this family needs both of us." "You silly boy," Maggie said as she closed her eyes. That was the first real night's rest either of them had had since DJ was kidnapped. Moses stood in the doorway looking in on them as they slept. Benny walked up behind him. "It's time we head home tomorrow, son."

"I know Dad, I know. But just think, we helped save one of them this time."

* * * * *

Jane was sitting in her cell crying. "But the dog can talk, I swear, that dog can talk."

Floyd walked back out in the outer office. "Boy that is one crazy woman. What do you think they'll do with her?"

"Don't know, and I don't care," Les said. "Just as long as they move her out of here, I could care less what they do with her."

CHAPTER TWENTY FOUR

Name Cleared

The headline in the Whitworth Morning News read, **Dr. Bill Thomas Cleared of all Charges**. The article was written by Bill Thomas. The editor allowed Bill to write the article because Bill wanted to try and prevent people from feeling resentment and anger toward Irina. In the article he told how Jane had lied to Irina and then how she threatened to kill her daughter if she didn't cooperate with her. The article also told how Dr. Thomas was going to assume Dr. Pittman's position while he was out sick and that if the doctor felt that Dr. Pittman wasn't able to return to work then Dr. Thomas was going to assume that position permanently in addition to teaching a few classes.

Robert Lee threw the paper down, stepped on it, and cursed. "That was mine, and now that…, that fool has stolen it once again from me. I'll stop him from taking it, even if it's the last thing I do. I might be out, but he isn't going to enjoy my job or his family for very long." Robert Lee walked across the living room floor of his house. His job was gone and he wasn't going to be able to teach any more now that the board had filed charges against him. He might even have to face charges over pushing Dr. Pittman around. It seemed there were more people on campus at that time of day who witnessed his assault than he thought there would be.

* * * * *

Jonathan sat there reading the article in the paper. His cup of coffee was getting cold as he read and reread the article. Why didn't Irina come to him with the truth? Why didn't he stop to think things over before he hit Bill that night? Jonathan got up and walked over to the window. He felt sick inside over losing the best friend he had ever had. He had allowed his past to cloud his judgment, and he didn't stop to think things through. If he had, he would have known that Bill Thomas would never have done anything like that. How could he have been so blind? Jonathan just stood there thinking to himself and wondering what, if anything, he could do to make things right. He knew he had class in an hour, and there was a good chance he might run into Bill. What would he do? The bell over the door rang. As Jonathan turned around to see who it was, he stood there shocked.

* * * * *

Clara was sitting beside the bed when Dr. Pittman woke up. "Hey, he said very weakly, tell me again how this is going to make me feel better."

"Shush, you old goat. You shouldn't be moving around a lot, and you need to rest more than you need to talk."

"But the school, they can't give it to Robert Lee Locklear. He isn't the man for the job."

280

"Dear, Clara said so tenderly, Robert Lee Locklear isn't on staff any longer, and they have appointed Bill Thomas as the New President of the University. Your school is in good hands now, dear."

Dr. Pittman's face lit up, "But how? I mean when did all this happen?"

"Oh, while you were in surgery, Irina came forward and told the whole truth. It's a long story, but I'll tell you when you are feeling stronger." Dr. Pittman held out his hand, Now, you know me better than that. I'll die just lying here wondering what happened. Why, I won't even get one minute's rest."

Clara picked up the paper, "Now, I'll read you what Bill wrote in this morning's paper, and then I'll fill you in on all the details that aren't in the paper."

Dr. Pittman started to speak, but Clara held up her hand. "No, I'll read and then I will tell you everything else that happened, now that's the deal, or I'll go and get myself a cup of coffee."

"Deal," Dr. Pittman said. He laid there with a broad smile across his face, and tears running down his checks.

Clara looked worried. "Are you all right?" She asked.

"Oh yeah, He did it, dear. He did it."

"Who did what?" Clara asked, wondering if maybe all this was too much right now.

"God, he did it and just at the right time too. He's always on time, honey. The school is in the best hands now."

Clara reached over and lightly kissed Dr. Pittman on the cheek. "Bill Thomas would agree with me on this. The school was in the best hands when you were the President."

"But my time is finished there now. Bill can continue working for years. God did it again."

Clara knew her husband, and she knew how he felt about Bill Thomas. What's more, she knew how Bill Thomas felt about her husband. They were friends, lifelong friends. The type that of friends that don't come around very often, but they enrich the heart when they do.

* * * * *

Yolanda Weir was answering the phone just as fast as she hung it up. "Boy, it seems like everyone in town is calling to ask how Dr. Pittman is getting along."

"Well, how is he getting along this morning?" asked Paula.

"Oh, good morning Mrs. Thomas, Oh you know Dr. Pittman. Why he's a tough man for his age. He's getting along just fine. Do you want to go and see him? I'll ring CCU and see if you can go up."

Paula just patted Yolanda on the arm. "Dr. Adcock has given me authorization to go back there anytime I want to, so there's no need to ring anyone."

Yolanda looked around, "Where's your husband?"

Paula smiled, "Why dear, he is at work, didn't you read the paper this morning?"

"Yolanda picked it up and read the headlines, "Oh sweet Jesus. Why this is just wonderful. I never did believe any of that junk about Dr. Thomas. I knew he wouldn't do anything like that. Why, my Lord, he has the most beautiful wife in the whole county."

Paula smiled, "Thank you, dear. But we have decided not to look backward, but forward. We are going to let the past be the past and move forward in our lives."

* * * * *

At the Heartland Grill you could hear the shouts all the way to the East Coast. No one could ever remember when they saw May and Fay so happy. Fay held the newspaper up for all to see. "Now everyone who thought Dr. Thomas was guilty, I hope you like crow for lunch." May stood there with tears running down her face. "Fay, this isn't a time for talking like that. Now we need to put it all behind us and get back to being the loving town Dr. Thomas came home to."

There were some amen's shouted and everyone felt that the town needed to pull back together again, but no one knew just how to begin. One thing was for sure, Fay and May were both happy to see the restaurant full again. It seemed like ages, even though it had only been a few weeks. Strange how the town was torn apart in such a short time. One would have thought that with everyone knowing everyone else so well, there would have been a closer bond between the people of the town. But that's how people are. When something negative gets out about someone, no one takes time to ask any questions. Many just take it and run with it, as if it was the Gospel truth. How many lives have been damaged by such short sightedness? Only time will tell the truth of that.

* * * * *

Bill stood up before the staff of the university. "I called this meeting so that I could let everyone know what the board has asked me to do." All at once everyone stood and begin to applaud. Bill stood with his head bowed. He wasn't sure the staff would accept him. Now he had his answer.

Jonathan stood and clapped louder than anyone there. He wasn't sure if things would work out between Irina and him or not, but he was thankful to have his friend back. Bill held up his hands. "Wait, you might want to hear what I am going to say before you clap. With my having to be stuck in an office most of the day, that means some of you are going to have to teach more classes until we can fill my spot and the one left open by Robert Locklear."

Jonathan spoke up. "I'll do my part. I can hire more help at the café and that way I can teach more."

Dr. Sam Balius spoke up also. "I've talked with the church board and they are agreeable to my taking on a few more classes."

"How did you know I was going to ask you that?" Bill said with a puzzled look on his face.

Sam just chuckled, "My boy, you have been hanging around Dr. Pittman far too long not to pick up some of his ways." Everyone laughed when Dr. Balius said what they all knew to be true.

Bill smiled, "Thank you sir for that. I count my years here as some of the very best years of my life. And as far as what happened, I am asking everyone here to put that behind us. And please, don't feel hard or resentful toward Irina. She was being used by a very mean and wicked woman. If I had been in her shoes, I might have done the same thing. So please, be kind to her and show her the kind of love this town is known for."

Jonathan stood there not knowing what to say. For what Bill asked of them hit him with its full force. This was the kind of man Bill Thomas was. Why hadn't he seen it when all this junk happened? He knew it, but he had forgotten it. He allowed his anger to color his eyes and his heart. He no longer listened to his heart, but instead he had listened to his own anger. He walked forward to where Bill was standing. Tears were running down his face as he spoke. "I did you such wrong. I judged you wrongfully and if I had only taken the time to stop and think, I would have known you were not capable of doing such a despicable act. Why, you're one of the most decent men I have ever met." Jonathan dropped his head as he cried.

Bill reached out and hugged Jonathan around the neck. "My friend, it has all been forgiven. Someone far greater than I forgave you long ago. Who am I to hold on to something? It's all in the past my friend." Bill whispered to Jonathan, "And I think I know someone who is going to need a job right now." Bill smiled as he looked into Jonathan's face.

"But how do I, what do I say?" Jonathan asked.

"It will come to you when you need it. Trust me, it will." Bill hugged his friend again and everyone there began to hug one another. A healing took place there that day. It was a start to what the whole town needed.

* * * * *

Bob Boswell had stopped washing the table to read the paper. "Hey honey, come here quick."

"What is it?" Mary Ann asked.

He handed her the paper. "Read for yourself." Mary Ann read the headlines and smiled. "You know what this is going to mean, don't you?"

Bob looked puzzled at her. No, what does it mean?" "Why the crowds will pick back up of course." Mary Ann's face was just beaming. Bob jumped up and grabbed Mary Ann around the waist and lifted her off the floor. "Hey, be careful, you are going to hurt the baby."

Bob put Mary Ann down very carefully. "You mean you're…?"

"Yes," Mary Ann said. "I hope you're not mad. I know we talked about not having any more children, but this just kind of happened."

Bob laughed. "Yeah, I know." He hugged her and kissed her. "So, we're only having one this time?"

"Honey, I don't know. Twins run in our family, so it could be twins again."

"Oh no," Bob said sitting down. "What if we have two more boys? They'll tear the house down."

"We could have," Mary Ann said smiling, "two beautiful girls."

"I'll have to teach them how to fight if they are going to survive with those two boys."

"No, you're not. If we have girls, then you are going to teach our sons not to hit their sisters."

Bob placed his hand on his face. "I'll have better luck teaching them to believe in the Easter bunny when they are twenty five."

* * * * *

Irina was working in the cleaners alongside Wayne and Cindy. It seemed everyone in town had brought their dry cleaning in. "Gosh, I have never seen anything like this," Cindy explained.

Irina was so happy the nightmare was over. And from what she was told by the police, Jane didn't have time to call anyone. Also with her acting the way she was saying that Bill Thomas' dog's talked and all, well, they weren't giving her a phone call.

Brad said, "I talked it over with the judge, and she isn't getting a phone call. You don't give crazy folks phone calls. She might try to call the White House or something stupid like that. No sir, unless the court orders me too, she is just going to sit in there until they come and take her out."

Wayne could tell Irina was much happier, but he knew that she also had lost her only chance of ever finding her daughter again. Wayne took Irina by the arm, "You can stay here forever if you like. We'll be your family, if you'll let us be, and Irina, I don't have much, but whatever I have is yours. I don't care if it takes every last penny I have. We'll find some way to find your daughter."

Irina's eyes were full of tears as she hugged Wayne and Cindy. "I love you both more than you could ever know. And yes, I would like to stay here if you don't mind. This is the closest thing I have had to call home since I left my own country. But don't worry about my daughter. I've placed her in God's hands. One day, she'll come walking through my door and tell me 'you are my mother.' She might even have children of her own by then."

Cindy just hugged Irina tight. "And we'll love them just as if they are our own, too."

Irina's heart was full, but there was still the pain she felt for the way she treated Jonathan. Would he ever be able to forgive her? She hoped that one day he would find it in his heart to understand what drove her to do what she did.

* * * * *

Father Grissom was waiting in his office for Sam Balius. They had been planning a way to maybe pull their little town completely back together again. Their plan was to meet with the City Council and then propose what they believed would bring a healing to their community. There was a light knock on the door. "Come on in Sam, the door is open."

Sam walked in and took a seat. "The Council will meet with us this afternoon after I finish my last class, but they are only going to give us ten minutes of their time. It seems they have more important things to discuss than how to help a hurting town."

Father Grissom smiled, "Well, I guess I can't blame them for the way they feel. I mean look at the way we handled things. I doubt they are jumping up and down waiting for us to show up with our words of wisdom."

Sam chuckled as he pictured in his mind the entire council jumping up and down. "Well, it wouldn't hurt them to at least listen to us. Besides, it's not going to cost them one red cent."

"And that is where we are going to get them," Father Grissom replied. "They're tight as Dick's hat band when it comes to money. And they are still mad at the loss of revenue during the yearly town flea market. But Sam, I agree, this is the only way to bring this town back to where it needs to be quickly." Smiling, Sam nodded. "And it's still going to take a miracle to pull this off. But we serve a miracle working God." Sam rose from his chair. "I need to get back to the school now. I have a class coming up soon."

Together they prayed before Sam left. After Sam walked out of Father Grissom's office, Father Grissom walked into the church to be alone for prayer. He knew it was going to take a big miracle to pull this thing off. There were a lot of hurt feelings in this town and only God could set things right.

* * * * *

Dr. Pittman was resting quietly as Bill walked into the CCU room. He walked up to the bed and reached out and lightly touched his friend's arm. "I'm not asleep my boy, I thought you were my wife. She has been hounding me all day to sleep, and I keep telling her that I have slept already."

Bill chuckled at his good friend. "Yeah, what would we do without them to watch over us?"

"By the way," Dr. Pittman asked, "Where is my wife, anyway?"

"Oh, I saw her going down the hall to get a bite to eat, so I told her to take her time. I'll stay in here and keep an eye on you."

Laughing, Dr. Pittman said, "And who is going to keep an eye on you?" They both chuckled at the thought of what was said, and when it hit them again, they both started laughing again at the very thought of it. "Bill, do try to get Clara to go home with you tonight. She doesn't need to stay out there in the waiting room all night. I have tons of nurses watching over me, and if I even act like I am going to do something I shouldn't, they chime in, 'We're going to tell your wife.' The bunch of old nags," Dr. Pittman said laughing.

Kim Adcock walked in and said. "You know Dr. Pittman, I would never have told on you, but since you just called me an old nag, wait till I see your wife."

"Oh no, dear," Dr. Pittman pleaded. "I wasn't talking about you, dear."

Bill was standing there trying hard not to laugh. "And just what are you laughing at?" Kim asked.

"Oh, nothing, nothing at all."

"I thought so," Kim replied.

Clara walked back in the room. "I swear, I think I would forget my head if it wasn't attached."

"Dear, you're going to stay with Bill and Paula tonight, and that's final."

Clara threw her head back and laughed. Bill thought to himself, "This isn't a good sign." Clara looked over at Bill. "So, you told me to take my time so you two could plot behind my back?"

Bill's mouth fell open. "No, I mean, no...Clara, I wasn't plotting behind your back." Bill was trying to maneuver himself out of the quicksand he felt he was standing in.

Clara just looked at him and handed him her money. "Get me a salad, please." He knew she meant it for every time Clara was upset, her accents were much more obvious. You knew she came from England, that's for sure. "Yes, Mrs. Pittman," Bill said.

"Mrs. Pittman," Dr. Pittman said, "My boy, where's your backbone?"

Smiling Bill responded. "I learned everything I know from you sir, and one thing I learned a long time ago, was not to cross that woman when she has her mind made up."

Kim Adcock was trying to take Dr. Pittman's blood pressure, but she was laughing too hard. "I'm sorry, I'll have to come back and do this later. I have to go and find my sister right now and tell her about this." Kim turned and ran out of the room laughing.

"Now look what you've done," Dr. Pittman said. "Why we'll be the laughing stock of the entire hospital."

Bill walked to the door. "Well, at least it won't be the whole town," holding both of his hands up in the air.

Clara smiled trying hard not to laugh. "Run along Bill, and get my salad."

Bill turned and walked out of the room just as Dr. Pittman and Clara both erupted into laughter.

* * * * *

Irina sat in her room looking out the window. She had worked hard all day and was just bone tired. She had heard that Bill and Jonathan had made things right again. For that, she was glad. But what about her, she wondered. Was she ever to have things made right? Would she always live with things in her life out of place? Wasn't it bad enough that she would never find her daughter, must she also never have the man she loved? Then the realization hit her with such force. She loved Jonathan.

CHAPTER TWENTY FIVE

Hope Renewed

Tuesday morning was still cool, but there were signs of spring everywhere. Irina was working in the back of the cleaners helping with the clothes that came in that morning. "Whew," she blew. "I didn't know there were so many dirty clothes in this place."

Cindy was wiping the sweat off her face. "Yeah, and if you work back here long enough, you won't have a weight problem. You'll sweat it off."

Irina laughed, "Then maybe I should live back here."

"Oh my gosh child; why you don't have a weight problem at all. I wish I didn't weigh anymore than you do."

Irina smiled. She was happy to see things back to normal for Wayne and Cindy, but her heart was still so heavy. If only she could talk with Jonathan. Maybe she could make him understand why she did what she did.

"Irina," Cindy called out. "Child, are you all right? You're just standing there looking off into space."

"Oh yes, I'm fine. I was just thinking how wonderful everything is for you now. It makes me happy to see how good the people are being to you now that they know the truth."

"Irina," Wayne called back. "Could you come up here for just a second, dear? I could use your help for just one minute."

Cindy smiled, "Run along, dear. I can handle things back here."

Irina walked to the front of the cleaners. As she walked into the room, her mouth fell open and her eyes filled with tears.

* * * * *

Moses and Benny were sitting with Bill and Paula before Bill left for work. "Well sir," Moses said, looking at his dad. "I think it's about time we headed toward home."

"No, y'all don't have to leave just yet, do you?" Bill asked.

"Surely you could stay just a day or two more?" Paula implored.

"Benny was laughing as he spoke. "My, you two sure know how to make a body feel right at home. I told Moses last night that we had our own business to get back to, but we were honored that you called and asked us to help."

"Oh yes," Smokey said walking into the room. "I wouldn't have missed this for the world."

"Well, I could have." DJ remarked. "Remember, I was the one in a cage, and with a gun pointed at me."

"Y'all get ready; he is going to ride this thing for a long time." Maggie said grinning.

DJ pushed her with his body, "And you wouldn't?"

Moses laughed out loud. "Man, I have missed you two, and that crazy Rocky. Boy now those were some good times." "No son," Benny spoke softly. "These are the best times. Why, here we sit with DJ, Maggie, and Smokey. What more could a soul hope for?" Moses reached over and patted his dad's arm. "You're so right, Dad. These are the best times. But if we don't get back home, Lady might think Smokey has done run off on her."

Smokey laughed, "Well, I know Lady, and she might be wondering right about now."

"I wish I understood better how you two communicate; I mean with Lady not being a guardian and all," Bill asked with a puzzled look on his face.

DJ was standing by Maggie with his head next to hers. "Bill, you know, with your heart first and foremost, different, but not different."

Maggie smiled as her head was resting next to DJ's.

Bill reached out and took Paula by the hand. "Yeah, I see, different, but then again, it's not so different. We all have to start with our hearts, don't we?"

"It does help," Smokey piped in.

"Well, let's get going," Benny said.

Smokey picked up Benny's small bag in his mouth. "I'll carry your bag for you, Benny," he said. Smokey saw Benny rubbing his chest before he laid down the night before. Before they came up to help Bill, he had seen Benny placing a small pill under his tongue one day. When he questioned Benny about the pill, Benny told him that he should mind his own business, and then he made him promise that he wouldn't say anything to Moses about it. Smokey couldn't help but worry about Benny. Paula noticed it, but thought to herself that there wasn't anything strange about it. After all, Moses and Benny had given Smokey and his family a safe place to live. As they drove off, Bill was standing by Paula and DJ was standing by Maggie. He felt that somehow they were going to see Smokey and Moses soon, but he couldn't understand why he felt that way. "I must still be tired," DJ said.

"You are," Maggie chimed in. "So, let's go back inside and get something to eat, and then we can rest some more."

* * * * *

May and Fay were working as hard as they could to keep up with the crowd they had for breakfast. "Man," Fay bellowed as she wiped her face. "We haven't been this busy in weeks."

"Yeah, but just think how good it's going to look at the end of the month," May said. "Why we might be able to keep the lights on."

Fay ginned at her sister, she knew this was May's way of letting her know that they had spent too much time worrying over things, and not enough time praying. Fay walked up and hugged her around the neck, "I'm glad you're my sister." With that, she lightly kissed her on the check.

May just laughed and pushed her back, "All you want is for me to wash the dishes, I know what you're up to." They both started laughing and went back to work. Everyone there knew things were getting back to normal in their lazy little town.

* * * * *

Irina was walking beside Jonathan without saying a word. She was shocked when she walked into the room and there he stood. He asked if she had time enough to walk down the street with him so they could talk. But as they walked, neither one of them said anything which made Irina a little nervous. "Jonathan, you said you wanted to talk?"

"Yes, and I do, but, well, I had everything worked out in my head, but when I saw you, it all went away. I missed you, first let me tell you that. And, that I am sorry about your daughter. I can't imagine how you must feel right now. I know I haven't been there for you and I am sorry for that too."

Irina looked at him as they walked, "But I pushed you away. I knew what I was doing was wrong, and that it would hurt you. So I pushed you away, thinking that maybe it wouldn't hurt you as badly. But now I see that I was wrong in thinking that." Her voice trembled as she spoke.

Jonathan put his arm around her and held her close. "Shush," he said quietly. "You don't have to explain. I know everything. I understand why you did what you did. And as Bill said, if he had been placed in that same position, he would have done the same thing himself."

Irina looked back at Jonathan with a shocked look on her face. "Dr. Thomas said that?"

"Yeah, he did. I hate to admit it, but I misjudged him so badly. Bill is one of the nicest men I have ever known."

"And he was your best friend too, that is, until I came along."

Jonathan grinned, "He still is."

Irina's were eyes filled with tears. "You worked it out, I mean, you talked to him?" "No, he came to me. That's the kind of man he is. He knew I didn't know anything, and he knew that our friendship was as important to him as it was to me." Jonathan stopped walking and held Irina close to him. "He was the one who told me it was about time I grew up and came to see you. He said that any woman who loved her daughter so much that she was willing to throw everything away to find her, had to be worth something."

Irina laid her head against Jonathan's shoulder and started crying. "I didn't want to do what I did. I was going to let my daughter go and try to find happiness with you, but then that hateful woman came with pictures and she said that she could hire men to hurt my daughter before they killed her. I was so afraid, I wanted to run to you but I knew if I did, my daughter would be killed." Irina was crying almost out of control now as she held onto Jonathan tightly.

Jonathan held her as they stood on the sidewalk. "It's ok, I'm sorry for the way I acted and I want you to forgive me."

"No," Irina said shaking her head. "It's I who needs to ask forgiveness from you. I love you so, and I threw it away."

Jonathan held her face in his hand, "Who said it was over? I didn't."

"You mean?" Irina couldn't even finish saying what her heart was daring to believe. "Yes, if you will have me," Jonathan said. "I don't ever want to lose you again. Life has been a nightmare without you. Irina, I can't live without you. Please, let's never allow anything to come between us again."

Irina reached up and kissed Jonathan, "I promise, never again."

* * * * *

Father Grissom was standing about two blocks down the street watching. He had received a phone call from Bill Thomas telling him that Jonathan was going to talk to Irina that morning before he came to class. Since Bill knew that Irina was going to Father Grissom's church, he asked him to please be praying. Father Grissom felt that this was one of those situations where you needed to watch and pray. He wiped the tears from his eyes as he turned to walk back to his church. Yes, his days were numbered here, he knew that. Already, he felt a tug of the Holy Spirit upon his heart. It was time he returned to the prison ministry. He knew that, but he was hoping he'll be able to go to one special place. There was one soul he felt the Lord leading him to. He would sit down and write his bishop this afternoon, that way he would have time to see things finally back in order here before he moved on to his next place of ministry. Surely the bishop would understand, why he had said the last time they met, that he sure missed having him working in the prisons. Yes, it was time to go back to where his heart belonged.

* * * * *

Sam Balius was walking to his next class. He liked teaching. He was also wondering if Jonathan was going to try and talk with Irina, but he wasn't going to pry. Jonathan turned onto the sidewalk just ahead of him. "Hello, Dr. Balius. Good to see you this morning." "Why, hello yourself; tell me something, when are you going to talk to that poor girl? My boy, you should give her another chance." There, he had done what he said he wasn't going to do, but it was the right thing to do. Jonathan laughed, "And I always thought you were the type of fellow who would never pry into someone else's business."

"Well, I'm not," Sam, said, trying to sound like he really meant it. "But I just remember how happy you two looked together, and I would hate to see you both throw that away."

Jonathan reached over and patted Sam on the shoulder. "Don't worry doc, we're good. I had a long talk with Irina this morning before I came to class."

Sam's face was beaming with joy, "Why, that's wonderful news, wonderful news, indeed." They continued to talk as they walked. If anyone had seen them walking together, they would never had guessed that just a week ago, Jonathan wouldn't even speak to Sam.

Things were slowly getting back to normal, but Sam and Father Grissom had an idea to help speed things up a bit. It all depended upon timing. The one sad fact that no one had taken into account was the one dark cloud that was still hanging over the head of Bill Thomas. He didn't know it was there, and with everything going so smoothly, why should he? That's when we let our guard down, when everything looks as if it's running smoothly. That's when we need to keep on praying, for our enemy never takes a day off.

Chapter Twenty Six

One Last Attack

The sun was shining and everyone talked about how wonderful the classes were that day. Bill was busy in his office and had already called Paula to tell her he was going to be late coming home. He never knew there was so much paperwork with this job. The sun was starting to set when Jonathan stuck his head in the door, "Hey, how about going with me down the road a piece? There's a flea market going on about ten miles out of town and I'm told they have an old English table that I would love to have."

Bill looked up at his friend. Truly God's grace was amazing; here Jonathan stood asking him to ride with him to a flea market, when a week ago he wouldn't even speak to him. Yes, amazing indeed. "Hmm, let me call Paula and tell her that I am going to be even later than I told her."

"No," Jonathan said. "I'm not trying to keep you from going home to your wife."

Bill laughed, "That's quite alright, in fact, why don't you come home and eat with us when we get back to town?"

"You really mean it!" Jonathan said with very deep feelings. "Bill, I was so mean to you, maybe Paula wouldn't want me in her house just yet."

"Nonsense, you're welcome there any time. Besides, just the other day she asked me when we were going to have you and Irina over for a meal."

"No joke? You're serious." Jonathan said almost nervously. "Look here," Bill said as he stood up from his chair. "We all make mistakes in our life; I know I have made my fair share. A lot of people were hurt because of Jane, and I deeply regret that. But there isn't anything we can do about the past. All we can do now is move forward, and not allow the hatred of one woman poison our lives. Yes, my friend, you and Irina are always welcome in our home."

Jonathan took Bill's hand as he held it out to him, and then he grabbed Bill and hugged him close. "You are, by far, the very best friend I have ever had."

* * * * *

Anyone walking by might not have noticed an old car sitting there in a side parking lot. It was late in the afternoon and everyone was headed somewhere. Yes, no one noticed it and evil always depends on the good folks not noticing what is happening around them. But what evil never seems to remember, is that heaven is always watching. DJ walked into the room where Maggie was laying down. "Hey," He said with an urgency in his voice.

Maggie sat up, "What's the matter? Do you feel alright?"

"Yes, but we need to pray. Bill's life is in danger."

Maggie shook her head. "DJ, Jane is in jail. Are you sure you didn't have a bad dream?"

DJ's eyes flared with emotion. "Yes, I'm sure. I don't know what, or who it might be. But if we sit here, Bill could die today."

Maggie knew DJ well enough to see that he was dead serious about this. "Ok, do you want to me go and get Paula?" "No," he said as he shook his head, "It might be too much for her. This is our charge, my Love, let's get busy about our work." Together they walked toward a back bedroom where they could be alone. It was there that they stood in the gap for Bill Thomas.

* * * * *

Irina was working at the Morning Blend when all of a sudden it hit her. Jonathan and Bill were in trouble. She ran to the phone, but they had already left the campus. Irina locked the door and called Father Grissom. "Hello," Father Grissom said as he picked up the phone.

"I don't know what it is, I have never felt this way before, but everything inside of me tells me that Jonathan and Bill's lives are in danger now." Her voice was filled with tears as she spoke.

"Ok, let's pray together on the phone and then you go and stay in prayer until we hear from them."

After he hung up the phone with Irina, Father Grissom called Sam. "My friend, pray. Bill and Jonathan's lives may very well be in danger right now."

He told Sam about Irina's call and how she had never felt that way before. "I believe it's the Holy Spirit speaking to her heart." Sam said. "I'll start praying now. Call me when you hear something."

Sam picked up the phone and made one call, and from there it spread all over town. Without Bill or Jonathan knowing it, their lives where being covered in prayer.

* * * * *

Bill was talking and laughing with Jonathan as they drove down the mountain. Neither of them noticed the car that was trailing behind them. Why should they, no one wanted to hurt them. As far as Bill was concerned, all of his troubles were behind him. That's when the car behind then turned its lights on bright. "Hey," said Bill. "I don't know who this person is behind us, but he is blinding me with his bright lights."

Jonathan thought to himself, I wish we had made this trip in my car. I would leave him sitting in my dust. "Speed up Bill, maybe that will send him a message."

Before Bill could speak, the car behind them hit them in the rear. It almost made them lose control. "What in heaven's name is he doing?" Bill yelled.

Jonathan looked back but the bright lights kept him from seeing who was driving the car. Then it hit them again. Bill's car almost went off the mountain, but he was able to get it back under control. "He's trying to kill us," Jonathan yelled out.

"You think!" Bill said back, His voice filled with fear.

"Well, speed up," Jonathan said.

"I can't, this is the most dangerous part of the road. We could fly over and it's a five hundred foot drop."

"Oh my God," Jonathan cried out. "What are we going to do?"

"I don't know," Bill said. "You pray, and I'll drive."

Every time Robert Lee's car hit Bill's, he just knew it was going over the cliff. "What's keeping that fool from going over? I'm going to drive him over the cliff if it's the last thing I do." He sped up and hit Bill's car again. Bill's car went too close to the edge of the road. He was just inches from going over the cliff.

Robert Lee cursed as Bill was able to get his car back on the road.

Jonathan was praying. His voice was shaking, and his heart was pounding so hard he felt like it was going to burst. "Oh God, help us please," he called out.

"Amen," Bill said.

* * * * *

Paula walked to the back room to see what DJ and Maggie were up to. She heard them singing, but this song was different than any she had ever heard them sing. "Hey, I never heard that song before."

DJ opened one eye and looked at her and shook his head, as if to say, "We can't talk now."

It was then that it hit Paula, recognition of what was happening. "Oh my God, it's Bill and Jonathan. They are traveling down the worst roads in these mountains." Paula sat on the bed and cried. She held her hand across her belly.

Maggie got up and spoke to DJ in a tongue Paula had never heard. *"Heerth telme keeth deloup.* We do not cast forth our young before time," is what Maggie said. She jumped up on the bed beside Paula and placed her head next to Paula's hands. With that, Maggie started singing another song. It was different from the one DJ was singing. There was such sweetness in her voice that it seemed to flow right through Paula. The baby grew calm. Paula found herself growing calm also. She lay on her side as Maggie kept singing. Before she knew what was happening, Paula had fallen asleep. DJ kept singing, as he watched how Paula had grown so calm that she fell asleep.

He thought to himself. "Now she is going to have to tell me where she learned that." Even now, DJ realized that he was still learning things about his Love. A lifetime wouldn't be enough, he thought.

* * * * *

Bill's car went out of control again, just missing going over the edge. "Curse them," yelled Robert Lee Locklear. "I'm going to kill them both; they took everything away from me. I had it all and they took it away." He ran up on them and hit Bill's car again. Once more Bill was barely able to keep his car in the road. What Robert Lee Locklear wasn't noticing was that every time he hit Bill's car it went faster, which in turn, made him have to drive faster.

"Bill," Jonathan yelled. "If we don't slow down, we are going to go over the cliff."

"I know, but I can't. He keeps running into me and causing me to go faster." Then it came to Bill what he had to do. "Pray, my friend. This might kill us both, but we're dead one way or the other." Boom! The car hit them again; Bill almost went over the edge with the impact, but he held it steady and hit his brakes lightly, which slowed him down just a little.

"I have him now," Robert Lee Locklear cried out. And with that, he put his foot on the gas. Bill watched in his side mirror and just before they were hit, he pulled to the other side of the road and hit his brakes. They were approaching a curve in the road, and as Bill pulled to the other side of the road, Robert Lee went over the cliff. Bill had to fight to hold the car in the curve, but with a strength that came from outside of him, he was able to hold it in the road. Bill stopped his car by running into the side of the mountain. He and Jonathan got out. As they looked down the mountain, they could see the fire where Robert Lee Locklear's car went up in flames.

"Bill," Jonathan said quietly. "I think that was Robert Locklear who was driving the car. I saw him as he flew by. My God, he was trying to kill us."

Bill pulled out his cell phone, "Let me call the State Police, and then Paula. I need someone to come and get us. When I drove my car into the side of the mountain to stop us, I trashed it."

"Don't worry, I'll buy you a new one," Jonathan said. They both stood there, sensing that they were not alone. They knew God had spared their lives that night.

* * * * *

Paula was crying as she hung up the phone, but these were tears of joy and thanksgiving. "They are safe, DJ and Maggie, they are safe," Paula picked up the phone and called the Morning Blend. When Irina answered the phone Paula began telling her everything that had happened. Both women cried and thanked God for watching over the men they loved. Paula called the tow truck to go out and pick up Bill's car. She then called Sam Balius and asked him if he wouldn't mind going to pick up Bill and Jonathan.

"Mind, why my dear, it would be an honor. Please call Father Grissom and tell him though. He has been praying also." "But how did he know?" Paula asked. "Oh, well, Irina called him, and then he called me, and I called someone who called someone. That's how it happened, my dear. Now let me get going to retrieve those young men."

Paula stood there with such a sense of peace. "We were not alone in this, DJ, Maggie, and most of the town was praying along with us."

Smiling, Maggie nodded, "That's how the Creator works, Paula. He is always calling on those who will listen and respond to his call."

Paula sat down in a chair. "I need to think about something to cook."

"Oh dear, just send out for something, I'm sure Bill won't mind."

Paula reached down and patted Maggie's head. "You are such a sweet little soul. But Jonathan and Irina are going to eat with us too, so maybe I should."

"Call Fay and May," DJ chimed in.

"Good idea," Maggie said in agreement. "Now let me see, you two want chicken, right?" Maggie grinned.

"Well Love, only if you say so." DJ couldn't keep from laughing as he spoke. Paula started laughing too and Maggie joined right in with them.

When Paula called Fay and May to ask them if it wouldn't be too much trouble to cook their meal, she found that they had stopped everything in the Heartland Grill, and had everyone in there praying. "Child," Fay said, "when we got the phone call, we told everyone in here that we had to pray, and pray right now. So if they were not of the mind to pray, now was the time to leave. Everyone stayed and prayed, Paula. Everyone in this town loves you two kids." Fay told her what the special was and that they would get someone to run it right over.

"Do you have any baked chicken," Paula asked. "I could use a couple of pieces if you have it."

"Lord yes, and I'll send over four or five." Fay told her.

DJ licked his lips, "I wanted fried, but I can eat baked."

* * * * *

Bill arrived home and Jonathan with him. Irina came in just a few minutes behind them. Paula held out her hand to Irina, "You could have come on and waited here with us."

"Oh thank you, but I had to go and wash my face. My eyes were all red from crying." Jonathan walked over and held her close to him.

Bill held Paula, "I pray to God that now, maybe there isn't someone out there, who is wanting to kill me."

306

"It's over Bill," Jonathan said. With a knowing in his voice, "Your past is behind you now for good."

"Please dear God," Paula said as she buried her face into Bill's shoulder.

Maggie stood by DJ as they both just watched. "How good it is for people to dwell in unity," DJ thought to himself. Paula looked up and took some chicken and placed it in their bowls. "Here, you two deserve this." Maggie grinned and DJ walked up to his bowl, trying not to look as if he was running.

"Did you see that?" Jonathan exclaimed. Maggie looked as if she was grinning when you placed her chicken down for her to eat. I would swear she understood every word you spoke."

Irina patted Jonathan on the back. "Sweetheart, you just had a very bad experience. Your mind is just playing tricks on you, that's all."

Bill turned and walked out quickly so as not to laugh, "I need to get something out of my office," he said.

Paula hugged Irina around the neck and whispered in her ear. "Welcome to our family, and thank you for keeping our secret." Irina winked at her as she backed up.

"Hey, I saw that. What are you two up to? Hey Bill, get back in here. These two are up to something."

"Friendship," Maggie thought. "Long after we're gone, Bill and Paula will have this friendship with Jonathan and Irina."

* * * * *

Dr. Pittman sat in his office at his house reading over the papers that Brad brought to him. They were papers that were found in Robert Lee Locklear's house. In those papers Dr. Pittman found evidence that Locklear had paid a man to kill Bill years earlier, but instead had killed his wife and daughter. He rose up from his seat and walked over to the fireplace. He threw the papers into the fire and watched them burn. "Bill has his life back, and he is where he needs to be, knowing this will only cause him pain, no, it goes to the grave with me."

Clara walked in. "Honey, aren't those the papers Brad brought over for you to look through. I don't think he meant for you to burn them."

"I didn't burn all of them, just the ones that needed to be burned."

Clara looked at her husband. She knew he would never burn papers like that without there being a very good reason. "What did they say; I mean what was in those papers that caused you to burn them?"

Dr. Pittman smiled and walked over and lightly kissed Clara on the cheek. "They said Robert Locklear was madly in love with you."

Clara put both her hands on her hips. "Now you know you're telling a big lie. What did they say?"

Dr. Pittman walked back to his desk chair and took his seat. "My dearest, that is something that no one will ever find out, and don't you go and say anything to Bill about me burning those papers. He's free from his past, let's leave it that way." Without saying what it was Dr. Pittman told Clara enough to know that the truth of those papers could do more harm than good.

"I'm sorry dear," Clara said. "I think I must have misunderstood. I thought you were burning papers you received from Brad. Those were old tax records, my mistake, dear." With that Clara walked out of the office of the man she loved. She knew that what he was doing was for the good of Bill Thomas. She could live with that.

* * * * *

The FBI came to pick up Jane and transport her back to Atlanta. The man who was working for her was taken to another location. He had turned State's evidence for a lighter sentence. When the psychiatrist came up from Atlanta to review Jane's case, she just about took his head off, and called him every name under the sun, all of them bad. She kept insisting that Bill's dogs could talk. "Just give me five minutes with those dogs and I'll make them talk for you." When the psychiatrist came out of the room, Jane was yelling at him to go and talk with those dogs.

Brad asked him, "Well doc, what do you think?"

"Jane is in no shape to stand trial, I'm heading back and first thing in the morning I will have the judge sign the papers stating that she isn't fit to stand trial. Then she will be taken to a woman's prison where she will be locked away from the rest of the inmates. That woman is very dangerous. She just might kill someone."

Now Jane was in the hands of the FBI. She was chained and had two big men on either side of her. Her days of roaming free were over. It was night. They transported her then so that no one would know when she left town, just in case she had some more men working for her.

* * * * *

Father Grissom hung up the phone in his office. It was a friend of his from his days as a chaplain. There was an opening in one of the prisons in Atlanta, and it turned out to be the same one they were transporting Jane to, maybe God wasn't finished with his work in the prisons after all. He picked up the phone and called his bishop. He knew him to be a fair man, and one who truly loved God. Yes, he felt sure he would approve his going back into the prison system to work as a chaplain.

"Yes Bishop, Father Grissom here. It's good to hear your voice too. I have something I need to talk over with you. Something the Lord has placed upon my heart."

Chapter Twenty Seven

Healing

Sunday afternoon was a clear cool day. The City Council was a little nervous about allowing this town meeting, but since it was being held in the high school gym, there wasn't much they could do about it. Brad was there with Les, both men were hoping nothing would happen since Bill's name had been cleared and he wrote that piece in the paper. The gym was packed and they had put extra chairs on the floor, it seemed the whole town was there. Dr. Sam Balius was sitting on the platform along with Father Grissom. No one knew just what to expect or why the meeting had even been called, but it was announced in all the churches that morning and in the local paper as well.

Mable King walked up to Les, "How's the jaw?" she asked with a smile.

Les jumped back a little. "Mable, you just about scared the very life out of me. Everybody is nervous here today, no one knows why this meeting was called and I just hope nothing bad is brought up again. This town can't stand much more."

Mable reached over and patted Les on the side of his face. "Boy, that's not why this meeting was called, don't you know anything?"

Les looked surprised, "How do you know what it's about? I mean, who told you?"

Mable smiled that smile she could give you when she knew you wanted to know something, and she knew she wasn't going to tell. "You just sit back and take it easy, there isn't going to be any trouble here today." Pastor Frank Robbins was sitting with his wife Christa when Greg Vice walked up with his wife Tiffany. "Could we sit with y'all?" Greg asked.

"Sure, have a seat," Frank said as he moved over just a little bit to give them more room. Greg and Frank both started speaking at the same time each one asking the other one to forgive him for the way he had acted.

Christa laughed along with Tiffany, "Well," said Tiffany, "It seems you two have the same thing on your mind."

"Yes it does," Frank said with deep feelings, "I'm sorry for the way I acted."

"No," Greg replied. "I'm just as much in the wrong, maybe more so."

Even before the meeting began, the power of God's love was moving through the hearts of everyone there.

* * * * *

Sam and Father Grissom both stood up, Sam walked to the microphone and asked everyone to bow their heads while he prayed. After he had prayed, Father Grissom walked up and stood beside Sam. "We are here today," he said, "Dr. Balius and I, to address this community about the trouble which has divided so many in our fair town. This has always been a loving community and a place where people liked to come and visit. I hate to admit this; however, over the last month or so, we haven't been that friendly little mountain community. We were drawn into something that was meant to destroy us, and it was born out of hell itself. Although this town has suffered, I believe the ones who suffered the most were the ones who were being used by a very disturbed soul. We allowed the evil in that one person to divide us, even to the point where friendships, long standing friendships, were broken up over this. If we can't take the time to sit back and reflect upon something before we act, we will always be easily lead down this path. I know I was, and I am ashamed of myself for the way that I acted. Dr. Balius and I, were also caught up in this web, but I am here to tell you that today our friendship is stronger than ever. We both have been praying together each day asking God to heal this community and to bring folks back together. Well, that's all I have to say, I'll turn it over to my good friend, Sam Balius."

Sam stepped up to the microphone, "I don't know what I can add to what Father Grissom has already said, but let me ask you this one thing. Haven't you missed the people you have been avoiding? Don't you miss the way this town use to be so friendly and open? I believe we can get that back, but it isn't going to just happen. We are going to have to do something for it to work. We are going to have to forgive each other and realize that we were all wrong in this thing. I believe it can start here today if only we will open our hearts to one another and forgive each other as God has called us to do." Sam bowed his head and asked God to help every heart there to forgive those who might have said something or even done something to cause hurt or pain.

When he finished praying the whole place was filled with a sense of peace. Everyone felt it and everyone began getting up and going to someone to ask forgiveness. The gym was filled with noise, but it was the noise of repentance, a sound that is the very sweetest to heaven. Mable walked over to Les and hugged him around the neck, "I'm sorry I hit you that day, Les. I shouldn't have lost my temper that way with you. You were only doing your job."

Les smiled back at Mable, "Well, I know one thing about you now, stay away from your right hook." They both laughed and hugged each other again.

Philip reached over and took Polly's hand and pulled her to his side, "I feel like a fool acting the way I did."

"No," Polly said. "I'm the one who acted like a fool, you were right, and I was wrong about Bill Thomas. I should have listened to you instead of getting so mad at you."

Philip put his arms around Polly, "Let's just say no one was right or wrong, and just put this whole mess behind us."

As Polly brought her lips to his, she whispered, "I like the way you think, dear."

Jonathan was standing there by Irina, both of them were watching in awe as the town was being healed right in front of their eyes. One person after another came up to Irina and asked her to forgive them for the way they acted toward her. Irina's eyes were red from all the crying, but it was good crying. It was healing tears which flowed down her cheeks that day. Jonathan reached over and held her hand, "You know, you never told me what you are planning to do now that all this is cleared up. I guess what I am trying to ask is, you're not planning on leaving now are you?"

Irina reached over and kissed Jonathan on the cheek, "No, I was planning on staying here. This place has become a new home for me. For the first time in a very long time, I feel like I have a place where I belong."

Jonathan looked at this woman who had turned his world so upside down. "Would you stay here forever? Would you stay here with me?"

Irina looked at him, her eyes filling again with tears. Her hand went over her mouth as she tried not to break down and really cry. "Yes," Jonathan said, "I want you to marry me, if you can forgive me for being such a fool. I want you to stay here forever and build a life with me. Irina, I don't want to lose you ever again."

She grabbed him and held onto him, "Yes, yes, I will marry you. I want to stay here with you, and grow old with you. I never want to leave you again. I love you Jonathan, with all my heart."

As they stood there holding onto each other, Father Grissom walked up and put his arm around them both. "I still have time to do one more wedding before I leave," he said.

"Father," Irina said with such sadness in her voice. "You can't leave now; I have so much to learn."

"Oh child," he said as he patted her on the shoulder, "I think you're in good hands. Besides, I have something I have to do. God is calling me to try and reach a lost soul for Him, and so I have to move on."

Jonathan held out his hand to Father Grissom, "Sir, it's been an honor knowing you. When can you do the wedding?"

"When can you be ready, is more the question?"

Bill walked up, "Give us five days, Paula and I can help." Bill waved to Fay and May, "We need help with a wedding, it has to be done in five days. Can you help?"

"Is the Pope Catholic?" asked Fay, "Oh sorry Father, I didn't mean that to sound..," Father Grissom laughed. "Hmm, I'm going to have to remember that one."

"Ok, said Jonathan, "What time this coming Friday, then?"

Irina looked up, "Six in the evening; I think that is the prettiest time of day here. I love the sunsets in the mountains."

"Alright then, let's get ready for a wedding," Bill exclaimed.

* * * * *

Later that day Sam and Father Grissom were playing chess in Father Grissom's office. "I'm going to miss our games of chess, my friend," remarked Father Grissom as he made his next move on the board.

Sam stopped and looked up, "What do you mean, you are going to miss our games. You're not leaving are you?"

"Yes, Father Grissom said shaking his head. "It's time for me to move on, besides, there is someone I have to try to reach."

Without saying anymore, Sam understood who Father Grissom was talking about. "I'll be praying for you, my friend."

"Thank you, I'm going to need the very wisdom of God to reach this poor soul." They went back to their game, neither of them said a word, nothing needed to be said. Theirs was a friendship that would last, no matter the time or distance.

* * * * *

Friday evening came and the Church of St. Paul's was filled to capacity. There wasn't even standing room available. Father Grissom asked Sam Balius to help with the service, so together they performed the wedding ceremony. Fay and May sat with Paula, for Bill was Jonathan's best man. By the end of the service, there weren't many dry eyes left in the church. Everyone remarked about how beautiful the wedding cake was. Fay and May were proud of it, said it was the best one they had ever made. And afterwards, why the food in the fellowship hall, one person said there was enough food there to feed an army; which is about how many folks showed up for the wedding.

Bill held Paula close to him as they walked through the line to greet the new couple. "Honey," Paula said. "Look at what God has done for our little town. Here we have Jonathan married to the woman he deeply loves, you have your new job at the school, and Dr. Pittman is going to start taking better care of himself. I stand back in wonder at God sometimes."

"So do I, my dear, so do I."

CHAPTER TWENTY EIGHT

Good-byes

Sam was standing on the sidewalk of St. Paul's church. Father Grissom was finishing loading up the U Haul. "Well, I guess that's about everything, hmm, I don't think I have forgotten anything."

"Please promise me that you won't forget to write, call, and e-mail, everyone is doing it these days."

Father Grissom grinned, "I promise. Here's my phone number and address where I will be living. My e-mail address will stay the same; so you should be able to reach me anytime."

Sam reached out and hugged his friend, "I'm going to miss you my friend, do take care of yourself down there in the big city."

Father Grissom's eyes were full of tears, "You have been a God send in my life, my friend. I thank God everyday for bringing me here to Whitworth. I'm going to miss you as well. I talked with my bishop last night, and I suggested a friend of mine to be sent here. He's a Spirit-filled priest, so he should fit right in here. We both went to school together. He's a good man, and a fine Christian to boot."

317

"If you say he's ok, that's all I need to know, I'll see to it that he receives a good welcome here."

"I never had any doubts about that for one minute, my friend," Father Grissom said as he hugged Sam one last time.

Sam, Bill, Paula, and just about everyone who attended St. Paul's Church was there waving their good-byes as Father Grissom drove off.

"There goes a very good man," said Irina, as she waved good-bye. "He helped me at the worst time of my life. I'll never forget him."

"None of us will, dear," said Jonathan as he held her close to him.

Everyone just stood there even though the U Haul was out of sight; they stood there remembering a friend who had helped them and prayed with them through a very dark hour. "He was one of the most honest souls I have ever met in the ministry," said Sam. "He wasn't concerned about everyone seeing him, but more concerned about people seeing Christ in him, a lesson we all need to learn."

* * * * *

It was nine that evening when the phone rang. Bill walked over to pick it up, wondering who would be calling at this hour of the night. "Hello, why Moses, yes, I understand. We'll leave first thing in the morning."

As Bill hung up the phone Paula stood there waiting to hear why they were leaving in the morning. But the look on his face told the story. DJ looked at Bill and said, "It's Benny, isn't it?"

"Yeah," Bill said trying to hold back the tears. "Smokey said to bring you two; he said the guardians need to gather for Benny." "Yes," said Maggie, "That's a wonderful idea, but we need Rocky to be there as well." "For what?" Paula asked. "What does he mean the guardians need to gather, and why do you need Rocky to be there?"

"You'll see," said DJ, but that's all I can say about it now."

318

"I'll make the call and see if I can get Rocky to be there, but it might take some imagination on my part."

"You can handle it," DJ said, "If anyone can, Bill, you can."

* * * * *

Moses was waiting outside as Bill, Paula, DJ, and Maggie arrived. Rocky was already there sitting outside with him. "Rocky smiled as he saw DJ, "My main man DJ, how have you been, Maggie hasn't been leading you a dog's life, has she?"

Maggie's eyes flamed as she started to speak, but Paula reached down and lightly patted her on the head. "Now you know all he is trying to do is get a rise out of you, so don't let him."

With that, Maggie held her head up high and walked right past Rocky.

"Man, not even a comeback, boy, people can sure mess up your fun."

Moses laughed as he walked past Rocky, "She might have saved your hide too, if you know what I mean."

Bill walked up and took Moses by the hand, "I'm so sorry Moses, do they know what the cause of his death was?"

"It was his heart. He kept it hidden from everyone. I think he knew his time was coming and he was ready to go. Dad told me a few weeks ago that he could die a happy man. He had seen guardians and even helped save DJ's life, which he felt was repaying Maggie for saving mine. But bottom line, Bill, Dad was just ready to move on to his heavenly home. I think there were times he missed Mom so much that it hurt. Can you understand?"

"Yeah," Bill said softly, "Before Paula, I lived that way every day. Yeah; I can understand how he felt."

DJ walked up to Moses and placed his head against Moses leg, "I am so sorry for you Moses, but so very happy for Benny. Have you made the arrangements yet?"

Moses shook his head, "Tonight we are going to the funeral home by ourselves. I had to do a lot of talking to get the director of the funeral home to go along with this, but we can do it tonight."

"What are we going to do?" asked Bill.

"You will see," DJ remarked, "This is for Benny, it is something we want to do for him."

* * * * *

It was eight o'clock when they arrived at the funeral home. The director opened the door to let them in, and then he left, as was arranged. "Ok, we have only one hour, so whatever you four have on your minds, now is the time to do it."

Smokey walked up to DJ, "Sir, you're the senior guardian here, would you lead us in our service?" DJ stood, "It would be my honor." He looked at everyone and said softly, "Tonight we are going to hold a service for Benny that hasn't been held for a human being in hundreds of years. It's the service guardians hold for one who has been their friend and who kept their secret safe. Benny was such a friend to us, so tonight we are here to honor him one last time. This service and these songs have never been seen or heard by any living human to our knowledge, so what you see and hear tonight must never be spoken of again." With that, DJ stood in front with Maggie just a little past his right side. Rocky stood over to his left with Smokey to his right. They sat there for a few minutes in complete silence. Then DJ started to sing very softly. Maggie joined in with him, and then Rocky, and Smokey. With each one joining in, the song became a little louder; it was a very moving song.

Paula thought to herself that part of the song sounded very gentle, while other parts sounded like a rushing wind breaking in on you. The one thing everyone knew was that it was meant to tell something about Benny's life as their friend.

At one point Moses sat there with tears running down his face freely, he looked up to heaven and said, "This is for you Dad, this is for you." For forty five minutes they sang. The songs changed, but you could tell there was something very similar in each of them. The peace that filled the room was unlike anything anyone there had ever felt. Moses knew his pastor was going to perform a good service tomorrow, but nothing could ever surpass tonight. When they finished singing, it stopped like it started. Smokey stopped singing, then Rocky, Maggie, and finally DJ. He turned toward Moses and said, "Your Dad was our friend, and we will always hold him in our hearts as long as we live." Maggie stood up and whispered softly, "Goodbye Benny, you dear sweet soul." Moses stood and started singing Amazing Grace. Everyone joined him, guardians included.

CHAPTER TWENTY NINE

Favors

School was out and Bill was taking a week off to help Paula with the baby. He had rocked and fed his daughter, then laid her down for a nap. Paula was already sleeping, so Bill quietly walked outside. Maggie stayed in the room with the baby to watch and make sure she was alright. Everyone knew how Maggie could worry, but DJ had to talk with Bill about something. "Hey Bill," He said walking up behind him. "Could I talk with you for just a minute, please?"

Bill smiled, "Sure anything you want, you know that."

"Boy, that's great, and I don't even have to ask for that new car I saw on TV last night," DJ teased.

"Now wait a minute, I mean within reason, anything within reason, DJ, you know I'll do whatever you ask. So, what's on your mind?"

DJ walked up and sat down beside Bill, "You know, there are times I still miss Sally, and well, one day, we're not going to be here with you either. I would really like to get Maggie something for Christmas, but it might cost a lot, and I need your help. I'll do whatever you want, just please say yes."

Bill placed his arm around DJ, "Sally is in heaven because of you two, Moses and his Dad's lives were brought back together because of you two, not to mention how y'all have repeatedly placed your lives on the line for us. No, my friend, you owe me nothing, command me and if I can do it, I will."

"Wow," DJ said, "all I was hoping for was a simple yes."

"No," said Bill shaking his head. "For you there will never be just a simple yes, I owe you far more than that."

DJ looked around to make sure Maggie wasn't walking up behind him. "I don't want Maggie to hear what we are talking about, you know." "Don't worry, she is in the room with little Rachel Ann, watching over her."

"I like that name, tell me why did you and Paula choose that name?"

Bill stopped and smiled, "I told Paula that she could pick the name and she said that she wanted to name her Rachel Ann. Rachel is the name of her grandmother she loved so, and Ann was the name of my daughter who died with her mother," Bill stopped speaking. It was still hard for him to talk about them.

"How do you feel about it?" DJ asked.

"At first, I wasn't sure I was going to like it, but when I held her in my arms, I don't know, something about it made it right. I know that doesn't make sense."

"No, no," DJ said, with such feeling in his voice, "It makes perfect sense to me, and I can see how you came to realize that yourself. It's something to hold your child that contact for the first time, it bonds us to them." "So, you do understand," Bill sat there amazed at DJ and how much he knew and understood. "So, what do you want?" DJ whispered softly so that in case Maggie happened to walk outside, she wouldn't hear what DJ wanted to get her for Christmas. "We'll have to make some phone calls," DJ said, and we still might not be able to find what I want."

Bill rubbed his head, "Yes we will, even if we have to go across the country, we'll find it."

"But we can't call from here DJ stated, Maggie will try to listen if she thinks we are up to something. We'll have to make the call from your office."

"So, when Paula gets up, you can go to the office with me. I have some papers I need to get, and that will take care of that."

"You can't tell Paula either, Bill. I love her, but she will let it slip out."

"Right, now it's going to be hard, but here we go, us men, need to get out for a while and let the womenfolk have the house to themselves."

"Yeah, DJ said, "We feel like an old shoe shut up in a box."

"Wait a minute," Bill said, "If you say that, the only place we are going to go is one of our funerals."

DJ just grinned, "Ok, what you said then, we'll go with that. You know," DJ said, "I think I have been a good influence on you."

"Yeah, just don't let it go to your head, my friend."

They sat outside for an hour just talking. Bill knew these times would be the ones he would always remember. DJ looked up at him with a sparkle in his eyes, "This Christmas is going to be great." "Yes it will, and I will have a small part in something good."

Grinning DJ smiled up at him, "You have a greater part than you know, trust me."

"What do you mean," Bill asked.

"Wait for Christmas," DJ said.

* * * * *

It was cold and dark in her cell, but Jane sat there not saying a word. She couldn't figure out how that dog could talk, or was she really losing her mind after all? She was so deep in thought that she didn't hear the cart being pushed up to her cell door. "Good afternoon, I'm Father Grissom, and I will be the one bringing you books to read. So, here are a few that I picked out for you to start with."

Jane's eyes were filled with fury, "Why don't you go somewhere else and leave me alone," she said with such hatred in her voice.

"Hmm, I see we need to work on our people skills."

Father Grissom unpacked the books he brought Jane and set them on the tray in her cell door. "I didn't ask for you to bring me anything."

"I know child," he said smiling, "But it's my job, and besides, no one else is allowed to come around you. They think you are a dangerous person."

"Yeah, and what do you think?"

Father Grissom looked at Jane feeling his heart going out to her. "I think you're a soul in need of help, my child, that is what I think." Jane laughed, "Then you're a fool Father, for I would just as soon kill you as look at you."

"Maybe, but then you would never know the truth, would you?"

Jane stood and stared, "Yeah, and what truth is that?"

Shaking his head, Father Grissom had Jane right where he wanted her. "Maybe you're not ready to hear the truth yet. I think we need to spend some time talking first."

Jane picked up the books Father Grissom brought her. "A Bible, and who is C. S. Lewis? I don't want these to read. Bring me something with sex in it."

"I am very sorry, but we don't have those kinds of books in the library. You see, I'm the librarian here as well, and when I came here the first thing I did was to go through all the books and I threw out those kind of books. This is all you are going to get from me, Jane. But the Bible you can keep, it's a gift."

"You can burn in hell priest; I'm not reading this trash. Why, it will drive you crazy."

"Really," Father Grissom said with a smile, "I thought it was the talking dogs that drove you crazy."

Jane grabbed the bars of her cell, "What do you know about them?"

Slowly walking away, Father Grissom said. "First, read those books and then I will bring you some more, and maybe, if you show me that you are hearing what you are reading, I'll tell you what I know. I'm the only one who is going to do you any favors child, just remember that."

If you haven't read the first books, than please check them out as well, DJ, Maggie and I know you will enjoy them also.

The Guardians: Loving eyes are watching
The Guardians: Lost in the City

CPSIA information can be obtained at www.ICGtesting.com
Printed in the USA
BVOW081141300912

301765BV00001B/179/P